REPLACED

A THRILLER

STEPHANIE KREML

ISBN: 978-1-955921-18-3 (paperback); 978-1-955921-15-2 (ebook)

www.stephaniekreml.com

1

———

The October sunshine blazes overhead with an almost cruel intensity, its golden rays streaming down mercilessly through the sparse overhang of half-bare trees. It feels like nature is mocking us with this radiant, cheerful light that refuses to acknowledge our grief. Why can't the sun dim itself out of respect for our devastation? The warmth on my face seems wrong when everything inside me has turned to ice.

Around me, the dark cluster of mourners stands in stark contrast to the brilliant day, their black clothing absorbing heat while their faces remain pale and drawn. They shift uncomfortably, dabbing at perspiration that mingles with tears, their formal funeral attire suddenly too heavy for this day that Peter will never see.

"Mommy, is Daddy asleep in there?" Lucy whispers. Several nearby mourners turn their heads.

My throat tightens, the words sticking as they form and then slip out. "No, sweetheart." I search for an answer that won't shatter us both. "Remember what we talked about? Daddy's body is there, but the part that made him Daddy

—his thoughts and love and everything that made him smile—that's somewhere else now."

It's the best explanation I can offer, when I barely understand it myself. Peter was forty-three. Healthy. Until he wasn't.

The polished mahogany casket gleams under the sun, its surface impossibly bright. I focus on its brass handles, the arrangement of white lilies cascading over one end. Anything but the hollow space inside.

"You're doing great," my friend Alison murmurs beside me, her hand briefly touching my elbow. "Just breathe."

I nod mechanically. I've been breathing, eating, speaking, moving through these awful days like I'm following someone else's instructions. For Lucy's sake, I maintain the composure everyone expects of me. Juliette Samson: always put-together, always appropriate, always in control.

Even now, I've dressed the part in a conservative black dress and the pearl earrings Peter gave me on our tenth anniversary. My hair is pulled back, makeup concealing the dark half-moons under my eyes without looking like I tried. The perfect grieving widow.

The cemetery spreads out in geometrically precise plots of green and stone. Ancient oaks spread their canopy above us, their leaves fading from green to copper, matching the penny someone has left on a nearby headstone. A gentle hill sweeps up to our right, where generations of families rest in elaborate mausoleums.

The minister's words float past, something about Peter's spirit living on. Lucy shifts beside me, her patent leather shoes scuffing against the artificial turf laid around the grave. I squeeze her hand gently—part reminder to stand still, part desperate grip on the only person keeping me from collapsing.

"In addition to being a loving family man, Peter

Samson built a successful business, along with a legacy of integrity and innovation in our community," the minister continues. "As the founder of SD Title and Escrow, his vision transformed how property transactions are conducted throughout many states."

I nod as a fresh wave of grief washes over me. Peter was indeed a loving father. My heart aches thinking about all the moments he'll miss—Lucy's graduation, her first heartbreak, walking her down the aisle someday.

But then the rest of the minister's words fully register. *Founder?* Not *co-founder?* We built it together, Peter and me. My MBA and market research, his sales expertise and connections. It was our shared vision, our shared risk, our shared late nights planning at our kitchen table. The memories replay in my mind's eye, rendered in painful high definition against the blurred background of my present reality.

"And now," the minister gestures solemnly, "we'll hear from Sebastian Dorsey, Peter's business partner and closest friend."

Sebastian steps forward in his tailored charcoal suit, shoulders squared. His silver-streaked hair catches the light as he positions himself beside Peter's casket. The corners of his mouth turn down precisely, his eyes narrowed just enough to suggest sorrow without disturbing the lines of his face.

"Peter was more than my business partner," he begins, his voice resonating without need of amplification. "He was my brother in all but blood."

I study him as he speaks, this man who has been woven into the fabric of our lives for the past five years. The careful placement of his hands when he gestures. The practiced pauses in his eulogy. The occasional glance in my direction—one second of eye contact, then away.

Sebastian describes the Peter I knew—brilliant, driven, compassionate—but his eulogy crafts a narrative I know is incomplete: a Peter who supposedly made all the decisive moves in our business, who single-handedly navigated the company through the last recession, who was the sole driving force behind our expansion into digital services. As he speaks, I note with a mixture of gratitude and unease how he amplifies Peter's contributions while artfully erasing mine—relegating my involvement to a footnote, as if I'd merely been a witness to Peter's genius rather than the architect of half our success.

Lucy leans against my side, picking at a loose thread on her black tights. I wrap my arm around her shoulders, as much for my stability as hers.

After the minister concludes the service, Sebastian approaches us. His cologne—sandalwood with hints of something citrus—reaches me before he does. He takes both my hands in his, his grip dry and warm.

"Juliette," he says, his voice dropping to an intimate tone. "If there's anything you need, anything at all—"

"Thank you, Sebastian." I slip my hands from his grasp. "Actually, I wanted to talk to you about coming back to the office. Now that Lucy's started first grade, it's time I returned. Peter and I always planned that I'd come back once she was in school full time."

Sebastian nods as a flash of calculation crosses his eyes —so brief I almost miss it. His face softens, brows drawing together in what looks like rehearsed sympathy.

"Let's not worry about that right now," he says. "You've got enough on your plate with... everything." He gestures vaguely at the grave, the mourners, the burden of it all.

"I don't want to wait too long," I press. "The transition will be easier if I—"

"We'll discuss it later," Sebastian interrupts, his tone

gentle but firm. Then his expression shifts, lips relaxing into something more solicitous. "I'm sure you need time—take care of yourself and Lucy for now. We can talk more about it next week."

He pauses, then adds, "You know, my lake house is available if you and Lucy need to get away. Sometimes being surrounded by too many memories can be difficult."

"That's kind, but we'll be fine at home," I say, with a little more edge to my voice than I'd intended.

Sebastian nods, squeezing my arm before moving away so I can accept condolences from other mourners.

Mrs. Greene from church squeezes my shoulders too hard. Someone from Peter's golf club pats my back three times, exactly three. A distant cousin, whose name I should remember, offers a casserole. I say "thank you" so many times, the words lose all meaning and become just sounds escaping my mouth.

"Take comfort in knowing Peter provided well for you and Lucy, dear," says my great-aunt Eleanor, patting my arm with her paper-dry hand. "That's something to be thankful for."

I smile, but it doesn't come easily. Another comment that reduces me to a dependent rather than an equal partner in our business and marriage. Another implication that I should be grateful for financial security, as if money could possibly fill the Peter-shaped hole in our lives.

"Yes," I say. "We were always a good *team*."

She blinks at me with rheumy eyes, already turning to make room for the next person waiting to deliver their synthetic sympathy. At least she came to the funeral. My only other family, outside of Peter's, is my sister Lena. But after what happened, it's not surprising she didn't show.

As the crowd begins to thin, a woman I don't recognize approaches Peter's mother, Margaret, as she's being escorted by an attendant to a car from her assisted living facility. The stranger is perhaps in her late thirties, with soft brown hair framing a face that is both plain and striking. Her black dress is understated but hangs with the perfection that only comes from custom tailoring.

Margaret's face transforms when she sees the woman—grief melting into something almost like relief. They embrace fully, not the awkward shoulder touches I've been receiving all day.

I watch as Margaret reaches into her purse and withdraws what appears to be a photograph. She hands it to the woman, who studies it with parted lips before carefully tucking it into her handbag.

"Who's that lady with Grandma?" Lucy asks, following my gaze.

"I'm not sure," I admit. My instinct is to walk over and introduce myself, to ask the obvious question of how this stranger knew Peter. But the funeral director is tapping his watch.

"Shall we go, sweetheart?" I ask, turning her gently toward the waiting car.

"But who is she?" Lucy persists, craning her neck to look back.

"I don't know," I say, helping her into the backseat of the black sedan. "But I'll find out."

As we pull away, I look back through the window. The mystery woman and Margaret stand side by side, watching our departure, with identical postures—shoulders aligned, heads tilted at the same angle—like two people who have honed their grief together. My skin prickles despite the warmth of the day.

Lucy presses her small palm against the window, then waves goodbye to her grandmother. "Grandma looks sad," she observes.

"Yes, she does." I stroke Lucy's hair, her dark waves so like Peter's. "She misses Daddy very much."

"Me too," Lucy says simply, and leans her head against my side.

I wrap my arm around her as the cemetery recedes behind us. The questions about the unknown woman will have to wait. Right now, my priority is getting Lucy home, maintaining whatever semblance of normalcy I can manufacture.

But as we drive through the iron gates, everything has tilted on its axis, and not just because of Peter's death. The secretive exchange between Margaret and the stranger. Sebastian's synthetic sympathy. The eulogy's careful revision of history.

Foreboding takes root as I watch them fade in the rear window. I've been so consumed with heartache, with logistics, with keeping Lucy's world from completely unraveling, that I haven't had space to notice anything else. But now, as the cemetery disappears around a curve in the road, my senses sharpen through the fog of grief.

A sliver of doubt creeps in, persistent and unwelcome. *What else haven't I seen? What other truths have been hidden from me while I've been drowning in despair?*

2

The procession of casserole dishes continues long after the funeral. By evening, our kitchen counters groan under aluminum-wrapped offerings, each bearing handwritten labels: "Tuna Noodle from the Hendersons," "Mrs. Klein's Famous Lasagna," "Chicken and Wild Rice—Freezes Well!" Food as proxy for comfort, as if grief could be smothered beneath a blanket of bechamel sauce.

I stand at the kitchen island, running my finger over the corner of Mrs. Klein's lasagna pan, trying to figure out where I'm going to put all of this food. The house has finally emptied of visitors, though the air still feels crowded with their whispered condolences. Lucy is upstairs taking a bath—she insisted on washing her hair herself tonight, a small declaration of independence I lacked the strength to contest, even though I'll have to do a thorough rinse before she gets out of the tub.

Through the window, porch lights flicker on down the street as the sun sets in perfect suburban synchronicity. Our house looks unchanged from two weeks ago when Peter was still alive—the trim shrubs, the fall wreath on the front door, the crooked-smiled jack-o-lanterns he and Lucy carved together the weekend before he collapsed.

I rest my fingers on the cool granite of the countertop. Peter and I spent three months debating this very slab. He wanted something darker, and I pushed for a lighter veining. We met in the middle, just as we always did.

The doorbell chimes, startling me enough that my hip bumps against the counter. Through the window in the door, I see Alison's silhouette, arms laden with what appears to be more provisions.

"I brought real food," she says when I open the door, brushing past me without pausing for a hug. "Not another casserole. Thai from that place you love."

"You're a lifesaver." The scent of lemongrass and ginger cuts through the bland miasma of cream-of-something soups permeating the air. "I couldn't face another noodle bake."

Alison moves through my kitchen with familiarity. She finds plates in the cabinet, silverware in the drawer, wine glasses above the sink—her brisk efficiency both comforting and slightly intimidating.

"Lucy asleep?" she asks, spooning green curry onto a plate.

"Bath. I should check on her soon." I accept the plate and the glass of merlot she pours. "Thank you for today. For everything."

Alison dismisses my gratitude with a shake of her head, settling onto a barstool. "That's what friends do." She takes a sip of wine, her eyes fixed somewhere past my shoulder. "How are you? Really?"

The question catches me off-guard, puncturing the script I've been reciting all day: "Holding up" and "Taking it day by day" and other empty phrases that let people nod sympathetically and move on.

"I don't know," I say, answering honestly for once. "It doesn't feel real. Like he's just away on business."

Alison nods and waits, giving my words space. After almost a decade of friendship, she knows exactly when I need silence.

"The house feels wrong without him," I continue, pushing curry around my plate. "Too quiet. Too empty. And yet somehow suffocating at the same time."

"That's normal," she says. "Whatever you're feeling— or not feeling—it's all normal."

"Is it normal to be angry?" My voice catches on the question. "Not just at the universe or God or whatever for taking him, but at Peter himself? For leaving us? For—" My words dissolve, the first real crack in the veneer I've maintained all day.

"Yes," Alison says simply. "Anger is part of it."

I take a gulp of wine, more than I meant to, and wince as it burns down my throat. "At the funeral today, when Sebastian was speaking—"

"I noticed your face," Alison says. "When he kept referring to Peter as the founder."

My shoulders drop an inch. "You caught that too?"

"Of course I did. I mean, yes, Peter's name came first on the paperwork, but—"

"We built it together," I finish. "I wrote the business plan in grad school. I secured our initial funding. I designed our entire service approach."

Alison nods. "Before Lucy, you two were practically joined at the hip in that office. Neither of you went anywhere without the other."

"And then I stepped back when she was born," I say quietly, twisting my wedding ring. "That was the deal. I'd focus on Lucy for the first few years, and once she started school, I'd return to the office full-time. Peter and I decided that together."

The memory materializes—Peter and me in this very kitchen, my eight-months-pregnant belly pressed against the counter, mapping our future on a legal pad. Equal partners dividing responsibilities differently for a season, not forever.

"At least no one can take what you two built together," Alison says, refilling my wine glass.

Something in her phrasing snags in my brain—*take what we built together*—but before I can examine it, she continues.

"Speaking of the office, I stopped by yesterday to drop off that donation our firm collected for Lucy's education fund." Alison twirls noodles around her fork. "Sebastian's made a lot of changes since Peter got sick."

"What kind of changes?"

"Moving things around, mostly. Your and Peter's office has been boxed up—he said they're converting it into a conference room." Alison hesitates, her fork pausing midway to her mouth. "It seemed fast to me, but I figured maybe you'd discussed it."

"No," I say, my jaw tightening. "No one's discussed anything with me."

"I thought it was odd. The nameplate was already gone from the door." Alison's eyes meet mine. "Have you been to the office at all since Peter went into the hospital?"

I shake my head. "I've been with him every day since he got sick." A cold realization trickles down my spine—I've been completely cut out of business communications while focusing on Peter's rapidly declining health.

"Sebastian mentioned he's taken over Peter's client portfolio. For continuity, he said."

My appetite vanishes as suddenly as if someone had snatched the plate away. "I need to get back there. Soon."

"Don't rush it," Alison warns. "Give yourself time to—"

"I can't afford time," I interrupt, pushing my stool back. "If Sebastian's already making substantial changes, I need to be present. The business is half mine."

Alison looks like she's weighing her words, as she taps her fingernail against her wine glass. "Just... be prepared. Things might not be as straightforward as you remember."

"What does that mean?"

Before she can answer, Lucy calls from upstairs. "Mommy? I'm done with my bath!"

"Coming, sweetheart!" I call back. To Alison, I say, "Hold that thought."

After rinsing her locks clean, I help Lucy into her pajamas and brush her damp hair, breathing in the fresh fragrance of her strawberry shampoo. Her eyelids grow heavy as I tuck her in, surrounded by the stuffed animals arrayed like sentinels around her pillow.

"Will you stay until I fall asleep?" she asks, her small fingers clutching her favorite rabbit, Nibbles.

"Of course." I stretch out beside her on the twin bed, my feet dangling off the edge. She curls against me, fitting perfectly into the curve of my body.

"I miss Daddy," she whispers into the darkened room.

"I know, baby. I miss him too."

"Does he miss us?"

The question makes my chest constrict. I swallow hard before answering, "Yes. Very much."

Lucy falls asleep quickly, exhausted by the day's emotions. I extract myself carefully from her bed, adjust her blanket, and return downstairs to find Alison loading our plates into the dishwasher.

"You didn't have to clean up," I say.

"Force of habit." She wipes her hands on a dish towel. "Lucy okay?"

"As okay as can be expected." I sink onto the sofa in the adjoining family room. "She asked if Peter misses us."

Alison sits beside me. "What did you tell her?"

"The truth. Or what I hope is the truth."

We sit in silence, the dishwasher humming in the background.

Then Alison takes a deep breath, her eyes lighting up.

"Speaking of the truth," she says, a mischievous grin spreading across her face, "you won't believe what I heard about Karen Russell from the mom group."

I brace myself, knowing this is how Alison often navigates her own discomfort, by distracting herself with someone else's drama.

"Apparently," she continues, lowering her voice conspiratorially as if we might be overheard, "her husband has been cheating on her for months. Total shocker, right? I mean, they always seemed so perfect together..."

As she rambles on, I find my mind wandering. Alison's idle chatter grates like a blunt blade against the mounting pressure in my heart, with memories of Peter occupying my thoughts. I mechanically nod, pretending to listen.

"Anyway," Alison presses on, oblivious to my distraction, "she caught him at a bar downtown with some blonde bimbo. Can you imagine? And now she's saying she wants to file for divorce! I mean, honestly, why do men always think they can get away with it?"

My eyes glaze over as I picture the perfect lives of others—families unblemished by tragedy. I can't help but think about my own situation as I envision Karen's heartbreak that will soon be a minor echo of my own. Alison's voice becomes a mere background buzz, easy to ignore as I slip further into my thoughts about Peter.

"And poor Karen! She's so upset, but honestly, I think this will be good for her. She's always been too accommodating anyway, always catering to his needs."

I let her words wash over me, feeling a strange mix of annoyance and understanding. She continues her gossiping spree, giving me a sense of normalcy tangled in chaos.

"Oh, before I forget," Alison says, seamlessly transitioning from Karen's marital woes, "I'm flying to Phoenix on Friday for that real estate conference I mentioned. You know, the one with the keynote on market forecasting? Should be fascinating, though I'm dreading the dry desert air."

She checks her phone. "But I'll be back next Tuesday night, so I won't miss the luncheon on Wednesday. You're still planning to go, right?"

I blink, trying to catch up. "Luncheon?"

"At the country club. We talked about it last month—well, before..." Her voice trails off, then she takes my hand. "Juliette, you should come. Really. It would be good for you to get involved with things again. See people. Get out of this house."

"I don't know if I'm ready for—"

"You need this," she interrupts, her tone shifting to what I recognize as her professional persuasion voice. "Sitting here surrounded by casseroles isn't helping anyone. Besides, these women have known you for years. They'll understand if you're not quite yourself yet."

I nod absently, my mind still caught between Peter's absence and the pile of sympathy cards stacked on the mantel. "Of course. Yes, I'll go."

"Wonderful," she says, then she leans closer. "Oh, and

Juliette, there's something else you should know about the office."

The shift in her tone makes me sit up straighter. "What?"

"Sebastian's been holding meetings with all the department heads. Strategic planning sessions, he called them. But they seemed... preparatory. Like he's setting wheels in motion."

"Setting what in motion?"

"I don't know exactly. But when I dropped by, Carol—your old assistant—seemed nervous. She started to say she had concerns about Sebastian's plans for restructuring, then stopped herself when he walked in." Alison touches my wrist. "It felt like she wanted to tell me more but couldn't."

A shiver races up my spine, each vertebra tingling with unspoken warning. There's trouble brewing here. I can feel it. "I need to check our financials. And the client accounts."

Alison squeezes my hand. "Just be careful. Sebastian's been Peter's right hand for years now."

"And I've been out of the loop," I acknowledge. "But that's changing tomorrow."

After Alison leaves, the house falls into that peculiar quiet where silence itself becomes an inhabitant. I wander into our study, a space I've avoided since Peter's death. His presence lingers here—the leather chair still holds the impression of his body, a half-empty coffee mug sits on the desk, the faint scent of his cologne hangs in the air.

I lower myself into his chair, wake up his computer, and type our anniversary date—the password he used for everything. Our digital lives have always been open books to each other—shared passwords, shared accounts, shared everything.

The screen lights up, illuminating the stack of mail I'd collected from the hall table. Bills, sympathy cards, financial statements that arrived while Peter was in the hospital. I begin sorting, making piles with mechanical efficiency.

A credit card statement catches my eye. Our joint Platinum card—the one we use for business expenses and larger purchases. I unfold it, expecting the usual charges— Peter's business lunches, my Target runs, the monthly insurance payment.

I stare at the transactions, my fingertips going numb against the paper.

$258.43 - Carmelina's, Boston, MA

$329.17 - La Perla, Boston, MA

$1,873.22 - The Peninsula Hotel, Boston, MA

Peter hasn't been to Boston for over a year. And he was supposed to be in Chicago that week. The dates align with his quarterly meeting with our midwestern affiliates—a trip he made religiously every three months.

I search backward through the statement, but nothing else looks amiss. However, I'm still shaken.

Behind the perfect husband, the devoted father, the man who would buy flowers for no reason, who never missed a school play, who insisted on family dinner every Sunday—was there another Peter lurking in the shadows? One who crafted elaborate lies about business trips, who lived a double life in expensive hotel rooms with another woman, who could look me in the eye each morning and pretend our marriage was everything I believed it to be?

The thought makes my stomach lurch, bile rising in my throat. I picture him at that restaurant, Carmelina's, leaning across a candlelit table toward someone else.

Laughing at her jokes the way he used to laugh at mine. His hand covering hers while I sat at home, probably helping Lucy with homework or folding his laundry, completely oblivious to his deception.

Or is there a simpler explanation? Credit card fraud, perhaps. A stolen number used by strangers. That has to be it.

But the transactions are all card-present purchases. Physical swipes, not online fraud.

I pull open the desk drawer, searching for past statements. The drawer sticks slightly, as it always has. Peter kept meaning to fix it but never got around to it. I give it a harder tug, and it finally yields with a woody groan.

Inside, I find precisely organized files—Peter's military-neat method of record keeping. One thing is conspicuously absent, though. Every other financial document is in its place, but the rest of the credit card statements are missing.

My throat tightens as possibilities spiral through my mind. Peter hiding evidence. Peter lying about his where-abouts. Peter with another woman—the woman from the funeral?

I close my eyes, inhaling deeply to steady myself. There must be an explanation that doesn't shatter the foundation of our marriage. Peter wouldn't betray us like that. Not the man who held my hand through twenty hours of labor. Not the man who cried when Lucy took her first steps. Not my Peter.

I continue looking, pulling books from shelves, checking the false bottom of his humidor, even searching beneath the desk.

As I run my fingers along the underside of the central drawer, I feel something. Not paper, but metal. A key, secured with duct tape. Small, bronze, with some numbers stamped on it.

I peel it carefully from its hiding place, the adhesive reluctantly surrendering its grip. Not a house key. Not a car key. Perhaps a safe deposit box?

Why would Peter hide a key from me? And what does it unlock?

I slip the key into my pocket and continue my search, finding no other irregularities. But as I replace the last stack of files, the certainty of my past begins to crumble. The man I married, the life we built, the trust I never doubted—everything now wears a question mark.

Grief transforms in me, reshaping itself into something with edges and points. I turn off Peter's computer and leave the room. Tomorrow, I'm going to the office. I need answers. And someone there must know the truth about my husband.

3

____

The asphalt is still wet with dew as I pull into the parking lot of SD Title & Escrow. I turn off the engine and sit, gathering my thoughts. Our company. Our legacy. The life I stepped away from when Lucy was born, expecting it would still be waiting for me.

I am mentally reeling, grappling with each new revelation like a swimmer caught in a rip current. After finding the credit card statement and the mysterious key, sleep had become impossible—my mind constructing and demolishing theories about Peter, about Sebastian, about our company until dawn painted our bedroom walls.

Employees filter into the building, many faces unfamiliar. When I'd stepped back, we had twenty staff members. Now, according to our website, there are over fifty. The growth should make me proud. Instead, it heightens my sense of alienation, like returning to your childhood home to find strangers living in it.

The lobby has been redesigned since I last visited to have lunch with Peter before he got sick. Sleek white marble replaces the warm wood floors I chose after weeks of deliberation. Abstract art hangs where photos of staff members once created a welcoming atmosphere. Nothing remains of my touch, my vision.

I'm reminded of why we'd originally brought Sebastian into our company. Peter liked to call it "connections"—Sebastian's friends in the county clerk's office who could make filings happen faster than any lawyer can send an email. When Lucy was born and I stepped back, those quiet favors smoothed over the bumps on our deals. At the time it felt practical, but now those informal back channels felt less like help and more like Sebastian collecting invisible strings he could pull whenever he needed them.

A young woman with pin-straight blonde hair sits at the reception desk, tapping away at a computer. Her crisp white blouse and professional demeanor project efficiency. She doesn't look up as I approach, though the click of my heels on marble announces my presence.

"I'm here to see Sebastian Dorsey." My voice sounds steadier than I feel.

"Do you have an appointment?" Her fingers hover over the keyboard, eyes still fixed on her screen. Not even the courtesy of eye contact—as if I'm any random visitor.

"No, I don't need one." I lean slightly forward, into what should be my space. "I'm Juliette Samson."

This gets her attention. She glances up, her lips tightening almost imperceptibly, the professional mask slipping to reveal a flash of recognition—followed by deliberate dismissal.

"I'm sorry, Mrs. Samson, but company policy requires all visitors to have appointments. Even..." She hesitates. "Family members."

Family members. As if I were just Peter's widow, not the woman who wrote the business plan for this company, who secured our first major client, who designed the very logo displayed behind her head.

The glass doors behind the reception desk swing open, and Sebastian emerges, immaculate in his signature charcoal suit. Surprise flashes across his face before he quickly rearranges his features into something resembling concern.

"Juliette!" He strides forward, arms outstretched. "I wasn't expecting to see you here today, especially so soon after the funeral."

Before I can step back, his arms engulf me in a hug that smells of his sandalwood and citrus cologne. When he pulls away, his hands remain on my shoulders, pressing down just enough that I have to resist the urge to hunch beneath their weight.

His tone is smooth and reassuring. For a moment, I question my own misgivings. Then I remember the credit card statement, the mysterious key, and my suspicion crystallizes, hardening my uncertainty into purpose.

"Thank you, Sebastian." I shift away, breaking his grip to stand taller, refusing to be diminished. "We need to talk."

His eyes flicker to the receptionist, who looks profoundly relieved at his arrival. "Of course. Let's use my office."

He places a light hand on my elbow, guiding me through the main workspace. Everything feels different—new faces look up curiously as we pass, familiar furniture rearranged, the energy altered. We turn down the corridor that once led to the office Peter and I shared.

The nameplate reads "Conference Room A." Our office, converted just as Alison said. I stop abruptly, staring at the door.

"You've been busy," I say, my voice tight.

Sebastian's hand drops from my elbow. "We needed the space. With the eastern expansion—"

"When did this happen?"

"Last month. After Peter..." He doesn't finish, gesturing instead toward another hallway. "My office is this way now."

I follow him, a fresh wave of anger washing over me as I realize he now has a corner office, the old conference room, the one with the view over the creek that all of us used to enjoy together. The space now screams masculine power—dark leather, sleek tech. A large framed photograph hangs prominently: Peter and Sebastian at some ribbon-cutting ceremony I don't recognize, both smiling broadly.

"Please sit." Sebastian indicates a chair opposite his imposing desk. "Can I offer you coffee? Water?"

"No." I remain standing. "I want answers, Sebastian."

His expression shifts into something contrived—sympathetic yet subtly patronizing. "Of course. Though I'm concerned about you being here so soon after Peter's passing. Grief requires time."

"Don't worry about my grief. Worry about these." I pull the credit card statement from my purse and spread it across his pristine desk. "Explain these irregularities to me."

Sebastian's expression doesn't change, but his fingers freeze in the act of aligning a pen with the edge of his desk. "Irregularities? What kind?"

"These credit card charges. Hotel stays. Purchases that don't match Peter's business trips." I force myself to hold his gaze. "Expensive purchases."

"Ah." He lowers himself into his chair. "Yes, there were some unusual expenses in the last year. Peter explained those to me."

My throat tightens. "Did he? And what was his explanation?"

Sebastian leans back, spreading his hands. "Client entertainment. Gifts for major accounts. Some travel for our expansion efforts."

"Expansion to where?"

"New England primarily. Boston."

The city on the credit card statement. I can't decide if his answer makes me more or less suspicious. "Peter was supposed to be in Chicago when these charges happened. He never mentioned expansion plans to me."

Sebastian's lips turn down in hollow sympathy. "Juliette, I know this is difficult. Peter tried to shield you from business concerns while you were focused on Lucy. He didn't want to burden you."

The condescension in his tone makes my jaw clench. "I stepped back temporarily, Sebastian. I didn't surrender my stake in this company."

"Of course not." He answers too quickly, too smoothly. "No one's suggesting otherwise. But things evolve, businesses grow. Peter made certain decisions in your absence that moved us forward."

"Decisions like removing my name from my office door? Boxing up my belongings?" My voice rises despite my efforts to control it.

His smile wobbles. "That was premature. The facilities team misunderstood my instructions. I wanted to prepare a new space for you, something more suited to your eventual return."

He lowers his voice. "Look, this is obviously stressful for you. You should take some time for yourself. The offer still stands: my lake house is available if you need a place to find peace and regroup. It would be good for you and Lucy to get away from all the reminders here."

For a split second, the overture tempts me. Sebastian's lake house is lovely, with the wraparound deck overlooking calm water, the gentle breeze playing the wind chimes hanging from the eaves. He'd invited us out a few times and had even hosted a couple of company retreats. I can almost hear the loons calling across the water at dusk, feel the cool evening air that made us pull our chairs closer to the fire pit.

The memory tugs at something exhausted inside me. Lucy would love the dock, the chance to feed ducks from the wooden planks. We could disappear for a few days, let the silence wash away the chaos of the last few weeks.

But then I look at Sebastian's face—too eager, too hopeful—and the spell breaks.

"That's generous," I say carefully, "but I'm not going anywhere until I understand what's been happening here."

His smile tightens almost imperceptibly. "Of course. I just thought—"

A light knock on the doorframe interrupts us. Sebastian's expression shifts as a woman in her thirties enters carrying a stack of files.

"Mr. Dorsey, I have the Urban Canvas report you requested." She glances at me with polite curiosity. "Also, the Morrison Group is here for your ten-thirty."

Sebastian stands immediately, smoothing his tie. "Thank you, Andrea." He turns to me with apologetic hands raised. "Juliette, I'm so sorry. This meeting's been scheduled for weeks. But I absolutely want to address all your concerns—"

"You don't have a choice. Sebastian."

The words cut through his charlatan charm. Andrea freezes in the doorway, sensing the tension.

"Excuse me?"

"This is my company." Peter and I had each reduced

our shares to forty-five percent to give Sebastian ten when he joined. Now, with Peter gone, it truly was mine.

Sebastian's smile returns, professional and controlled. "Of course. Why don't we set up a proper meeting for next week? I'll have Andrea prepare all the quarterly reports and bring you up to speed." He locks eyes briefly with Andrea, who acknowledges his request and rushes off.

I nod stiffly and allow myself to be escorted back through the office, his hand hovering near but not touching my back, a shepherd guiding a potentially disruptive element away from the flock.

"Take care of yourself, Juliette," he says. "Peter would want that." Invoking Peter's wishes—a calculated move to end the conversation.

I drive away from SD Title with my hands trembling on the steering wheel. The reception I received wasn't just surprising—it was strategic. Sebastian's too-smooth reassurances, the receptionist's cold deflection, the complete transformation of the space I helped create. He's been erasing me from my own company.

Of course he wants me safely tucked away at his lake house instead of asking questions.

I grip the steering wheel tighter. I need to get into our bank accounts, trace these transactions myself. To find answers before I'm completely erased.

4

Before heading home, I swing by the post office, requesting delivery confirmation receipts for all our packages—personal and business—for the past year. The clerk's sympathetic smile tells me she's heard about Peter. Next stop: the grocery store for Lucy's favorite apple juice and goldfish crackers. Small comforts in our upended world.

Our neighbor Mrs. Henderson meets me at her door before I can knock. "Lucy was darling as always," she says, squeezing my arm. "How are you holding up, dear?"

I manage what I hope passes for a grateful smile. "One day at a time."

A police car screams past the end of our street, lights flashing. Mrs. Henderson shakes her head, lips pursed in disapproval.

"Third one this week. This neighborhood isn't what it used to be." She leans closer, lowering her voice. "The Millers had their garden shed broken into last month. Power tools, all gone. And that nice couple on the corner— someone went through their mail." She clutches her cardigan tighter. "You just can't trust anyone anymore, Juliette. Not even people who seem perfectly respectable."

Her words hit closer to home than she could possibly know. I think of Peter's credit card statement and Sebastian's evasiveness.

"No," I say. "You really can't."

Lucy appears in the hallway, crayon drawings clutched in her small hands. Her face holds a fragile brightness, as if she's found a way to process her grief through art. "Mommy! I made pictures of us!"

She's drawn a picture of a stick figure man with angel wings and a halo, floating above a smaller stick figure girl with tears bigger than her face. There's a house with a mommy stick figure standing alone by the door, and a big yellow sun in the corner with a frowning face.

My heart feels like it's being squeezed by an unseen hand as I take in the raw emotion on the page—her grief laid bare in crayon strokes. Even the sun is mourning with us. How is a six-year-old able to capture such profound loss when I can barely articulate it myself?

"They're beautiful, sweetheart." I kiss the top of her head, inhaling the scent of strawberry shampoo and childhood. "Ready to go home?"

At our house, I settle Lucy in front of *Wild Kratts* with her snack. "Mommy needs to do some work. Come get me if you need anything, okay?"

She nods, already absorbed in animal facts and colorful animation.

Once alone, I slip into our study. The computer hums to life, and I navigate to our bank's website. Peter always insisted we maintain joint accounts—a symbol of our partnership.

I type in our username, then the password. After a few moments, our account dashboard comes up on the screen.

But there's a red banner at the top: "This account has been temporarily frozen. Please contact customer service."

What is this? Frozen? How can that be?

There has to be some sort of mistake.

I grab my phone and dial the bank's customer service number with trembling fingers. Six menu options and two transfers later, a human voice answers.

"Northland Bank, this is Stephen." After verifying my identity, he asks, "How may I assist you today?"

"My checking account appears to be frozen. I need to know why."

"Let me check that for you... hmm, I'm seeing something... yes, the account has been frozen pending probate proceedings."

"Probate? This is a joint account with rights of survivorship. It shouldn't be subject to probate." The legal terminology comes back to me from my MBA classes. We'd made sure everything was clear when we set up these accounts—specifically to avoid this very situation if one of us passed away.

"I understand your frustration, ma'am, but I'm seeing a flag here that indicates a third party has made a claim disputing ownership of these accounts."

My pulse hammers against my throat like it's trying to escape. "A third party? Who?"

"I apologize, but I don't have that information available. The note simply indicates that documentation was provided that puts the ownership in dispute."

"That's impossible. This is a joint account. My name is on it." My voice rises despite my efforts to remain calm. "I need to speak to a manager immediately."

"Ma'am, I understand this is upsetting, but a manager will tell you the same thing."

"Put your manager on the phone. Now."

After another eternity on hold, a woman with a clipped, efficient tone introduces herself as Diane Reynolds, Assistant Branch Manager.

"Mrs. Samson, I've—" she clears her throat, "—I've reviewed your accounts, and Stephen is correct. We've received formal documentation questioning the right of survivorship on these accounts, which requires us to freeze access pending legal resolution. This is standard procedure."

"There's nothing 'standard' about this. My husband and I established these accounts together. I've been a customer for fifteen years. I need access to my money to pay bills, to care for our daughter."

"I sympathize with your situation, truly I do, but I suggest you visit our branch in person with identification. We can discuss your options then, though I must emphasize that until the legal dispute is resolved, access will remain restricted."

After disconnecting, I check the time. Just past three. If I hurry, I can make it to the bank before closing.

"Lucy," I call, finding her in the living room arranging her stuffed animals. "We need to run an errand. Can you get your shoes on?"

Her eyes narrow the way they do when she's solving a puzzle. "Your face is doing the angry thing, Mommy. Did I do something?"

I kneel beside her, summoning a reassuring smile. "I'm not mad at you, sweetheart. Mommy just needs to talk to some people at the bank. It's boring grown-up stuff."

"Can I bring Nibbles and Bun-Bun and Captain Whiskers?" She clutches the trio of well-loved animals to her chest.

"Just one, honey. We won't be long."

Twenty minutes later, Lucy sits in the bank's waiting

area. The oversized chair swallows her as she hunches over her coloring book, her shoes dangling inches above the floor. Meanwhile, I'm escorted into the office of Mark Treadwell, Branch Manager. His office smells of leather and coffee, with framed sailing photographs and family gatherings decorating the credenza behind his desk.

"Mrs. Samson." He rises, extending his hand. "I wish we were meeting under better circumstances. Please have a seat."

I remain standing. "I'd like to understand why my checking account has been frozen."

He gestures again to the chair. "This might take a few minutes to explain."

I lower myself to the edge of the chair, keeping my spine straight, refusing to settle into its comfort. Placing my identification and a folder with my papers on his desk, I say, "I've brought copies of the original documents from when we set everything up, proving I'm Peter's wife and co-owner of our accounts."

Treadwell examines the papers, his expression neutral. "I appreciate your thoroughness, Mrs. Samson. However, we've received formal legal notification questioning the survivorship rights on these accounts."

"I want to see these documents."

Treadwell smooths his already-perfect Windsor knot, his watch catching the light from his desk lamp. "I'm afraid I can't share those with you directly. They're part of a legal proceeding."

"Then who submitted them? I have a right to know."

"I'm sorry, but all I can tell you is that we've received a formal notice from a third party regarding your joint account with Peter Samson. Until we resolve the claims about rights of survivorship, we must temporarily restrict access."

My foot taps a violent rhythm under the desk, each evasion adding another beat to my mounting rage. "So someone walks in with some paperwork, and suddenly I can't access my own money? Money I need to pay our mortgage, utilities, buy groceries—"

"Mrs. Samson." His tone remains so carefully measured I want to reach across the desk and shake the concrete composure from his face. "I understand this is distressing. However, we must follow legal protocols. I strongly suggest you contact your attorney immediately."

"I want copies of everything that was submitted."

"I'm not in a position to provide those documents. Again, my recommendation is to seek legal counsel." He stands, a clear signal our meeting is over. "They can file the appropriate motions to access those materials through proper channels."

The controlled mask I've worn slips, just enough that Treadwell takes a small step back.

"I've been banking here since before my daughter was born. Peter and I chose this institution specifically because you promised personal service and care."

"And we value your business, Mrs. Samson. Truly. This isn't a decision we've made lightly." He pauses, then adds, "I'm sorry I can't help you any further."

I shake my head as I get up. But as I turn to leave, a final question stops me. "Has Sebastian Dorsey contacted this bank regarding our accounts?"

Treadwell's expression remains carefully neutral, but something flickers in his eyes. "I couldn't comment on that even if I knew, Mrs. Samson. Client confidentiality."

His non-answer is answer enough.

I'm livid as I go out into the lobby. Lucy looks up from her coloring as I approach, her innocent face a stark contrast to the adult turmoil swirling inside me. I take a deep breath, closing my eyes for a second to reset myself.

"Are we all done, Mommy?"

"For now, sweetheart." I take her hand, forcing a smile. "For now."

In the car, I dial Michael Bennett's law office. Our attorney for both personal and business matters, Michael has handled everything from our wills to the company's contracts for over a decade.

His receptionist answers with familiar warmth. "Bennett Legal Services."

"Sarah, it's Juliette Samson. I need to speak with Michael immediately. It's urgent."

Her tone shifts subtly. "Oh, Mrs. Samson. Let me check if Mr. Bennett is available."

Sarah. The woman who sent hand-knitted booties when Lucy was born now sounds like she's reading from a script written by someone else.

After a minute of hold music, she returns. "Mr. Bennett can see you tomorrow at nine."

"Tomorrow isn't good enough. I need to see him today. My bank account has been frozen."

After a pause, she says, "Let me check with him again."

Lucy fidgets in the back seat while the hold music plays once more. "Mommy, I'm hungry."

"Just a few more minutes, sweetie." I twist to smile reassuringly at her while Sarah comes back on the line.

"Mr. Bennett says he can stay late to see you at five-thirty. Will that work?"

"We'll be there."

I end the call and count the ornate columns flanking the bank's entrance, a trick I learned in therapy to ground myself when panic threatens. The foundation I thought was stable has turned to quicksand, and I'm sinking while everyone watches from solid shore.

"Mommy, can we get chicken nuggets?"

Lucy's voice pulls me back to the immediate present, to her needs that won't wait for legal battles and frozen accounts.

I check my wallet. It contains exactly seventy-three dollars. My credit cards carry balances I need to watch before I max them out. Our future seems to be crumbling between my fingers.

"Of course we can, sweetheart." I turn the key in the ignition, determination hardening inside me. "And then we're going to see Mr. Bennett. He's going to help us figure this out."

As we pull away from the bank, each revelation clicks into place like tumblers in a lock, securing me further from the life I thought was mine. I've been cut off—from the company, from our finances, from the life Peter and I built. I'm sure somewhere in the midst of this calculated assault is Sebastian Dorsey, with his too-smooth reassurances and careful deflections.

I glance at Lucy in the rearview mirror, singing softly to herself, blissfully unaware of how quickly our security is unraveling.

For her sake, I need answers. And I need them now.

5

The digital clock on my dashboard reads 5:24 p.m. when I pull into the parking lot of Bennett Legal Services. My jaw tightens as gray clouds gather above in the darkening sky. Lucy clutches her stuffed rabbit to her chest, chicken nugget crumbs still clinging to her sweater.

"Remember what we talked about, sweetheart?" I wipe a smudge of ketchup from her cheek. "Mommy needs to have a grown-up conversation with Mr. Bennett. You'll sit quietly with your coloring book."

"And then ice cream after?" Her eyes brighten with hope.

"Sure," I chirp with false brightness. Then I add quickly, grasping for anything that might keep the conversation normal, "We'll stop at Marble Slab on the way home."

The law office occupies the ground floor of a renovated Victorian. I grip the sturdy iron railing as we climb the wide brick steps, searching for reassurance in its solidity. I've visited this office dozens of times over the years, from drafting our wills to reviewing property purchases. Michael has been our trusted advisor through it all.

Lucy drags her feet, the weight of the day finally catching up with her.

Inside, the reception area's warm lighting and familiar scent of coffee now feel like a stage set—all appearance, no substance. Sarah, Michael's long-time receptionist, looks up from her computer with a tight-lipped smile that vanishes the moment our eyes meet.

"Mrs. Samson." She emphasizes my title, continuing the formality she expressed on the phone—something she'd never done before. "Mr. Bennett will be with you shortly. Would... would Lucy like some juice?"

"No, thank you," I answer before Lucy can respond.

I guide Lucy to the leather sofa, unpacking her coloring book and crayons. The waiting room walls are lined with framed magazine articles and professional awards. Michael's face smiles from a chamber of commerce photograph, his arm around Peter at a charity golf tournament three years ago. Their easy camaraderie captured forever in glossy print.

Seeing Peter during happier times makes my heart ache—how could everything have changed so drastically?

Sarah's phone buzzes. She picks up, murmurs something, then looks at me with a wary expression.

"Mr. Bennett will see you now."

I squeeze Lucy's shoulder "Be good. I won't be long."

Sarah doesn't offer to watch Lucy as she normally would. Instead, she busies herself with paperwork, carefully avoiding my gaze.

Michael's office has always conveyed the image of successful reliability: oak bookshelves lined with leather-bound legal volumes, his undergrad and law school diplomas, a massive desk that's witnessed countless contracts and agreements. I've always found comfort in its orderliness.

Today, it feels like entering a stranger's office.

Michael stands, adjusting his tie. His handshake is brief. No warmth, no "Juliette"—just "Mrs. Samson, please have a seat."

Once more, I remain standing. "What's happening, Michael? Why are my accounts frozen?"

He gestures to the chair again, more insistently. "This isn't a simple explanation. Please sit."

I lower myself into the chair, keeping my back straight, my spine rigid. "My daughter's out there. I need answers quickly."

Michael's fingers drum against a manila folder on his desk. The wedding band on his left hand catches the light —I attended that wedding with Peter eight years ago. We brought the champagne that Peter had been saving for a special occasion.

"I understand this is difficult, Mrs. Samson." He exhales slowly, the sound seeming to fill the space between us like a confession he doesn't want to make. "However, certain... developments... have emerged regarding Peter's estate that require careful legal navigation."

"Developments?" The word tastes bitter in my mouth. "Like someone freezing our joint accounts without warning? Like treating me as if I'm some stranger trying to access money that isn't mine?"

Michael removes his glasses with deliberate precision, his movements measured and calculated. He polishes them with a monogrammed handkerchief—white with his initials embroidered in navy blue thread, a gift from his wife. It's a delay tactic I've seen him use countless times with difficult clients, the ones who refuse to accept unfavorable terms. Never with me. Never with someone he's known for over a decade, someone whose husband was one of his closest friends.

"Three months ago," he begins, his voice taking on the formal cadence he reserves for depositions, "Peter made substantial changes to his estate planning documents. Significant modifications that affect the distribution of assets."

The words hit me like a physical blow. I grab the edge of his desk, my knuckles going white against the dark wood grain. "That's impossible. We make those decisions together. Always. Every financial decision, every legal document—we discuss everything. Peter wouldn't have done something like that without telling me."

"I'm bound by attorney-client confidentiality regarding the specific contents until the formal reading of the will." His voice remains steady, but he won't meet my eyes. "I've scheduled that for next Tuesday at 10 a.m."

"Confidentiality? I'm his wife, Michael. We've known each other for twelve years. You were at our house for dinner last Christmas."

Michael replaces his glasses, his expression remote. "I understand this is confusing. But I must follow proper legal protocols."

"Did Sebastian Dorsey contact you about our accounts?"

A muscle twitches in Michael's jaw. "As I said, I'm bound by confidentiality."

"What about the joint accounts? Those should pass directly to me regardless of any will changes."

Michael shuffles papers on his desk. "Normally, yes. However, when there's a dispute about the ownership or survivorship rights, banks typically freeze access until legal clarity is established."

Something in his careful phrasing catches my attention. "A dispute? From whom?"

His eyes flick toward his office door before returning to the papers before him. "That will become clear next week. I suggest you prepare yourself."

"Prepare myself? For what, exactly? Stop being evasive, Michael."

He exhales slowly. "Mrs. Samson, my hands are tied in what I can disclose before the formal reading. But I would strongly advise you to secure independent legal counsel."

My stomach drops as his meaning becomes clear. "You're my attorney. You've been our family attorney for over a decade."

"I represent Peter's estate." Each word is carefully measured. "Given the... circumstances, having your own representation would be prudent."

I lean forward, studying his face. "You know something. Something you're not telling me."

Michael aligns the edges of the papers on his desk. "The will reading is scheduled for Tuesday at 10 a.m."

"I want copies of the documents disputing my accounts."

"You can obtain those through proper legal channels. Your attorney can file motions to—"

"My attorney?" I stand, palms flat against his desk. "You've been our attorney for twelve years."

Michael's expression remains maddeningly blank. "Mrs. Samson, please understand my position. I must perform my duties as executor of Peter's—"

"Wait, you're the executor of his estate?" Sweat breaks out along my hairline as my breaths come faster, shallower. "Peter and I had decided we would be the executors of each other's estate, should it come to that. You know this."

Michael grimaces. "As I mentioned, there have been

changes, and I'm duty-bound to follow his documented wishes."

"What documented wishes, Michael? What exactly did Peter change?"

"That will be addressed at the reading. Tuesday, 10 a.m."

"You keep saying that like it's an answer." My voice rises despite my efforts to control it. "I can't pay our mortgage. We have bills due. What am I supposed to do until next week?"

Michael's left eye twitches—the first crack in his professional veneer. For a moment, I glimpse something like guilt, maybe even fear.

"I wish I could be more helpful." His voice drops. "I truly do."

The sincerity in those words frightens me more than all his evasions. Whatever is coming next week is bad enough that Michael Bennett—our trusted friend and advisor—can't bring himself to warn me directly.

"Do you have any recommendations for attorneys who specialize in estate disputes?"

Michael pulls a business card from his drawer. "Patricia Torres. She's excellent with complex cases."

I take the card without looking at it. "I hope tomorrow brings you clients you're actually willing to help."

A flush creeps up his neck. "Juliette—"

"It's Mrs. Samson." I mirror his earlier formality. "According to you."

I turn toward the door, then pause with my hand on the knob. "One more question. The bank mentioned documentation disputing ownership. Does that have anything to do with the changes Peter supposedly made?"

Michael's silence is answer enough.

"I'll see you next week." I straighten my shoulders. "With my own attorney."

Like at the bank earlier, Lucy glances up from her coloring book when I enter the waiting room, her face lighting up briefly before she reads my expression. "Are we done, Mommy?"

"Yes, sweetheart." I gather her things, avoiding Sarah's gaze. "We're done here."

Outside, fat raindrops begin to fall as we rush to the car. I buckle Lucy into her booster seat, my fingers slipping twice before the clasp clicks into place.

"Did Mr. Bennett fix the problem?" Lucy asks, clutching her rabbit.

I bite the inside of my cheek hard enough to taste metal. "Not yet, honey. But we're going to figure it out."

Before I pull out of the parking lot, I glance at the card Michael gave me. Patricia Torres, Estate Litigation. Her office address is downtown, likely an expensive high-rise with views and hourly rates to match.

I check my wallet again. Seventy-three dollars minus twenty for our fast-food dinner leaves barely fifty-three. Not enough for a retainer, probably not even enough for a consultation.

In the rearview mirror, Lucy's eyes are already drooping, exhaustion finally claiming her, her request for ice cream now forgotten. How many more days can I shield her from the reality of what's happening? How long before our carefully constructed life falls completely apart?

I dial the number on the card, keeping my voice low as Lucy drifts to sleep. The call goes to voicemail.

"This is Juliette Samson. I need to speak with Ms. Torres regarding an urgent estate matter. My husband recently passed away, and I've discovered... complications with his will and our accounts. Please call me back as soon as possible."

I leave my number and end the call, then press my palms against my thighs to stop my hands from shaking.

Whatever Michael couldn't bring himself to tell me, whatever is waiting at next week's will reading, I'll face it. Not just for my sake, but for Lucy's. For the little girl sleeping in the back seat, who's already lost her father and doesn't know she might be losing everything else.

I'll spend this evening researching law firms—who knows if this referral from Michael will pan out. How can I trust anything from him now? But someone in this city must be willing to help me unlock the secrets Peter has left behind, the changes no one seems to be willing to explain.

Rain pelts the windshield as we drive home, the wipers struggling to keep pace with my racing thoughts. Letting Lucy sleep as we sit in our driveway, I make three more calls, leaving nearly identical messages for attorneys specializing in estate disputes. Lucy doesn't stir as I unbuckle her, gathering her limp, warm body against my chest and carrying her inside. I tuck her into bed, still in her clothes, too drained to wrestle with pajamas and teeth brushing.

Standing in our kitchen, surrounded by flowers and sympathy cards, I spread the remaining cash from my wallet on the counter. Fifty-three dollars and eighteen cents.

My phone buzzes with a text from Michael: *Juliette, I apologize for our difficult meeting today. Please know I'm doing everything within my professional obligations. See you next week.*

I don't respond. Instead, I search our cabinet for the emergency cash envelope we keep for unexpected expenses. Three hundred dollars. Not enough for an attorney, but enough for groceries while I figure out my next move—assuming I still have access to our investments.

On the refrigerator, Lucy's drawing of our family—now one member short—stares back at me. The stick figure of Peter floating above us with his angel wings. The crying stick figure of Lucy. And me, standing alone by the door of our house.

Except the house doesn't feel like ours anymore. It feels like another thing that could be taken away at any moment.

I pull out my laptop, entering the words "estate litigation patricia torres" in the search bar. Her website appears, professional and sleek. Twenty years of experience. Former prosecutor. Specializes in high-conflict estate disputes. Overall, client reviews are positive.

I send an email detailing my situation again, adding "URGENT" to the subject line. Maybe I'll get a faster response with both the email and voicemail. Then I search for information about joint accounts and survivorship rights, about spouses contesting wills, about what might constitute "documentation disputing ownership."

Each search leads to more questions, more legal complexity, more unease about what next week might bring.

Outside, rain lashes against the windows, drumming a chaotic rhythm that matches my heartbeat. Inside, I stand guard over my sleeping daughter, our diminishing resources, and the crumbling foundation of the life Peter and I built together.

I close my laptop and press my palms against my burning eyes. The will reading is one week away. One week to find an attorney. One week to prepare for whatever bomb Michael couldn't bring himself to detonate today.

One week to figure out how to hold our world together when everything is falling apart.

6

Condensation fogs the kitchen window, where the morning chill meets warm indoor air, blurring my view of the backyard, while the unpaid bills spread across the counter remain all too clear. My third cup of coffee sits cold beside me, my stomach too knotted to drink it. I check my phone again—nothing from Patricia Torres or any of the other attorneys I called in desperation last night. The microwave glows 9:03 AM, a reminder that time keeps slipping by.

My laptop sits open on Patricia's website. Her stern professional photo stares back at me—dark hair pulled into a tight bun, sharp jawline, penetrating eyes that seem to evaluate me through the screen. Her firm specializes in "high-conflict estate disputes" and "contested inheritance cases." The words swirl inside me like restless birds, their wings occasionally fluttering against my ribs.

My phone remains silent. Four attorneys contacted, zero responses.

Lucy shuffles into the kitchen clutching Nibbles by one ear, still wearing yesterday's clothes, her hair a wild nest of tangles. The threadbare stuffie dangles precariously from her small fingers.

"Morning, Mommy." Her voice still rough with sleep.

"Morning, sweetheart." I close the laptop with a soft click, forcing a smile. "Want some cereal?"

She nods, climbing onto a stool at the counter. Her eyes drift to the spread of papers—bank statements, credit card bills, and printed copies of our joint account information.

"Is that homework?" she asks, poking at one of the pages with her small finger.

"Sort of. Grown-up homework." I slide the papers into a folder and reach for her favorite cereal bowl—the blue one with stars around the rim, the one Peter bought her after she memorized all the planets.

The doorbell rings, its chime cutting through the kitchen's morning quiet. Lucy's head swivels toward the sound.

"Is somebody bringing more casseroles?" Lucy asks, her voice tiny and sleepy, tugging at her rabbit's ear.

"I don't think so, honey." My heart stutters as I cross to the door, checking through the window. A woman in a navy pantsuit stands on our porch, leather briefcase in hand. Her dark hair is pulled back exactly like in her website photo, not a strand out of place.

I open the door. "Ms. Torres?"

She extends her hand. "Mrs. Samson. I received your messages." Her grip is firm, her gaze direct. "I apologize for not calling first, but given the urgency of your situation, I thought an in-person consultation would be more..." She pauses, choosing her words carefully. "...efficient."

No trace of the sympathetic head tilt I've grown accustomed to since Peter's death. Just cool assessment and practicality. It's strangely refreshing.

"Please come in." I step aside, suddenly aware of my unwashed hair and the coffee stain on my sleeve. "And it's Juliette."

"Patricia." She enters, her heels clicking against the hardwood floor—a sharp, authoritative sound. Her eyes scan the foyer, taking in the family photos on the wall, the stack of sympathy cards on the side table, Lucy's purple unicorn backpack by the stairs. A professional assessment of her new client's life.

Lucy peeks around the kitchen doorway, Nibbles dangling from her hand, watching this stranger in our house with wary eyes.

"That's my daughter, Lucy." I gesture toward the kitchen. "Lucy, this is Ms. Torres. She's here to help Mommy with some grown-up things."

Patricia's expression softens slightly as she catches sight of Lucy. "Hello, Lucy. That's a nice rabbit you have."

Lucy retreats back into the kitchen without responding, her bare feet silent against the floor.

"Again, I apologize for dropping in unannounced," Patricia says, lowering her voice. "After reviewing your messages, I had an opening this morning and thought we shouldn't waste time." Her eyes meet mine, serious. "Estate disputes move quickly. Waiting can be costly."

"I appreciate it." I lead her toward the dining room, my nerves both calmed and heightened by her presence. "Would you like coffee?"

"Black, please."

While I prepare the coffee, she unpacks her briefcase at the dining table. Lucy sits at the kitchen counter, spooning cereal into her mouth, eyes fixed on the stranger who's invaded our morning.

"Lucy, why don't you take your cereal to the living room and watch some TV?" I suggest, pouring steaming coffee into Peter's favorite mug before thinking better of it. I switch to a plain white one instead.

She slides off the stool without argument, balancing her bowl carefully as she leaves. She's been so compliant since Peter died. Too compliant. Another worry to add to my growing list.

When I return with two mugs of coffee, Patricia has arranged several documents in neat piles. A yellow legal pad sits beside them, already containing notes in precise handwriting.

"Tell me about these frozen accounts," she says without preamble, accepting the mug with a nod of thanks.

I sink into a chair across from her, the wood hard against my back. "Peter and I have—had—joint accounts." The verb tense correction still feels like swallowing glass. "Yesterday, I discovered they've been frozen. The bank manager kept apologizing, saying some third party is disputing my ownership."

Patricia makes a note, her pen scratching against the paper. "What type of accounts?"

"Checking, savings, and a money market account." I push the bank statements toward her with unsteady fingers. "All joint with rights of survivorship. I have the documentation."

She examines the statements, eyes flicking over numbers and dates. "And your husband's attorney?"

"Michael Bennett."

A flash of recognition—and something else—crosses her face, but she says nothing.

I continue. "He's been our family attorney for years, but yesterday he treated me like..." I search for the right words. "Like a stranger. Or a threat. He said Peter made changes to his estate planning three months ago and refused to tell me what those changes were before next week's will reading."

Patricia's pen pauses mid-stroke. "Three months ago." Her voice sharpens slightly. "When did your husband fall ill?"

"About six months ago." My throat tightens around the words. "It started with numbness in his hands and feet. The doctors initially thought it might be a relapse of Guillain-Barré syndrome—he had that as a teenager after some viral infection. He got better off and on, but then... he developed pneumonia... in the final week." My voice falters, breaks. "It happened so fast. One minute we were discussing treatment options, the next..."

Patricia waits, giving me space to compose myself. When I don't continue, she says, "I'm sorry for your loss." Her voice softens slightly, the first crack in her professional demeanor. She taps her pen twice against the legal pad, then meets my eyes directly. "I need to ask you something difficult, and I need complete honesty." She pauses, giving me a moment to brace myself. "Is there any possibility— any at all—that your husband was planning to divorce you?"

The question lands like a slap. My coffee sloshes dangerously as I set the mug down too hard. "What? No. Absolutely not."

"You seem certain." Her eyes never leave my face, assessing, weighing.

"I am certain. We were happy. Ask anyone who knew us." I pause, the credit card statements flashing in my mind. "Well, at least I thought we were."

"What does that mean?" Her pen hovers over the pad.

I take a breath, steadying myself. "I found this in the mail after he died." My hands tremble as I slide the credit card statement toward her. "Charges from a fancy restaurant. A lingerie store. A hotel in Boston on a weekend that Peter told me he was at a meeting in Chicago." The words taste bitter as they leave my mouth. "I've been going over and over it in my head, trying to find an explanation that makes sense."

Patricia examines the pages, her expression neutral. "Have you spoken to anyone about these charges?"

"Briefly. Sebastian Dorsey, a partner we brought in to our firm after Lucy was born. He implied they might be business-related but changed the subject quickly." I take a sip of coffee to steady myself. "Why did you ask about divorce?"

She taps her pen against the legal pad again. "Joint accounts with rights of survivorship usually pass directly to the surviving spouse without going through probate. For someone to freeze those accounts, they would need to challenge either the joint ownership itself or..." she watches me carefully, "your status as the surviving spouse."

"My status? I don't understand."

She leans forward, the morning light casting sharp shadows across her face. "Mrs. Samson—Juliette—I need to check something quickly." She pulls out her iPad and types rapidly. The screen's light reflects in her dark eyes as she scans whatever information she's found.

"What is it?" I ask, dread pooling in my stomach, heavy and cold.

"One moment." She continues typing, her expression tightening almost imperceptibly.

I grip my coffee mug, cognizant of Lucy's laughter drifting from the living room. Whatever Patricia has discovered, I can't afford to fall apart. Not with Lucy in the next room. Not with so much at stake.

Finally, Patricia turns the tablet toward me. "I've searched the county records. I think you should see this."

The screen displays a legal document with the heading "PETITION FOR DISSOLUTION OF MARRIAGE." My eyes fix on the names: "In the matter of Peter Andrew Samson, Petitioner, and Juliette Marie Samson, Respondent."

"This can't be right." The words come from somewhere outside myself, my voice hollow and strange. The dining room seems to contract around me, the walls pressing closer as a high-pitched ringing starts in my ears.

"It was filed five months ago," Patricia says quietly.

"That's impossible." I scroll through the document, my hand shaking so badly I can barely control the screen. "I never received any divorce papers. I never signed anything."

"Keep scrolling."

At the bottom of the document is a signature. My signature.

"That's not—I didn't sign this." The tablet nearly slips from my fingers. I set it down before I drop it. "Someone forged my signature."

Patricia takes back the iPad, her expression grave. "This would explain the frozen accounts. If someone is claiming you were divorced before Peter's death, you may not have survivorship rights."

"But we weren't divorced! This is—" My voice catches, then rises. "This is forged!" I glance toward the living room where Lucy's cartoon plays, forcing myself to lower my voice. "Sorry, I just..." I press my fingertips against my temples. "This is insane. I never signed anything. I never even knew these papers existed. How could—?" I can't even finish the thought.

Patricia makes another note. "Was your marriage having problems?"

"No." I press my palms flat against the table, needing

the solid surface beneath my hands. "We had the normal stresses—work, raising a child. Peter traveled more these last couple of years. But divorce? Never. We were mapping out how I'd ease back into the business, which clients I'd take on first, how we'd manage the new dynamic of working together again—" My voice catches on the last word.

"Tell me about your business arrangement with Sebastian." Patricia shifts direction, giving me a moment to recover.

I take a deep breath, forcing myself to focus. "Peter and I founded SD Title & Escrow together." I pause. "Actually, it was Samson Title & Escrow back then. We changed the name to SD Title & Escrow after Sebastian joined. You know, SD for both our last names: Samson and Dorsey. This all happened when I stepped back from the day-to-day business after Lucy was born and with the understanding I'd return once she started school." I pause again, remembering the strange tension at the funeral. "Lucy started first grade this fall, but when Peter got sick, I delayed things to take care of him. But I told Sebastian at the funeral that I still plan to return full-time."

Patricia writes this down, her pen moving in quick, precise strokes. "What's your equity position in the business?"

"I own forty-five percent of it. At least, I should." Another horrible thought strikes me, making my stomach lurch. "Unless Peter somehow transferred my shares too."

"We'll investigate that possibility." Patricia continues writing. "Who is the executor of Peter's will?"

"According to Michael Bennett, he is. Which makes no sense. Peter and I always agreed we would be each other's executors. We put it in writing years ago."

Patricia's pen stills. "This is beginning to paint a

concerning picture, Juliette. Someone appears to be challenging your position as Peter's wife, which affects your rights to joint property, inheritance, and possibly your business interests."

"But who?" As I ask the question, Sebastian's face flashes in my mind. The credit card charges. The changes at the office. His calculated sympathy at the funeral. The way his eyes followed me as I left.

"That's what we need to find out." Patricia flips to a new page in her legal pad. "I'll request copies of the divorce papers and any documents the bank received disputing ownership of your account. We'll challenge the validity of your signature with forensic analysis if necessary. We'll also prepare for the will reading next week. That should reveal who's behind this."

7

———

The next week passes in a blur of forced ordinariness and mounting dread. I took Lucy to a classmate's Halloween party on Saturday, helping her transform into a butterfly with wings that shimmered under the porch light. But while Lucy collected candy and played pin the tail on the black cat, I found myself trapped in a series of stilted conversations with other parents who stumbled over their condolences, their eyes darting away when they mentioned Peter's name.

"If there's anything we can do..." they'd say, trailing off as if they'd forgotten the rest of the sentence. I'd smile and nod and thank them, all while the forged divorce papers burned in my brain. Standing in that cheerfully decorated living room, surrounded by plastic skeletons and paper bats, I felt like I was the one wearing a costume—playing the role of the grieving widow while underneath, I was drowning in questions about the man I thought I'd known.

The reading of the will loomed ahead like a storm front, and with each passing day, Patricia's warnings echoed louder in my mind. Each night I found myself checking Lucy's bedroom as she slept, needing to confirm she was still there, still safe, still mine.

This morning, as I await the reading of the will, I watch her absently twirl her cereal spoon, blissfully unaware of the anxiety eating away at me. The frozen bank accounts. Peter's "changes" to his will. The credit card statement. Each inconsistency with my old life crashes over me like another wave in this relentless storm. Patricia has been my anchor through the tempest, steadying me as I opened a new bank account and moved funds from investment accounts I still had access to—but the will reading approaches like a dark thunderhead on the horizon, promising even fiercer winds to come.

Over the past week, Patricia and I have forged an unexpected connection rooted in trust. After that first surprising house call, I visited her downtown office twice— a sleek space with floor-to-ceiling windows overlooking the financial district. Her assistant, Carmen, now greets me by name, and Patricia has started addressing me as Juliette instead of Mrs. Samson. The formal distance has melted away, replaced by something that feels almost like friendship, though I know it's built on the foundation of my crisis.

During one of these visits, as we sat across from each other at her glass conference table reviewing documents, I finally worked up the courage to ask the question that had been nagging at me.

"Patricia, why did you come to my house that first morning? I mean, I appreciate it, but lawyers don't usually make house calls, especially not to people they've never met."

She paused, her pen hovering over the legal pad where she'd been taking notes. For a moment, she looked like she was weighing her words carefully, the way someone does when they're walking through a minefield.

"Someone reached out to me," she said finally, her voice measured, "letting me know you might need assistance."

My stomach tightened. "Someone? Who?"

Patricia set down her pen and clasped her hands together on the table. "Juliette, I can't—"

"Was it Michael Bennett?"

The question hung in the air between us. I'd called Patricia after Michael gave me her card, and I'd sent emails, but the house call had caught me completely off guard. No lawyer just shows up at someone's door at nine in the morning without prior arrangement.

Patricia's silence spoke volumes. She didn't confirm it, but she didn't deny it either. Instead, she looked out the window at the city below, her expression carefully neutral.

"You can't discuss it," I said, understanding flooding through me. "Attorney-client privilege or something else."

"Something like that."

I leaned back in my chair, pieces of a puzzle I hadn't known existed starting to form a picture. "Michael was always our friend and confidant. Peter and I trusted him completely. We've known him for years—he handled our house purchase, our business incorporation, everything."

As Patricia turned back to me, I caught a glimpse of something that looked like sympathy intertwined with frustration on her face.

"Sometimes in the legal profession," she said slowly, "people are put in positions where they aren't always able to help those who need it, even though they know it's the right thing to do."

The weight of her words settled over me like a heavy blanket. Michael knew something. He'd known enough to direct Patricia to me, but he wouldn't—or couldn't—tell me directly. The man who'd been one of Peter's closest friends, who'd sat at our dinner table countless times, who'd held Lucy when she was a baby, was bound by some constraint that prevented him from helping me outright.

"Professional obligations," I said quietly, understanding.

"Among other things."

I nodded, though my chest feels tight with the implications. If Michael Bennett couldn't help me personally, if he had to work around some kind of restriction to get assistance to me, then whatever Peter had done—or whatever had been done to Peter—ran deeper than I'd imagined.

THE ELEMENTARY SCHOOL comes into view, its brick facade painted with murals of rainbows and cartoon animals that scoff cheerfully against my growing dread. My lips stretch into what I hope passes for a smile when another parent waves to me as I park the car to drop Lucy off.

I kept her home for almost two weeks after Peter's passing, but she returned to school yesterday with the start of the week. To my relief, she handled it well. The resilience of children never ceases to amaze me.

"You good for another day?" I ask as I wipe away a smudge of toothpaste on Lucy's face.

She nods, her small fingers twisting the straps of her backpack. She's wearing the butterfly barrette Peter gave her for her birthday last year, the one she's insisted on wearing nearly every day since his death.

As we join the line of children and parents at the entrance, the familiar sounds of shuffling feet and excited chatter echo through the open doors, while colorful construction paper projects line the walls inside. Lucy's teacher, Ms. Carter, stands greeting students, her cardigan as bright as her usual smile—a smile that falters when she spots me. Her face pinches into something tight and concerned. My stomach contracts, that same visceral warning I've felt countless times since Peter's death. Yesterday, her expression was laced with compassion. Today, there's a darker layer.

"Good morning, Lucy!" Ms. Carter crouches to Lucy's level, her voice brightening as she regains her composure. "Why don't you go inside and put your things away? The morning puzzle is already on your desk."

Lucy hesitates, her eyes darting between us, but the allure of the puzzle prevails. She gives me a brief hug before slipping away through the door, her dark braids bouncing against her backpack.

Ms. Carter straightens, her smile evaporating like morning dew. "Mrs. Samson, can I speak with you privately after drop-off?"

Acid rises in my throat. "Is everything alright?"

"Just a matter I'd like to discuss." Her eyes slide past me to the next family in line. "Perhaps you could wait in the conference room? Second door on the left after the office."

The steady stream of cheerful greetings continues as I step aside. The conference room is small and windowless, dominated by a scratched wooden table and mismatched chairs. Children's artwork lines the walls—handprint turkeys, cotton ball snowmen, tissue paper flowers. My fingertips trace the edge of the table as I circle it, the wood worn smooth by years of worried parents' hands. The tick of the wall clock counts down minutes until the door finally opens.

Ms. Carter enters clutching a manila folder, followed

by a man I recognize as the principal, balding, in a navy suit, who seems to fill the small room with his presence.

"Mrs. Samson, I'm sure you know Principal Hoffman," Ms. Carter says as she sets the folder on the table and sits down. "I thought it best he join our conversation."

Principal Hoffman extends his hand. "Mrs. Samson. I understand you're going through a difficult time. Please, have a seat."

The plastic chair creaks as I lower myself into it. "What's this about?"

Ms. Carter exchanges a glance with the principal before speaking. "Someone came to pick up Lucy yesterday."

My pulse pounds in my ears, drowning out the ambient hum of the building. "What? Who?"

"A woman." Ms. Carter opens the folder, sliding a visitor log across the scratched surface toward me. "She said her name was Eva Lerner."

The name sounds vaguely familiar, but I can't quite place it. The handwriting on the page strikes a chord of dissonance—oddly intimate in its curved letters, as if someone had studied my own hand.

"She claimed to be Lucy's stepmother."

The air vanishes from my lungs. "Her *what*?"

"She presented documentation claiming to be authorized to pick Lucy up." Ms. Carter's voice remains steady, but her eyes betray discomfort. "Of course, we didn't release Lucy to her. Our policy requires direct parental notification for any changes to the approved pick-up list."

Sweat prickles along my hairline as heat rushes to my face. "This woman—what did she look like?"

Ms. Carter hesitates, her fingers flattening the edge of the folder. "Mid to late thirties. Brown hair. Very put-together. Professional clothing, tasteful jewelry."

Recognition crystallizes, sharp and painful. The woman from the funeral. The one speaking to Peter's mother.

"Who is she?" My voice comes from somewhere far away, as if someone else is speaking for me.

Principal Hoffman leans forward, his cologne momentarily overwhelming in the small space. "She claimed to be married to your late husband, ma'am. She showed a marriage certificate."

I feel myself sway, caught between a startling clarity and a hazy confusion, as if time has stretched and warped around me. The frozen accounts. The divorce filing. Now, a marriage certificate? They're all connected—an elaborate fiction someone is constructing around my life, around Peter's death.

"That's impossible." The words scrape my throat. "I was married to Peter for twelve years. We were never divorced. This woman—whoever she is—is lying."

Ms. Carter slides another document across the table. "She also provided this."

My eyes fix on a school emergency contact form. My signature—or what appears to be my signature—authorizes Eva Lerner as an emergency contact and approved guardian for Lucy, dated last week. The pen strokes mock me, each loop and curve a near-perfect replica of my handwriting.

"I never signed this." My hands tremble so badly the text blurs before my eyes. "I've never heard of Eva Lerner. I never authorized anyone to pick up Lucy except myself, her father, and my friend Alison Cole."

The couple of months flash through my memory—coordinating with Alison to pick Lucy up several times while I kept vigil at Peter's hospital bed, the endless paperwork at the funeral home, the financial chaos—but I never signed any documents adding anyone as Lucy's guardian.

Principal Hoffman clears his throat. "Mrs. Samson, you can understand our position. We have conflicting documentation and claims about Lucy's family situation."

"There is no conflict." Bile rises in the back of my throat, metallic and bitter. "I am Lucy's mother. Her only parent now that her father has died. This Eva Lerner is a stranger—a fraud—and I want her nowhere near my daughter."

Those carefully forged curves and lines on the form seem to taunt me, challenging my very identity as Lucy's mother. The same careful mimicry I'd seen on those divorce papers.

Ms. Carter touches my arm gently. "Juliette, no one is questioning that you're Lucy's mother. We just needed to make you aware of the situation."

Pushing the form back toward her, I struggle to keep my voice from breaking. "I want this woman's name removed from all school records immediately. This signature is forged. I never authorized this."

"Of course." Principal Hoffman takes the form, his expression carefully neutral. "We'll update our records and flag any unauthorized pickup attempts. But given the... unusual circumstances, we'll need to see legal documentation confirming your status as Lucy's sole guardian."

The implication sends heat crawling up my neck. My hands shake as I pull out my phone and tap through to my email. "I have Lucy's birth certificate right here. And—" I scroll through photos, finding one of Lucy's passport. "These confirm I'm Lucy's mother."

They examine the documents, exchanging glances that make my stomach twist.

"We'll make copies for our records," Principal Hoffman

says finally. "And I suggest we implement a password system for Lucy's pickup—a word only you would know."

"Astronomy," I say. "It was Peter's passion. And Lucy knows all the planets by heart."

Ms. Carter scribbles a note. "We'll implement that immediately."

"And I need to know if this woman—or anyone unfamiliar—shows up asking about Lucy again." The zipper of my purse catches as I yank it closed. "I need to be notified as soon as possible."

"Of course." Principal Hoffman stands, chair legs scraping against the linoleum. "We take student safety very seriously, Mrs. Samson."

The hallway feels too bright compared to the conference room, children's voices echoing off the walls as they transition between activities. My legs carry me toward the exit on autopilot, driven by a desperate need to check on Lucy, to see her with my own eyes. But Ms. Carter's words stop me at the door.

"She's safe in class, Mrs. Samson. I promise."

Outside, the November air hits my flushed face, carrying the musty scent of fall leaves. I lean against the brick wall of the school, its rough texture grounding me as I try to regain my composure.

Across the street, a dark sedan with tinted windows idles at the curb. The hair on my arms rises as I notice the driver's silhouette becoming visible—a woman, her face obscured, watching the school.

My body moves before conscious thought forms. I push away from the wall, striding toward the street, phone in hand to capture the license plate. The sedan's engine growls to life. By the time my feet hit the curb, it's pulling away, turning the corner with deliberate speed.

I stand frozen on the sidewalk, heart hammering

against my ribs like it's trying to escape. There was no mistaking the intent—she was watching. Waiting.

For Lucy? For me?

My thumb finds Patricia's contact almost instinctively. Whatever game this Eva Lerner is playing, whatever she wants with my daughter, I need to stop her now.

As the phone rings, I glance back at the school building where Lucy sits inside, drawing or reading or practicing her addition, blissfully unaware of the battle beginning to rage around her. The playground equipment stands stark against the fall sky—the swing set where Peter pushed her every Sunday afternoon, the slide they raced down together on the day of her kindergarten orientation.

Something fierce and protective rises in me, displacing the fear. I squeeze my free hand into a fist, my fingernails pressing into my palm, allowing me to focus on the sharp sting rather than the trembling that threatens to overwhelm me.

Patricia answers on the third ring. "Torres."

"It's Juliette." My voice steadies with each word, charged with purpose. "Someone tried to take Lucy from school yesterday. She's claiming to be Peter's wife and Lucy's stepmother."

A beat of silence, just the sound of papers shuffling. "Where are you now?"

"Outside the school. I think she was just watching me from a car."

"Meet me at that coffee shop by Michael's office." Patricia's voice is clipped, practical. "Bring any documentation the school showed you. We can go over it before we head to the reading of Peter's will."

"This woman—Eva Lerner—she forged my signature on a school form."

"Get a copy of that document. We're building a pattern

of fraudulent activity." Patricia pauses, her breath audible through the phone. "Juliette, do you have any idea who this woman might be? Any connection to Peter you might not have considered?"

The questions settle in me like stones I can't swallow. "No."

"Alright. I'm heading to a meeting right now, but I'll see you soon."

8

The coffee shop near Michael Bennett's office buzzes with mid-morning energy. Patricia sits across from me, hair pulled into a tight bun, as usual, reviewing the copy of the school form bearing the forged signature through narrowed eyes. The overhead lights catch on her silver watch as she compares the form to a printed copy of the divorce decree. She exhales slowly, the first sound between us in nearly two minutes.

"The handwriting is similar." She places both documents side by side. "Whoever did this spent time studying your signature."

I lean forward, examining the curves and loops meant to mimic my own. "They're good forgeries."

"Professional level." Patricia's finger traces the signature on the divorce papers. "Notice the loops and the slight hesitation on the 't' crossing? Identical on both documents."

The chair feels less solid under me. Someone studied my handwriting, practiced it, perfected it—now they're using it to strip me of my identity piece by piece.

"We need a handwriting expert." Patricia slips the documents into protective sleeves with the precision of someone handling crime scene evidence. "But first, we need to get through this will reading."

I check my watch—9:47. "We should head over."

Patricia tucks the documents into her leather portfolio and fixes me with a steady gaze. "Remember what we discussed. Maintain composure regardless of what happens."

We walk the three blocks to Michael's office in silence, my mind churning through possibilities. What other surprises wait for me? Who is Eva Lerner, and what does she want with my daughter?

The Victorian facade of Bennett Legal Services stands before us, its gabled roof and ornate trim transformed from charming to sinister since my last visit. I pause at the bottom of the brick steps, slowing my breath—in for four, out for six—like Dr. Weller taught me after Lucy was born.

Patricia places a firm hand on my elbow. "Let them see nothing but strength."

Sarah, the receptionist, offers a tight smile. "They're waiting for you in the conference room, Mrs. Samson."

Despite the fact Sarah used to be less formal with me, after what we've discovered, the "Mrs." feels like a small victory. Sarah's eyes dart away when I try to meet her gaze, her fingers fidgeting with papers that don't need arranging. The same attendant who accompanied Margaret to Peter's funeral sits on the sofa across from Sarah's desk. I exchange nods with him as we walk past.

The conference room door stands half-open, voices spilling into the hallway. A woman's laugh—light, practiced, unfamiliar—cuts through the murmur of conversation, followed by Sebastian's deeper tones. Something about the sound raises the small hairs on the back of my neck.

Patricia squeezes my arm once before I push the door fully open.

The room falls silent. Four faces turn toward us. Michael rises from his chair at the head of the long mahogany table, his expression carefully neutral. Sebastian sits to his right, immaculate in a navy suit, fingers steepled before him. Peter's mother occupies the chair beside him, her silver hair arranged in its usual perfect coiffure, though her eyes are red-rimmed. She blinks at me twice, a moment of confusion crossing her face before recognition dawns.

And then—that woman.

She sits directly across from Michael in what would traditionally be the position of honor. Her posture is perfect, hands folded demurely on the table. Soft chestnut hair falls in gentle waves around a face constructed to display appropriate grief. The black dress she wears could have come from my own closet—conservative cut, subtle jewel neckline, three-quarter sleeves. A thin gold band gleams on her left ring finger.

The woman from the funeral. Eva Lerner.

Her eyes—a warm hazel that calculates even as they soften—meet mine. "Juliette. I'm so sorry we're meeting formally under these circumstances."

The familiar way she says my name—as though we've shared confidences, as though she belongs in my life— sends a chill radiating from my spine to my fingertips.

Patricia's hand at my back guides me forward. "Mrs. Samson and I apologize for the delay. I'm Patricia Torres, Mrs. Samson's attorney."

Michael clears his throat, tugging at his collar. "Yes, well. Please have a seat. Now that everyone is here, we can begin." He shuffles papers in front of him. "Before I read Peter's will, I should introduce everyone present. Sebastian Dorsey, business partner. Margaret Samson, Peter's mother." He hesitates, then continues, "And Eva Lerner Samson, Peter's legal wife."

My breath catches as the fragile scaffolding of my denial finally gives way. Despite the mounting signals, the scattered details, the fragments I'd unearthed since Peter's funeral, some part of me refused to believe any of it until now.

"Excuse me." Patricia's voice cuts through the buzzing in my ears. "But *my* client is Peter Samson's legal wife. There is no documentation of a legal divorce, making any subsequent marriage invalid."

Michael's expression tightens. "I have documentation indicating otherwise." He pulls several papers from a folder, sliding them across the table. "These divorce papers show the dissolution of Peter and Juliette Samson's marriage five months ago."

Patricia examines the papers without touching them. "These documents bear a forged signature. My client never signed divorce papers because no divorce was ever discussed or started."

"Peter explained Juliette's... difficulty accepting the end of their marriage." Eva's voice drops to a syrupy whisper. She pauses after "difficulty," the slight emphasis turning the word into something clinical, pathological. "He was very patient throughout the process."

From the corner of my eye, I catch Margaret nodding slightly.

Sebastian leans forward, hands spread in a gesture of reasonableness. "Perhaps we should simply proceed with the reading? Out of respect for Peter's final wishes."

My nails dig into my palms as I clench my fists in my

lap. Breathe. Stay calm. This coordinated performance—the calculated concern etched into every line of their faces, the synthetic sympathy dripping from their voices like honey laced with poison, the carefully constructed narrative they've woven around my supposed mental fragility—leaves me reeling, dizzy with a fury so pure and white-hot it threatens to consume me whole, while disbelief crashes over me in waves, each one more devastating than the last.

Patricia sits ramrod straight. "For the record, we dispute the validity of any divorce proceeding and, consequently, any subsequent marriage. We will be filing formal challenges to both."

Michael appears unmoved, though a faint sheen of sweat has appeared on his forehead. "Your concerns are noted. However, for today's purposes, we will proceed with the reading of the will as executed by the deceased."

He opens a leather portfolio and adjusts his glasses. "I, Peter Andrew Samson, being of sound mind and body, hereby declare this to be my Last Will and Testament, revoking all previous wills and codicils..."

Legal jargon fades to background noise as I study Eva. Her expression remains fixed in somber attention, her deceptive sympathy never wavering under my gaze. Through the window behind her, bare branches claw at a colorless November sky.

"...to my wife, Eva Lerner Samson, I bequeath the entirety of my estate, including but not limited to our family home on Oakwood Drive, all financial assets and investments, and my controlling interest in SD Title & Escrow."

The words knock something loose inside me—some fundamental certainty I'd never questioned until now. My existence distorts and recalibrates around this new impossibility.

"Additionally, I name Eva Lerner Samson as the guardian of my daughter, Lucy Elizabeth Samson, with all rights and responsibilities thereto—"

"Absolutely not." The words tear from my throat before Patricia can stop me. "Lucy is my daughter. My biological child. Peter cannot unilaterally assign guardianship to anyone."

Patricia places a restraining hand on my arm. "My client is correct. Under state law, a father cannot remove custody from a biological mother who has not been legally determined unfit. Regardless of the validity of these other claims, the guardianship provision is not legally enforceable without a separate court determination."

Michael removes his glasses, rubbing the bridge of his nose. "The guardianship will require separate proceedings, yes. However, the remainder of the will stands pending any legal challenge."

Eva's expression shifts minutely—a tightening around the eyes, a slight downward pull at the corners of her mouth. Disappointment glimpsed through a crack in her mask.

Sebastian breaks the tense silence. "I think we all want what's best for Lucy." His words sound reasonable, though his eyes remain cold. "A smooth transition would be easiest on her during this difficult time."

My pulse hammers in my temples. "There will be no 'transition.' Lucy stays with me. She has always been with me."

"Of course," Eva murmurs. "No one wants to upset Lucy *unnecessarily*." The slight emphasis transforms the word into a veiled threat.

Patricia straightens her papers. "For the record, my client contests every aspect of this will on the basis that the divorce proceedings were fraudulent, making the subsequent marriage void and the will invalid as it relies on that marriage."

"Your concerns are again noted." Michael begins gathering his papers. "The assets will remain frozen pending legal determinations. As for the house..." He hesitates. "Eva has legal claim as the named beneficiary, but given the dispute, I suggest maintaining the status quo until matters are settled."

Eva's lips curve into something that mimics compassion, but her eyes remain calculating, assessing my reaction. "I'm perfectly willing to be reasonable about the house. Lucy's stability is my primary concern."

The room shrinks. Sebastian, Michael, even Margaret —they all nod along as if Eva belongs here. As if I'm the intruder.

Patricia maintains her professional demeanor as the meeting dissolves into legal discussions about temporary arrangements and court filings. I sit frozen, watching these strangers dismantle my life with paperwork and measured tones.

As we prepare to leave, Eva approaches me. The others are engaged in conversation near the door, their voices a distant hum.

"Juliette." Her tone drops to a low whisper, just between us. "I know this is difficult. Peter told me about your episodes after Lucy was born. For her sake, please don't make this harder than it needs to be."

The oxygen vanishes from my lungs as if someone has sucked all the air from the room. My hospitalization for postpartum depression—two weeks of absolute darkness nearly seven years ago when Lucy was barely a month old. A chapter of my life that Peter and I buried deep, never discussed with anyone except my doctor and the therapists who helped me crawl back to the surface. The most vulnerable, broken, and terrifying period I've ever experienced.

Those sleepless nights when I couldn't bond with my own baby, when I questioned every maternal instinct, when the world felt like it was disintegrating around me. Peter held me through it all, promised me it would stay between us, that no one would ever use my struggle against me.

How could she possibly know? The medical records are private. Peter wouldn't have—couldn't have—shared something so personal, so sacred between us. Yet here she stands, wielding my deepest shame like a scalpel, cutting precisely where it will cause the most damage.

Eva's smile remains fixed, but something predatory flickers in her eyes—satisfaction at having landed a blow. She's revealing the depth of whatever Peter shared with her—or what she somehow learned.

"You don't know anything about my daughter or me." My voice emerges somehow despite the hurricane inside. "You won't get away with this."

"I already have." The words slide between us, barely audible as she turns away, rejoining Sebastian with a gentle touch to his arm.

Patricia guides me from the room. In the hallway, she speaks in hushed tones about emergency filings and expert witnesses. I nod mechanically, still reeling from Eva's words.

This isn't a random con or opportunistic fraud. This woman has methodically excavated my life, unearthing every private struggle and intimate detail. She hasn't just targeted Peter's assets—she's trying to replace me as Peter's wife and Lucy's mother.

And somehow, she's convinced the people around us—people who should know better—to help her do it.

Outside, the November wind slices through my coat.

Bare trees lining the street bend and sway, stripped of everything that once defined them.

"We have work to do," Patricia says, already dialing on her phone. "This is just the beginning of the fight."

I stare back at the Victorian building, its windows reflecting gray clouds. Whatever game Eva Lerner is playing, I'm now certain of one thing: she didn't choose me at random.

She wants my life. All of it.

And she's prepared to take it piece by piece.

9

____

Eva's offhand mention of my postpartum depression continues to steal the ground from beneath me, tilting the world sideways as my most guarded secret becomes conversation fodder. That sacred wound, still tender beneath its scars, now lies exposed in her casual possession.

How could Peter have told her something so private, so raw? That period—my darkest moments, where my thoughts were utterly mangled—now weaponized against me by a woman who has infiltrated my life.

Patricia and I walk back to the coffee shop, but my perception has fractured—everything around me undulates and shifts, solid ground transformed into something treacherous and uncertain. She continues strategizing beside me, but her words blur into white noise. All I can hear is Eva's voice: *Peter told me about your episodes after Lucy was born.*

Episodes. As if those weeks of gloom were mere fits of hysteria rather than a clinical condition I sought proper treatment for. As if being a responsible mother who recognized she needed help could be twisted into something shameful.

We walk past the coffee shop and make it to our cars in the parking lot. "We'll file the petition to contest the will first thing tomorrow," Patricia says. "The signature challenges will slow things down, but we need to move quickly on Lucy's custody—that's where they'll strike next."

I nod dumbly as I open the door to my car. "How did this happen?"

Patricia shakes her head. "Honestly, I've never seen a scheme this sophisticated." She places her hand on my shoulder. "When you get home, start putting together a timeline of your and Peter's activities."

I nod again. It's all I can do.

"I'll have someone in my office contact the county clerk's office to determine the paper trail for these documents Eva is using."

I plop into the driver's seat of my car. Patricia places her hand on my shoulder. "We'll figure out what's going on. I'll call you later with updates. Lock your doors, Juliette. And pack an emergency bag—just in case."

I SOMEHOW MAKE it back to our house. From the outside, it still looks like home—fall wreath on the door, Lucy's chalk drawings decorating the driveway, jack-o-lanterns grinning from the porch with smiles that have started to sag now that Halloween is over. But the house feels like nothing more than a theater set now, its familiar contours framing an unfamiliar narrative where I'm being written out of my own story.

The grandfather clock Peter inherited and spent months restoring chimes with mechanical precision as I come in from the garage, indifferent to the chaos engulfing me.

I need to gather proof of my life—our life—before someone steals more of it.

I head to our master bedroom first, retrieving our wedding album from the built-in bookcase. The corners are slightly worn from the many times Lucy has flipped through it, asking questions about "when Mommy was a princess." I place it on the bed, then pull out photo albums, tax returns, anniversary cards—anything that documents our continuous marriage.

In the closet, Peter's clothes still hang beside mine, his dress shirts arranged by color as he always kept them. I run my fingers along the fabric, finding a strange comfort in their presence. The scent of his cologne lingers faintly, like a ghost haunting the cotton and wool. I remove a stack of shoeboxes from the upper shelf, searching for old letters or cards.

A small noise from downstairs freezes me mid-reach.

I hold my breath, listening. The house creaks and settles, but underneath that familiar sound is something else. The unmistakable click of the front door closing.

Someone is in my house.

I move toward the bedroom door, keeping close to the wall. Voices drift up from below—male voices speaking in hushed tones. One of them is unmistakably Sebastian's.

"Just get the external drives and the laptop," he's saying. "The filing cabinet in the study has the lease agreements."

"What if she comes back?" another voice asks.

"She's meeting with her lawyer. We have time."

I edge to the doorway, peering down the hall. The tops of their heads are visible down below through the railing on the landing. I scan the room for a weapon, anything I could use to defend myself. The lamp on the nightstand is heavy crystal, a wedding gift from Peter's aunt. I unplug it, gripping its base, feeling the cold weight against my palm.

Clutching the lamp with both hands, I creep down the stairs as they disappear into our study. When I reach the foyer, the study door stands half-open, light spilling into the corridor.

I need to get my phone from the kitchen, but I bump into one of the many vases of flowers from the funeral still in the foyer.

Sebastian's shadow goes still. "Did you hear that?"

I abandon stealth and rush for the kitchen, my stockinged feet sliding on the polished wood. I'm almost there when Sebastian emerges from the study.

"Juliette! I didn't realize you were home." His voice is smooth, unruffled. As if he hadn't just broken into my house.

I stop, turning to face him with the lamp still in my hands. The other man appears behind Sebastian— younger, wearing a suit similar to Sebastian's but less expensive, his expression uncomfortable.

"What are you doing in my home?" My voice emerges from somewhere cold and hard within me.

Sebastian steps closer, his mouth turned down at the corners, his eyes wide with manufactured concern. "I should have called first, I apologize. Eva asked me to collect some documents from Peter's study."

"Eva asked you?" The words taste acrid in my mouth, like the time I accidentally bit into an aspirin. "She has no right to authorize anyone to enter my house or remove anything from it."

"Actually, as the beneficiary of Peter's estate, she does." Sebastian steps closer, but still maintains a careful distance from me and the lamp. "Eva received the keys from Peter before he died. She gave them to me so I could retrieve necessary company property."

"You're stealing from me."

Sebastian sighs, as if I'm being unreasonable. "Juliette, I understand this is confusing for you, but these are company materials." He shrugs. "And now Eva and I are majority owners of the business."

"If you needed those documents, you could have called me." I raise the lamp slightly. "Instead, you broke into my home."

The other man adjusts his grip on Peter's laptop and some external hard drives, while struggling to keep several folders secured under his arm.

"We didn't break in." Sebastian's tone hardens slightly. "We have a key and authorization from Peter's legal wife. I'm simply executing my responsibilities as managing partner."

"Put everything back." I step forward. "Now."

Sebastian shakes his head, a flash of something cold crossing his features before the mask of concern returns. "I'm afraid I can't do that. But I'll make sure Eva knows you're upset about the miscommunication."

Without taking my eyes off them, I step backward into the kitchen and reach for my phone on the counter. "I'm calling the police."

"Go ahead." Sebastian gestures to his associate, who heads for the door with Peter's belongings. "By all means, involve the authorities. They'll be very interested to hear how you're interfering with someone authorized to safe-guard company assets."

I hit the emergency call button. The signal vanishes with a beep.

Sebastian's thin smile spreads across his face. "Network problems? How unfortunate."

I lunge for the landline on the hallway table, the only one in our house, but Sebastian is faster. He rips the cord from the wall, letting it dangle from his fingertips.

"There's really nothing you can do about this, Juliette." His voice is almost gentle now, which somehow makes it worse. "Eva has legal standing. You don't."

"Get out of my house."

He holds up his hands in mock surrender. "Don't worry. We're leaving." He follows his associate to the door, then pauses. "You know, Peter was worried about you toward the end. He told Eva how obsessive you'd become, how you couldn't accept that things had changed. He was afraid of what you might do."

My fingers tighten around the lamp's base. "Peter would never say that."

"You'd be surprised what he shared with her." Sebastian steps outside, then turns back. "I'll tell Eva you're still having... difficulties. Perhaps she'll reconsider the custody arrangements for Lucy's safety."

His words about my daughter make my stomach drop, as if I'm free-falling through empty space. Resisting the urge to throw the lamp at his retreating figure, I set it down and hold up my phone instead.

"I've been recording this entire conversation." The lie comes easily. "Breaking and entering. Theft of personal property. Threats against my daughter. How do you think that will play in court?"

Sebastian's expression transforms to one of amusement. "You always were more clever than Peter gave you credit for. But recording or not, there's nothing you can do to stop what's coming."

He closes the door behind him with a quiet click.

I rush to lock it, then watch as they load the items into the back of Sebastian's sleek black Escalade. After they drive away, I slide down against the wall until I'm sitting on the floor, my limbs trembling like I've been standing in the cold too long.

They've taken Peter's laptop. His external drives. Most of his business files. Evidence I desperately needed.

I force myself to calm down and try my phone again. One bar of service flickers to life. I call 911 and report the break-in and theft.

While waiting for the police, I check what remains of our study. The ransacking was methodical—they knew exactly what they wanted

THIRTY MINUTES LATER, two officers arrive. Officer Davis, a woman with tired eyes and a neat bun, takes notes as I explain the situation. The other officer, Reyes, a towering figure with a military-style crew cut, stands nearby, observing.

"So this woman—Eva—has documentation showing she's… your deceased husband's wife?" she asks, her pen pausing mid-sentence. She looks confused and earnest at the same time.

"I know this doesn't really make sense," I say. "She claims to have divorce papers and a marriage certificate, but they're forgeries. I know because I never signed anything."

Reyes exchanges a glance with his partner. "And this business associate of your husband's—"

"Sebastian Dorsey," Officer Davis says.

"He had a key?" Reyes finishes.

"He says Eva gave it to him. But it's my house—she had no right. They stole my husband's personal effects," I say.

Officer Davis taps her pen against her notebook. "Ma'am, if he had a key and authorization from the estate's beneficiary, this becomes a civil matter rather than criminal. I understand you're disputing the estate proceedings, but until that's resolved legally..."

I catch the doubt in her expression—that careful neutrality that says she's not sure which party is telling the truth. "You don't believe me."

"We'll document everything in the report," Officer Reyes says. "But you'll need to address this through your attorney."

After they leave, I call Patricia and explain what happened. Her sharp intake of breath says everything.

"I'll add this to the filing for the emergency injunction," she says. "They're escalating faster than I expected. In the meantime, take photos and check if there's anything they overlooked. Anything at all."

I hang up and return to our study, photographing the empty spaces where his equipment should be. As I close the filing cabinet drawer, something catches my eye—a photograph on the carpet, partially hidden under the desk. I kneel to retrieve it.

The photograph pulls the air from my lungs like a vacuum.

It's Peter, smiling broadly with his arm around Eva on a beach. Behind them, palm trees lean toward the sunset. He wears board shorts I recognize—blue with a faint pattern of hibiscus. I bought them for him several years ago, before our vacation to Hawaii.

The room seems to shift around me, the walls appearing to breathe and pulse, the foundation beneath my feet destabilized. My vision blurs at the edges, and I grip the desk to steady myself as the pieces of evidence cascade through my mind like a relentless avalanche. I can't deny this photograph, which captures a moment of intimacy between my husband and Eva.

The evidence forms a constellation of betrayal, each point of light connecting to reveal a picture I'd been blind to see. Peter and Eva, together in ways that shatter everything I believed about my marriage, my life, my reality.

I turn the photo over. Written in Peter's handwriting: *Cabo.*

The date stamped on the back is from two years ago. I strain to recall what was happening during that time. Without Peter's laptop, I can't check his calendar. But I close my eyes, mentally scrolling back through those days. Lucy would have been four, in preschool. Then it hits me. Peter had told me he was attending a conference in Los Angeles.

I sink into the chair, the photograph trembling between my fingertips.

If Peter really was secretly seeing Eva... if he did introduce her to his mother... could the divorce papers be real after all? Could I have somehow blocked it from my memory, the way victims sometimes suppress trauma?

No. I touch the photograph, studying Peter's face. Whatever this is, whatever Peter was doing, I did not sign divorce papers. I did not forget our marriage ending.

I set the photograph on the desk and press my palms against my eyes. Everything I thought I knew about my husband, my marriage, my life, has been called into question. But one certainty remains: Lucy is my daughter, and no one—not Sebastian, not Eva, not even Peter's ghost—will take her from me.

I return to our master bedroom where my pile of evidence lies scattered across the bed. Our wedding album. Anniversary and birthday cards. Mementos of a shared life that might have been built on lies.

I need to reimagine my approach. If Peter betrayed me, I need to face that squarely. But first, I need to secure my daughter's future.

I gather everything and place it in a secure location—a locked cabinet in the closet of our guest room. Then I begin packing a bag for Lucy and myself, just as Patricia suggested. Clothes, toiletries, Lucy's favorite stuffed rabbit, her nightlight, her favorite pajamas.

Peter might have hidden things from me. Eva might try to steal my identity. Sebastian might raid my home.

But they all underestimate what they're up against: a mother who will do anything to protect her child.

I check the time. Two-thirty. Lucy will be done with school soon. I need to compose myself before picking her up. She can't see my fear, my uncertainty. For now, she needs stability, and I'm the only one who can provide it.

I place the beach photograph into a zippered compartment of my purse. One more piece of evidence in this twisted puzzle. One more reason for me to doubt everything I thought was true.

10

———

I barely make it to Lucy's school in time for pickup. I try to put on a smile when I see her, but it feels fixed and brittle. The drive home passes in a blur of red lights and turn signals, with my hands clenching the steering wheel as if it were the only solid thing in a world suddenly turned to quicksand. Lucy's eyes flick toward me in the rearview mirror, questions forming but never leaving her lips.

Once home, I shut the garage door with a click, and Lucy drops her backpack by the stairs. Her small fingers twist around the hem of her shirt, a nervous habit she's had since she was a toddler.

"Mommy, is everything okay?"

My heart sinks. I kneel down to her level, tucking a strand of hair behind her ear. "Of course, sweetie. Why do you ask?"

"You didn't sing along to the radio. You always sing, even when you say you can't."

I force a smile. "I'm just a little tired today. Nothing for you to worry about."

Lucy's eyes—so much like Peter's—search mine with a

wisdom beyond her years. She doesn't believe me, not completely, but she nods anyway.

"How about mac and cheese for dinner?" I ask, standing up and heading toward the kitchen.

"With the spiral noodles?"

"Is there any other kind worth eating?"

Lucy giggles and follows me, climbing onto a stool at the counter while I fill a pot with water. I measure pasta, preheat the oven for garlic bread, check her take-home folder—all the normal routines we've always had. But beneath every ordinary action, my mind can't let go of all that's happened today.

When bedtime comes, I read until my voice grows hoarse—princesses and dragons and happy endings— watching her eyelids grow heavy with each page turn. I'd give anything to have her innocence right now. To believe in fairy tales again.

Her breathing deepens into sleep, and I sneak out of her room. I circle the darkened house with the photograph of Peter and Eva in my trembling fingers. What am I even looking for? Some clue that this isn't real? I tilt it under every lamp, squinting at shadows and backgrounds for anything I might have overlooked, but all I can see is Peter looking back at me. Those eyes I trusted. That smile I fell for.

I thought I knew him. How could I have been so blind? We loved each other. Or was that just another lie? How could he betray me like this?

It's morning again, and my eyelids feel like they're lined with sandpaper as I navigate the traffic toward the court-house. The evidence Patricia requested sits on the passenger seat, in a folder containing the Cabo photo and other documents I'd gathered. My temples throb from lack of sleep—every time I'd closed my eyes, I'd seen Sebastian's smug expression as he walked away with Peter's laptop or imagined Eva reaching for Lucy.

The courthouse appears ahead—a blocky concrete structure with none of the grandeur promised by television legal dramas. Just a utilitarian building where lives are dismantled and reassembled according to statutes and precedents. Security waves me through the metal detector, my heels striking against the linoleum with each step, the sound bouncing off the cavernous lobby's walls.

Patricia waits by the elevators, her crisp navy suit making me suddenly aware of my own appearance. This morning, I'd spent forty minutes trying to make myself presentable—covering dark circles with concealer, applying mascara with shaking hands, blow-drying hair that refused to cooperate. Despite these efforts, the bathroom mirror had reflected sunken eyes and skin that looked almost translucent under the harsh lighting.

"Ready?" Patricia asks, shifting her briefcase to press the elevator button.

The question seems absurd. How could anyone be ready for this?

"As I'll ever be," I manage, smoothing my black pencil skirt. I'd chosen a conservative outfit—charcoal blazer, cream blouse, minimal jewelry—hoping to project strength and competence. The clothes feel like a costume now, an attempt to play the role of someone who hasn't had their life stolen from beneath them.

"Remember," Patricia says as we enter the elevator, "Judge Kemp is known for prioritizing children's stability. Focus on Lucy needing to stay in familiar surroundings. We have a strong case for the emergency injunction while the larger issues get sorted."

I nod, one hand resting on my purse, where I have a small photo album showing Lucy and me together through the years—tangible evidence of our bond that no forged document could erase.

The courtroom is smaller than I'd expected, with worn wooden benches that have absorbed decades of anxious fidgeting and whispered consultations. Patricia and I take our seats at one of the tables facing the judge's bench. I catch my foot bouncing under the table and press it firmly to the ground, channeling all that nervous energy into the solid contact between my heel and the courthouse floor.

The door at the rear of the courtroom opens. My spine stiffens as Eva enters, wearing a modest navy dress with her hair pulled back in a simple ponytail—the perfect picture of demure grief. But it's the woman beside her who makes my chest tighten—Karla Winters, whose reputation precedes her. I've read about her involvement in local celebrity cases, watched her post-trial interviews where she maintained a veneer of professionalism while systematically dismantling her opponents' cases.

This isn't a casual hearing anymore. They've brought in heavy artillery.

Eva keeps her eyes lowered as she sits at the opposite table. Her attorney leans toward her, whispering something that makes Eva nod solemnly.

"All rise," the bailiff announces, and Judge Kemp enters—a woman in her sixties with salt-and-pepper hair cropped close to her head and rectangular glasses perched on a prominent nose.

"Your Honor," Patricia begins after preliminaries, "we're seeking an emergency injunction to prevent my client's eviction from her family home while probate matters are resolved. Mrs. Samson has lived in this residence for eight years. Being forced out would cause significant trauma to her six-year-old daughter who has just lost her father."

Judge Kemp nods, making notes with a silver pen. "Ms. Winters?"

Karla Winters stands with deliberate slowness, her expensive suit rustling softly. Her eyes scan the courtroom before settling on the judge with focused intensity.

"Your Honor, we have no intention of creating instability for the child. However, Eva Lerner Samson is Peter Samson's legal widow and the rightful owner of the property." She reaches into her leather portfolio and withdraws a thick manila folder. "We've prepared documentation that speaks not only to the property rights but to serious concerns about Juliette Samson's fitness as Lucy's primary caregiver."

Patricia tenses beside me. "Objection, Your Honor. This hearing is specifically about the residential injunction. Custody matters—"

"—are inextricably linked to housing stability," Winters completes smoothly. She approaches the bench and hands the folder to the judge. "If you'll review these documents, you'll see why these matters cannot be separated. Your Honor, we have photographic evidence of my client with both Peter and Lucy Samson on outings and involved in other routine activities in family life. We also have sworn affidavits from two of Mr. Samson's colleagues who witnessed him with Mrs. Lerner Samson and his daughter on multiple occasions, referring to them in public as 'his girls'."

I feel the blood drain from my face. Peter didn't do that. Did he?

As Judge Kemp opens the folder, Winters pivots to face

both the judge and the gallery. Her voice modulates perfectly—authoritative without aggression, concerned without appearing theatrical.

"Furthermore, included in those materials are medical records documenting Ms. Samson's hospitalization for severe postpartum depression following Lucy's birth, including episodes that placed both mother and infant at risk."

A concrete block settles inside me, growing heavier with each word she utters. Those records are private—accessible only to me, Peter, and my doctors. My face flushes hot, then cold as the most vulnerable period of my life is displayed in this sterile room.

Patricia rises immediately, her chair scraping against the floor. "Your Honor, I object in the strongest possible terms. These medical records are confidential. Their inclusion violates HIPAA protections and my client's privacy rights."

Winters reacts before the judge can respond. "Your Honor, they were provided by Peter Samson himself before his death, as part of their divorce proceedings. Frankly, my client's main concern is the child's welfare. While Ms. Samson's grief is understandable, her recent erratic behavior, including numerous tearful and confusing voicemails, suggests that the instability documented six years ago may still be a present-day concern."

"There were no divorce proceedings!" The words escape me before I can stop them, my voice strained and too high.

Judge Kemp raises a hand. "Ms. Samson, please allow your attorney to speak for you."

Karla Winters tilts her head slightly, her expression shifting to one of calculated sympathy. "Your Honor, that emotional outburst is precisely the kind of instability that concerns my client. Mrs. Lerner Samson only wants what Peter wanted: a peaceful, stable environment for Lucy. She is willing to cooperate in any way to achieve that."

Patricia leans close to me. "Let me handle this," she whispers, then addresses the court. "Your Honor, my client categorically denies any divorce proceedings were initiated. Moreover, the alleged transfer of confidential medical records by her late husband still constitutes a violation of her privacy rights."

Winters responds, "With respect, Your Honor, Ms. Samson has a documented history of fugue states during her postpartum period. It's entirely possible she doesn't remember the divorce discussions." She gestures toward the medical documents. "These records clearly show episodes where she lost time and awareness, requiring hospitalization."

The courtroom blurs at the edges. Fugue states? There had been one terrifying night when, sleep-deprived and hormonally devastated, I'd found myself in Lucy's nursery with no memory of how I'd gotten there. I'd sought help immediately afterward. My nerves wind tighter than thread around a bobbin as I realize how Winters has transformed one frightening episode into a pattern of mental instability.

"That's a gross mischaracterization of my client's medical history," Patricia counters, her voice steady despite the slight reddening at her neck—the only sign of her fury. "She was diagnosed with postpartum depression, received appropriate treatment, and has been stable for years. There have been no subsequent mental health issues."

Judge Kemp adjusts her glasses as she reads through the documents, her expression giving away nothing. "Ms. Winters, how do you respond to the allegation that these proceedings never occurred?"

Winters produces another folder with the smooth efficiency of a magician revealing a card. "We have emails between the couple discussing their separation agreement, Your Honor."

She hands copies to Patricia and me. My fingers go numb as I look down at conversations I never had, discussing a divorce I never agreed to. The emails show my account address, but the words belong to a stranger. One particularly damning message shows "me" acknowledging Peter's relationship with Eva and expressing willingness to step aside for Lucy's sake.

I scan the document, my breath catching. The forgeries are meticulous—my habit of using ellipses mid-thought, my tendency to reference old movies Peter and I had watched together, even the sign-off I sometimes used with him. Someone had studied my writing patterns with obsessive attention to detail.

"These are fabricated," I whisper to Patricia, who nods once, sharply.

"Your Honor," Patricia says, "we contest the authenticity of these emails and will submit them for forensic analysis. My client didn't write them."

Judge Kemp sighs, setting both sets of documents aside. She removes her glasses, pinching the bridge of her nose for a long moment before speaking. "The court is faced with a difficult situation," she begins, her voice measured. "On one hand, we have Ms. Samson, the child's long-term primary caregiver. On the other, we have Mrs. Lerner Samson, who presents a valid marriage certificate and documentation—including photographic evidence— suggesting an established relationship with the child, endorsed by the deceased father."

She places her glasses back on. "The inclusion of Ms. Samson's medical history is troubling, but it, combined with her categorical denial of any marital problems in the face of contradictory evidence, forces the court to consider all possibilities. At this preliminary stage, the court's sole priority is the child's stability. Uprooting her from her home would be traumatic. However, leaving her solely in the care of a parent against whom such serious, though as yet unproven, allegations have been made is also a risk I am not willing to take."

A moment of hope flickers within me, but the judge's next words extinguish it immediately.

"Therefore, the least disruptive and most cautious path forward, *pending a full investigation*, is to maintain the child's residence while ordering a temporary shared custody arrangement."

My pulse pounds in my ears, drowning out part of her next words.

"—child, Lucy Samson, will remain in the family home to maintain her stability. Ms. Juliette Samson and Mrs. Eva Lerner Samson will alternate weeks of residence to care for her, with transitions occurring Fridays at 5:00 p.m."

Patricia's hand finds mine under the table, her grip firm and warm against my suddenly cold fingers. I try to inhale but my chest refuses to expand fully.

"Your Honor," Patricia objects, "this arrangement forces my client to leave her own daughter with a stranger—"

Judge Kemp holds up her hand to cut her off. "According to these documents, Mrs. Lerner Samson has been part of Lucy's life for some time. It appears she is not a stranger, as Mr. Samson seems to have introduced them prior to his death."

I focus on Eva across the room. Her expression remains composed—brows drawn together in an appropriate display of concern, hands folded neatly. But I catch the slight upward twitch at the corner of her mouth, so brief anyone else would miss it. The small tell of satisfaction beneath her mask of solemnity.

"Ms. Samson?" Judge Kemp's voice penetrates my fog. "Do you understand the terms of this temporary arrangement?"

Patricia leans close to me, her whisper urgent. "Accept it for now. It keeps you in the house and with Lucy. If you fight it, she might award Eva full temporary custody given those medical records. We can gather evidence during your weeks there."

My tongue feels swollen as I force out the words. "I understand, Your Honor."

"Would you like to speak to the arrangement?"

I push myself to standing, my knees threatening to buckle. The courtroom seems to tilt and straighten as I grip the edge of the table.

"I accept this arrangement solely for Lucy's wellbeing while these fraudulent claims are investigated. I want it on record that I maintain these documents are forgeries and that I never consented to a divorce."

After a moment, Judge Kemp nods. "So noted. This arrangement begins immediately. Ms. Samson will have the rest of this week, with Mrs. Lerner Samson taking residence beginning this Friday. We will reconvene in thirty days to assess the situation unless other legal proceedings resolve these matters sooner."

Her gavel strikes the sound block with a sharp crack that sends a jolt through my sternum.

Patricia gathers her papers quickly. "We'll file the signature authenticity challenges this afternoon. This buys us time to build our case."

The words register dimly as I watch Eva accept a

congratulatory squeeze of her shoulder from Karla Winters. My six-year-old daughter—who still sleeps with the nightlight on and needs her stuffed rabbit to feel safe—will be left alone with this woman for days at a time. A woman who has stolen my identity, my home, and now, partial custody of Lucy.

In the hallway outside the courtroom, Patricia outlines our next steps when Eva approaches, Winters trailing behind her. I straighten my back and lift my chin, every muscle tightening in preparation.

Eva's smile is soft, her eyes radiating what would look like genuine warmth to anyone who didn't know better. "Juliette," she says, her voice quiet and measured, "thank you for being reasonable about this arrangement. I know it must be difficult."

I stare at her, momentarily speechless at her boldness.

Eva steps closer, the scent of her subtle perfume— something with vanilla notes—reaches me. "I'm looking forward to our co-parenting arrangement," she says, lowering her voice as if sharing a confidence. "Lucy already knows me as Mommy Eva from the times Peter brought her to visit. This will be so much easier if we can be civil."

Before I can respond—before I can process the implication that Peter secretly introduced our daughter to this woman—Eva turns and walks away, Winters beside her.

Mommy Eva.

The two words settle in my stomach like lead weights. Not just Eva, not just Miss Eva, but *Mommy Eva*. The most sacred title I possess, shared without my knowledge or consent.

"She's lying," I whisper, though no one is listening. "Peter wouldn't have done that."

But the photograph of them in Cabo sits in my bag, a

reminder that I might not have known my husband as well as I believed.

Patricia touches my arm. "Juliette?"

I blink, focusing on her concerned face. "Two days," I say, my voice steadier than I feel. "I have exactly two days until I have to leave Lucy alone with that woman."

"We'll use every minute," Patricia promises. "Document everything in the house before Friday: Lucy's routine, her food preferences, her schoolwork. Document the patterns of care that Eva couldn't possibly know—the little details that make Lucy feel secure. When she disrupts those, we'll have concrete evidence of emotional harm to present to the court."

11

———

Two days. I have just two days until I'm forced to leave Lucy with Eva, and I'm not going to waste a single minute of them sitting by the phone, waiting for Patricia to call me back with her carefully crafted legal strategies and diplomatic maneuvers. She may have full faith in the glacial pace of the judicial process, in the measured cadence of motions and counter-motions, but I don't. Not anymore.

My jaw clenches until pain shoots through my temples as Sebastian's smug face flashes in my mind. The satisfaction gleaming in his eyes when he entered my home yesterday and claimed Peter's possessions.

I make a sharp left turn, abandoning my route home and aiming straight for SD Title & Escrow. If Eva and Sebastian are conspiring together—which seems painfully obvious now—I need answers that won't come from sitting at home. The coincidence is too perfect: Sebastian breaking in to take Peter's things right before Eva secures partial custody with mysteriously obtained medical records.

I pull into the parking lot, grab my purse as I get out of

my car, and stride toward the main entrance. Cool air washes over my heated skin as I push through the door. Today, I notice even more changes: the reception desk Peter crafted from reclaimed oak has been replaced with a floating glass monstrosity, and the abstract art seems to have multiplied, angular splashes of color that hold no meaning, no history. My fingers curl tighter around my purse strap. Not just my touch erased now, but the very soul of what we built, excised like a tumor. Even the air smells different—antiseptic, unfamiliar. As if the building itself is rejecting my presence, treating me as the intruder rather than its creator.

I approach the reception desk where the same young blonde woman from before watches me enter.

"Good morning," I say, forcing a smile that feels like stretching brittle plastic. "I need to see Sebastian."

She stiffens. "I'm sorry, ma'am, but I'm afraid I can't let you in."

Her words leave me momentarily speechless. "Excuse me?"

"I've been instructed that you no longer have access to the building." Her voice turns apologetic but firm. "I can call Mr. Dorsey to see if he's available to meet you in the lobby, but I can't allow you to go inside."

Blood rushes to my face, pounding in my ears. Fizz rises in my throat like a shaken soda bottle, pressure building behind the cap. I feel the same burning inside as I did when I presented to skeptical investors who assumed Peter is the only real talent. "This is my company. I founded it with my husband."

"I understand, but—"

Heavy footsteps approach from behind. I turn to find Jack, the building's head of security, walking toward me. His broad shoulders and serious expression have always made me feel safe before. Now, his presence feels like a threat.

"Mrs. Samson," he says, nodding politely. His eyes dart to the young woman, who gives him a barely perceptible nod. She called him the moment I arrived. "Is everything alright?"

"No, Jack, everything is not alright. I need to speak with Sebastian, and she's telling me I'm not permitted inside anymore."

Jack's shoulders hunch forward as he adjusts his security badge, his gaze fixed somewhere over my left shoulder. "I'm sorry, but there are new security protocols in place. Mr. Dorsey was very specific that you're not to be admitted without a scheduled appointment."

The words hit me with physical force, as if he's shoved me. "New security protocols? Since when?"

"Since yesterday afternoon." Jack won't meet my eyes. "I'm just following orders, Mrs. Samson."

Movement in the corridor behind the reception area catches my attention. Carol Matthews—our executive assistant who was one of our first employees—is walking quickly, arms laden with file folders. When her eyes meet mine through the glass partition, she freezes momentarily, then abruptly turns and hurries in the opposite direction.

"Carol!" I call out, stepping around the reception desk.

Jack moves with surprising speed for a man his size, positioning himself between me and the interior door. "Mrs. Samson, please. Don't make this difficult." His voice remains professional, but the implication is clear: he will physically prevent me from entering if necessary.

I stare at him, this man who'd wished me happy birthday every year, who'd once helped carry boxes of Christmas decorations to my car for the company party at our house, who shared his mother's recipe for peach cobbler with me.

"You know me," I say quietly. "You know this isn't right."

A flicker of shame crosses his face before he masks it with professional detachment, but he holds his ground. "I can ask if Mr. Dorsey will see you, but that's all I can do."

"Fine. Tell him I'm here."

Jack steps away to make the call while I retreat to the center of the lobby, pulse hammering against my throat. I scan the familiar space, looking for anything else that might have changed.

That's when I notice it.

On the far wall where a timeline of company milestones had once hung, there is now a single large portrait—Sebastian Dorsey, posed confidently in an executive chair, the company logo visible behind him. The plaque beneath it reads: "Sebastian Dorsey, Founder and CEO."

I grit my teeth as I stare at the portrait. They aren't just stealing my company—they're erasing our very existence, as if Peter and I had never created anything at all. Now that Eva supposedly has Peter's shares, she and Sebastian own a majority of the company. The company we'd built from nothing, the late nights hunched over financial projections, the clients we'd wooed with homemade cookies because we couldn't afford catering—all of it wiped away with a new brass plaque.

Jack returns, his expression telling me everything I need to know before he speaks.

"Mr. Dorsey is unavailable at the moment. He suggests scheduling an appointment through his assistant for next week."

Next week. When I'll be locked out of my own home

while Eva plays mommy to my daughter. The calculated cruelty of it makes my stomach lurch.

The urge to scream the truth crashes through me. I could make a scene right here—demand to see Sebastian right now, call the police, force everyone to acknowledge what's happening. The words burn in my throat, ready to explode.

Instead, I press my trembling hands against my thighs, steadying them, awareness spreading through me like ice water as Jack and the receptionist watch me. Each pair of eyes represents potential testimony, a possible report back to Sebastian. One outburst here would give Eva's attorneys ammunition to portray me as unstable.

I inhale slowly, forcing air into my lungs, tucking away the rage for when it can actually serve me.

"Jack," I say, my voice low so the receptionist can't hear, "could you at least tell Carol I need to speak with her? It's about a personal matter—something of Peter's she was helping me with before he died."

He hesitates before nodding once. "I'll pass along the message."

"Thank you." I turn to leave, then pause. "And Jack? When this is over, remember which side you chose."

Out in the parking lot, I slide into my car and press my forehead against the steering wheel. After a moment, I look up, mentally cataloging every object in my line of sight—fourteen parking spaces, three saplings, one security camera—until the pressure behind my eyes recedes and I trust myself to drive away without accelerating my car into the building's pristine façade.

How long had they planned this? How many years of smiles have concealed the knife being sharpened for my back?

My phone buzzes with a text notification. Unknown number. I open it.

Can't talk. They're monitoring everything. Check your old email from last year. I'm sorry.

Carol. It has to be. I stare at the message, my focus narrowing.

The realization crystallizes, sharp and cold, turning my fingertips numb as the implications spread through me. Whatever is happening has been in motion long before Peter died.

I turn the key in the ignition, theories and connections firing through my brain, each more disturbing than the last. The judge's ruling giving Eva partial custody, Sebastian's security lockout, Carol's warning—all of it points to a conspiracy far deeper and more calculated than I'd ever imagined.

12

—————

Before I pull out of the parking lot, a reminder pings on my phone: Women in Real Estate Luncheon, noon today at the Lakewood Country Club. The notification stops me in my tracks. I'd completely forgotten about it—a monthly networking event I've attended for years. And Alison will be there.

I stare at my phone, suddenly desperate for my old ordinary life and for someone who knows the real me. Alison has been away in Phoenix at a conference, and I haven't seen her since the day of Peter's funeral. She can help me work through this madness. I mentally rehearse what I'll tell her—about Eva's false claims, about Sebastian's betrayal, about losing access to my own company.

I arrive at the country club right on time, pausing to check my reflection in the rearview mirror. The earrings Lucy and Peter gave me last Mother's Day—tiny silver stars—catch the light as I tilt my head.

Drawing a deep breath that fills me all the way to my toes, I walk toward the entrance. The sprawling neoclassical building looms ahead, its manicured lawns and carefully pruned rose gardens dormant in the pale autumn sunlight. Just months ago, this place represented comfort and belonging. Maybe it still will.

The banquet room buzzes with conversation as I step inside. Round tables adorned with tasteful floral center-pieces fill the space, each setting complete with branded notepads and glossy real estate magazines. Women in tailored dresses and pantsuits cluster in small groups, wine glasses and business cards in hand.

I pause at the entrance, scanning the room. Several faces turn toward me, conversations falter, then resume with renewed vigor. Whispered comments. Sidelong glances. My stomach sinks. This is not the refuge I'd hoped for.

"Juliette? My goodness, I didn't expect to see you here!"

Marcia Townsend, head of the regional realtors association, approaches with a plastered-on smile.

"Hello, Marcia," I say, grateful that my voice emerges despite feeling like I've swallowed a hive of particularly agitated wasps.

"You're so brave for coming out. I mean, with every-thing that's happened..." She trails off, her eyes darting over my shoulder as if seeking rescue from our interaction.

"It seemed important to get back to normal," I reply, the phrase sounding hollow even to my own ears.

"Of course." She nods too emphatically. "Well, your usual table is over there—not that we've assigned seats, of course, but you know how we tend to gravitate to the same spots. Though I should warn you, there's been a bit of—well, a reshuffling—"

I touch her arm lightly, cutting off her rambling. "Is Alison here yet?"

Marcia's shoulders visibly relax, her smile shifting from strained to genuine at the change of subject. "Yes, I saw her by the bar. Catching up with everyone after her trip. She's been quite busy since she got back."

"Thank you."

I move past her, weaving through tables toward the bar area. As I navigate the room, conversations hush when I pass, only to resume in urgent whispers behind me. The hairs on my neck stand on end under the collective gaze.

And then I see her—Alison's unmistakable auburn curls pulled back in her signature messy bun, her animated hands gesturing as she speaks to a small circle of women. My first real friend in this industry, the person who brought me chicken soup when I was pregnant and on bed rest, the one who hosted my baby shower.

Alison looks up, meeting my eyes as I approach. Her face lights up with the warm smile I know so well. She raises her hand in a small wave, and the tightness in my chest eases slightly. She excuses herself from her group and moves toward me.

"Juliette," she says, reaching to squeeze my hands. "How are you holding up? I've been meaning to call since I got back."

The simple kindness of human touch sends a tremor through me. My vision blurs for a moment, and I blink rapidly, fighting the sudden burn behind my eyes. "It's been...complicated," I manage.

Alison's green eyes search my face with genuine concern. "I can imagine. Peter's passing was shocking enough, and now all this—" She stops herself, biting her lip.

"All what?" I press, desperate to understand what rumors have spread.

A flicker of discomfort crosses her face. She shifts her weight, glancing briefly toward the entrance. "Just... the whole situation. People are talking, of course."

"About what, Alison?" The room's walls seem to contract around us, the ambient chatter fading to static. "What have you heard?"

She doesn't answer, her gaze fixing on something over my shoulder. I turn to see what's caught her attention.

Eva Lerner stands at the entrance of the room, her soft figure draped in a moss-green wrap dress that portrays a maternal appearance. Dark waves frame a face arranged in serene dignity. She clutches a leather portfolio to her chest like a shield.

The room's reaction is immediate and bewildering. Several women move toward her, offering welcoming smiles and touches on her arm. Eva accepts their attention with demure nods, looking for all the world like a reluctant celebrity.

"What is she doing here?" I whisper, turning back to Alison. "She's not even in real estate."

But Alison's body has shifted, angling slightly away, and she looks at me strangely, as if I'd just said something in another language. The space between us has widened imperceptibly but undeniably.

"She's been very active in the community lately," Alison says, her voice oddly neutral. She fidgets with her bracelet, eyes darting between Eva and me. "Fundraising for the children's hospital. She joined the board last month."

"Last month? While she was stealing my life?" The words launch from my mouth before I can smooth their serrated edges.

Alison winces, taking another small step back. Her eyes dart between me and the door where Eva still holds court. "Juliette, I..." She trails off, seemingly at a loss.

I watch her internal struggle play across her face—the loyalty of our friendship warring with something else.

Fear? Self-preservation? The indecision in her expression makes my stomach knot up.

"It's just such a difficult situation, isn't it?" Alison glances toward Eva, then back to me, her fingers twisting her bracelet faster. "Everyone's so confused."

Confused. As if there are two equally valid sides to what is happening to me.

"I should greet some clients," Alison adds, already moving away. "We'll catch up properly soon, okay?" The promise hangs hollow between us as she retreats, carefully navigating to a position halfway between me and Eva.

I stand frozen, watching her strategic withdrawal. From my isolated position, I can see the invisible lines being drawn throughout the room—the formation of camps, the calculation of alliances. And I am being marked as toxic, dangerous to stand near.

Eva's gaze finds me across the room. Unlike our previous encounters, she doesn't immediately look away. Instead, she holds my eyes for one deliberate moment, her expression a masterpiece of compassionate regret, before turning back to her admirers.

I move to an empty table in the corner, my legs wobbling beneath me. A waiter appears with a glass of water, which I accept gratefully, while declining the offered wine. I need clarity now more than ever.

From my vantage point, I watch as the luncheon formally begins. Marcia welcomes everyone, makes announcements about market trends and upcoming regulations. Eva is introduced as a "special guest" with "a personal interest in our community's development." She doesn't speak, just smiles and nods appropriately, the perfect picture of humble grace.

Throughout the lunch, I catalog each interaction, each subtle response. Women I've known for years now approach me with cautious formality, their conversations brief and sanitized. Some avoid me entirely, suddenly fascinated by the contents of their salads when I glance their way.

Alison remains distant, professionally cordial when our paths cross but never alone with me for more than a few seconds. The betrayal stings worse than the outright avoidance of others. With each passing minute, I watch her laugh with the same women who whisper behind my back, her social instincts for survival overriding any loyalty to our friendship.

When the dessert plates are cleared, I make my way toward the exit, no longer able to maintain the facade under the weight of so many judgmental stares.

"Juliette."

Alison's voice stops me near the coat check. She approaches with quick steps, glancing over her shoulder to ensure we aren't observed.

"I'm sorry," she says in a rushed whisper, her eyes darting toward the main room then back to me. "This is just temporary insanity around here. People don't know what to think, and Sebastian's been very... influential lately. I need to be careful with my business, you understand."

The raw calculation in her admission hits me like a slap. This isn't my friend apologizing for a momentary lapse—this is someone actively choosing the path of least resistance.

"I thought I knew you better," I say quietly.

Alison's eyes flick around nervously. She takes a half-step back, hands clasped defensively in front of her. "Look, what matters is Lucy's well-being, right? Eva seems... devoted to her."

"What are you talking about?"

Alison's face crumples with uncertainty. She shifts from

foot to foot, her words tumbling out in fragments. "Well, the divorce, obviously. And how difficult the separation was for everyone involved—"

"There was no divorce." The words slice through her rambling.

She blinks rapidly, confusion replacing her nervous energy. "But Eva said—"

"Lucy doesn't know Eva. Hell, I didn't know Eva before this week."

Alison's mouth opens, then closes. Her brow furrows with confusion as she processes this information, and I watch the careful architecture of her assumptions begin to crumble.

"I thought you were my friend," I say, my voice barely above a whisper. "You know me, Alison."

"I never asked you about problems with Peter and the divorce because I thought it was too sensitive for you," she rushes to explain, her hands fluttering anxiously. "And then when Peter got sick, I figured it had brought you closer again. But I'm also friends with Eva, and she told me you were taking all of it very hard, so that's why I never brought it up. I thought you would talk to me about it when you were ready."

Her words thrust me backward like a child's push on a playground. Eva has been working her way into the community longer than I realized, weaving her narrative into my relationships.

"Maybe there's a way to make this situation work for everyone—"

"Work for everyone?" I repeat, incredulity sharpening my voice. "They're taking my daughter. They've locked me out of my own company. They're erasing Peter's legacy and mine. Please tell me which part of this you think should 'work' for me."

Alison steps back, affronted. "You're not being reasonable. There are aspects of this situation that—" She stops herself, pressing her lips together.

"What aspects, Alison? What exactly have you heard?"

She hesitates, then apparently decides she's already committed. "Your postpartum depression. The hospitalization. Your emotional state since Peter got sick." She lowers her voice further, leaning in despite her apparent desire to retreat. "People are concerned about stability, Juliette. For Lucy's sake."

The calculated precision of the attack leaves me breathless. They aren't just stealing my present—they're weaponizing my past.

"Who told you about my hospitalization?" I demand, my voice barely above a whisper.

"It's common knowledge now," Alison says, her expression suddenly guarded. "Look, I should get back. Let's talk when things calm down."

I watch her retreat, a hollow feeling spreading through me. Common knowledge. My private medical struggle, shared only with those closest to me, now circulating as gossip to undermine my fitness as a mother.

As I collect my coat, I catch a last glimpse of Eva across the room. She stands in a circle of women, her head tilted in that listening pose that radiates patience. She's positioned herself perfectly—the sympathetic figure, the reluctant replacement, the woman stepping into a void rather than the one creating it.

I step out into the bright afternoon, the country club's doors closing behind me with a soft, final click. The isolation I felt inside that room is complete, by design. One by one, my connections are being severed, my support system dismantled.

In my car, I crank the radio volume until the bass

makes the rearview mirror vibrate, drowning out my thoughts with noise. I've gone looking for allies and found only fair-weather friends. The disappointment is crushing, but clarifying. If I can't count on those I've considered friends, then I'll have to forge a new path forward.

Carol's text message resurfaces in my mind. I need to find out exactly how long, and how deep this conspiracy runs. And I need someone who isn't afraid to stand beside me while I do it.

For the first time in a while, I find myself thinking about my sister. Lena had warned me about Sebastian long before any of this happened. I didn't believe her then— perhaps now it's time to find out what else she knows.

13

Smooth asphalt gives way to potholed pavement as I drive across town, away from the manicured perfection of country club neighborhoods and into streets where buildings wear their histories without apology. My car's GPS guides me through sections of town I'd never seen before, each turn pulling me deeper into a world that exists beyond the ruins of what I once called mine.

I park and stare at the faded sign swinging in the breeze: "The Last Word." A fitting name for my sister's bar. Lena always did insist on having the final say in our arguments.

It's been three years. Three years since I chose Peter's reassurances over her evidence. How could I have been so blind? So desperate to believe in the life I thought we had? My stomach churns like I've swallowed a live fish, and I press one hand against it, willing the nausea to settle.

Inside my purse, my phone buzzes. Another text from Alison: *I hope you understand my position. This will all blow over. Let's meet for coffee next week.*

I delete it with a savage jab of my thumb. Cowards masquerading as friends are worse than honest enemies.

Drawing a deep breath, I step out of the car, slamming the door a little harder than necessary. The sound cracks through the quiet street, startling a pair of pigeons into flight. I track them until they vanish, wishing I could follow.

The bar's exterior is understated—weathered brick, a wooden door with peeling green paint, and a small window displaying a neon "OPEN" sign that flickers like a failing heartbeat. Nothing like the polished facades in the neighborhood I'm in danger of losing.

My hand freezes on the door handle. What right do I have to ask for her help after everything that's happened between us? But Lucy's face flashes in my mind, and I push the door open, the hinges creaking in protest, before I lose my courage.

The scent of whiskey, old wood, and lemon polish wraps around me. As my vision adjusts to the dimness, I make out a scarred wooden bar stretching along one wall, a few worn leather booths lining the opposite side. Low jazz filters from hidden speakers, providing a muted soundtrack for the handful of patrons scattered throughout the space.

And there, behind the bar, her back to me as she arranges bottles on a shelf, is my sister.

Lena looks different—sharper, harder. Her once-long hair is now cut in a severe asymmetrical style that accentuates her jawline. The sleeves of her black t-shirt are rolled up, revealing a tattoo winding around her forearm. As she turns, sensing a new presence, our eyes lock.

For a moment, we're frozen in place. Her expression shifts rapidly—surprise, vindication, anger, sadness—before settling into careful neutrality.

I force myself forward, each step of my heels against the wooden floor marking my approach like the ticking of a countdown.

"You didn't come to the funeral," I say, the accusation slipping out before I can frame a better greeting.

Lena sets down the bottle she's holding, each movement measured and precise. "Thought you wouldn't want me around." She wipes her hands on a towel tucked into her waistband. "Plus, Sebastian has a restraining order against me."

I flinch, my breath catching as though she'd reached across the bar and slapped me. "What? He—when did this happen?"

"There's a lot you never knew." She studies me, her eyes—so like mine—cataloging the changes in my appearance. "You look like shit, Jules."

I blink, and a sound that's a mix between a laugh and a sob bursts past my lips before I can stop it. "Thanks. You look... different."

"Different good or different bad?"

"Just different." I gesture to an empty bar stool. "Can I sit?"

Lena nods, reaching under the counter to produce a glass and a bottle of bourbon. She pours a finger's worth and slides it toward me.

"I don't usually—"

"Today you do." Her voice cuts through my protest.

I take the glass, swirling the amber liquid before taking a tentative sip. The bourbon sears a path down my throat, pooling hot in my stomach.

"So," Lena says, leaning against the back counter, arms folded across her chest. "What brings the suburban queen to my humble establishment? Last I checked, you didn't approve of my lifestyle choices. Or my journalistic integrity."

The barb hits its target. "I deserve that."

"You deserve more than that." She takes a glass for herself, pouring a measure equal to what she gave me. "But I'm guessing you're not here for my forgiveness."

The directness of her assessment cracks my carefully constructed composure. Words begin to spill out of me—about Peter's death, about Sebastian's betrayal, about Eva's appearance and her claim on Lucy. About being erased from my own life.

Lena listens without interrupting, her expression darkening with each revelation. When I finish, she drains her glass in one swallow and sets it down with a sharp click.

"I fucking knew it," she says, her voice low and fierce. "I knew Sebastian was dirty."

"You tried to tell me." My throat constricts around the admission. "Three years ago. You brought me evidence about Sebastian's business practices."

"And you told me I was being paranoid. That Peter trusted Sebastian implicitly, so I must be wrong." Her voice doesn't rise, but the resentment pours off her in waves. "You chose your husband's judgment over your sister's evidence."

I stare into my glass, unable to meet her eyes. "I was wrong."

"Yes, you were." Lena refills both our glasses. "But that's not even the half of it, Jules. After you shut me out, I kept digging. Found more evidence of embezzlement, offshore accounts, connections to money laundering operations."

My head snaps up. "What happened?"

"Sebastian sued me for defamation. Claimed I was conducting a personal vendetta, fabricating evidence." Her laugh scrapes like broken glass. "His lawyers buried me in paperwork. The magazine I was writing for couldn't afford the legal fight—they cut me loose. No one would touch me after that. My reputation was toxic. My career as an investigative journalist went up in flames."

My stomach drops, bile rising in my throat. "Lena, I had no idea."

"Of course you didn't. You were busy with your perfect life, your perfect husband, your perfect daughter."

"What about your reporting partner? Megan Rhodes, wasn't it?"

Lena's jaw tightens. "Megan had kids and a mortgage. So did Detective Adams—he was our inside source at the police department. When Sebastian's lawyers started circling, threatening their jobs..." She shrugs, but I can see the old hurt in her eyes. "I became the fall guy. Took the heat so they could keep their families fed."

She downs her glass of bourbon and refills it.

"The lawsuit was settled quietly," she says. "Very quietly."

"How? Sebastian doesn't seem the type to back down."

Something unreadable flashes across Lena's face. "Peter paid him off."

"He—what?" The glass slips in my suddenly numb fingers, bourbon sloshing over the rim. "Peter paid Sebastian to drop the lawsuit against you?"

"Not directly." She shrugs. "It was all very subtle—a lawyer approached mine, offering a settlement package that included dropping all claims if I signed an NDA and destroyed my notes. The money came through a shell company, but I traced it back to Peter eventually."

I shake my head, having trouble taking it all in.

"Peter didn't just pay Sebastian to drop the lawsuit," Lena continues, her voice carefully neutral. "I found out he also made some calls, smoothed things over with the detective's superiors at the department. Made sure Megan kept her job at the Tribune."

I press my fingertips against the cool wood of the bar, anchoring myself. "Peter never said a word to me. Not one word."

"Maybe he knew you wouldn't approve. Maybe he felt guilty for not believing me either." Her face softens slightly. "Or maybe he was trying to protect you from knowing the truth about his business partner."

A heavy silence falls between us, broken only by the soft music and the occasional clink of glasses from the other patrons.

"So Sebastian destroyed your career." I struggle to process this new piece of the puzzle. "And now he's trying to destroy my life. To take everything I have."

"Not trying. Succeeding." Lena's bluntness feels like a slap. "From what you've told me, he's executing a master class in gaslighting and social isolation. Classic abuser tactics, actually."

"But why now?"

Lena gives me a long look, her eyes suddenly tired. "Because Peter was in his way. And now he's not."

Her words hang in the air between us, their implication chilling me to the bone. Before I can respond, she holds up a finger and disappears into a back room. When she returns, she's carrying a worn file folder stuffed with papers.

"I kept copies," she says, sliding the folder across the bar. "Despite the NDA. It's an insurance policy, you might say."

I open the folder with trembling hands. Inside are meticulous notes, financial statements with highlighted irregularities, and photographs. My breath catches when I see the images—Sebastian in deep conversation with men I don't recognize, in restaurants and parking garages.

And then I see her—a younger woman standing half-hidden behind Sebastian in several photos. Her hair is different—shorter, lighter—but the face is unmistakable.

"Eva," I whisper, my voice barely audible even to myself.

"Evelyn Dorsey back then," Lena says, tapping the photo. "Sebastian's half-sister, though they kept that connection quiet in professional settings."

I snap my head up so fast my neck protests. "Half-sister? They're related?"

"Different mothers, same father. She's about ten years younger than him." Lena pulls out another photo—Sebastian and Eva sitting close together in a cafe, her hand on his arm, their heads bent in intimate conversation. "They've always been unusually close. Dependent, even. Look at how he watches her here."

I stare at the photo, noticing the possessive tilt of Sebastian's body toward Eva, the way his hand covers hers on his arm. Something predatory in his posture makes me shiver.

"This isn't a new scam, is it?" I ask, looking up. "They've been working together for years."

"That's right." Lena taps another document. "Evelyn Dorsey disappeared about two years ago. Changed her name, created a new identity. Eva Lerner emerged around the same time."

I flip through page after page of Lena's investigation, my bourbon forgotten.

"I don't understand," I say, looking up at my sister. "Why didn't you come forward with this again after the lawsuit was settled? Why disappear into..." I gesture around the bar.

Lena's face tightens, pain flashing briefly in her eyes. "Where exactly should I have gone, Jules? Back to you, who'd already chosen sides? Back to journalism, with my reputation in tatters?" She shakes her head. "This place was my fresh start. And a good place to lick my wounds."

I study my sister's face, really seeing the toll the past three years have taken. The fiery, ambitious journalist I grew up with has been replaced by someone more guarded, more cynical.

Heat crawls up my neck, my eyes burning as I force myself to hold her gaze. "I'm sorry, Lena. I should have believed you."

She stares at me for a long moment, her expression unreadable. Then she sighs, the rigid line of her shoulders relaxing slightly. "Yeah, you should have."

It's not forgiveness, but it's not rejection either. I'll take it.

"I was so blinded by my trust in Peter that I couldn't see what was happening. I failed you as a sister."

"And now it's coming back to bite you in the ass," Lena says, the edge in her voice softened by something almost like sympathy.

"I deserve that," I say again, pushing my half-empty glass away. "But Lucy doesn't deserve any of this. She's innocent in all of it. And she needs her mother—her real mother."

Lena studies me, her eyes searching mine, as if she's looking for something specific. Whatever she sees there causes something to shift in her expression.

"What exactly are you asking me for, Jules?"

The question hangs between us, weighted with years of hurt and this new, fragile truce. I could hedge, ask only for information, keep my walls up. Or I could risk everything.

"I need your help," I say, my voice breaking. "Not just

your information. I need your investigative skills, your contacts, your..." I swallow hard. "Your strength. Everyone else has abandoned me. You're the only person who saw through Sebastian from the beginning. The only one who wasn't fooled."

Lena's expression remains guarded, but something flickers in her eyes. "And if I say no? If I decide three years of silent treatment earns me the right to stay the hell out of this mess?"

"Then I'll understand." I meet her gaze steadily. "But I'm hoping you won't. Not just for me, but for Lucy. And maybe for yourself. For the justice you deserved three years ago."

A long silence stretches between us. In the background, the music has shifted to something slower, more melancholy. One of the patrons signals for another drink, and Lena holds up a finger in acknowledgment.

"Let me take care of this," she says, moving down the bar.

I wait, turning the pages of her investigation file, each document adding to my understanding of the elaborate trap that has been laid for me. By the time Lena returns, I'm trembling with a mixture of fear and rage.

"Sebastian's been planning this for years," I say, my voice tight. "Everything—Peter's death, my isolation, Eva's insertion into our lives—it's all been calculated."

Lena nods, leaning forward on her elbows. "Despite the settlement, I've still been monitoring the accounts I know about. About six months ago, there was a significant uptick in transactions—movements between accounts, large sums being transferred offshore."

I press my fingers to my temple, mentally scrolling through the timeline of Peter's decline. "Six months ago?

That's when Peter first started showing symptoms. Fatigue, numbness in his extremities."

"What was the diagnosis again?" Lena asks, straightening.

"Guillain-Barré syndrome relapse. He'd had it as a teenager after some viral infection." I frown as a terrible thought forms. "The doctors said it was unusual for it to recur, but not impossible They prescribed gabapentin for the neuropathy."

"Who was his doctor?"

"Dr. Wilson Grant. Sebastian recommended him when Peter first got sick."

Lena's eyes narrow to slits. "Wilson Grant. I know that name." She pulls out her phone, scrolls a bit. "Here—he was investigated five years ago for improper prescribing practices. The case was dropped for insufficient evidence, but..." She looks up, her expression grim. "Jules, what if Peter didn't die from complications of GBS?"

Air suddenly feels hard to come by. "No. They said it was pneumonia that killed him. He caught it in the hospital, and his weakened condition..."

"Pneumonia was the final cause, yes. But what weakened him in the first place?" Lena says, her tone softening but persistent. "Think about it. Sebastian recommends a doctor with a questionable history. Peter develops symptoms that mimic a previous illness, making diagnosis easier to accept. His condition worsens steadily, giving Sebastian plenty of time to position Eva and make financial preparations."

Nausea twists my gut as the timeline snaps together like a gruesome puzzle. "You think Peter was poisoned."

It's not a question, but Lena answers anyway. "I think it's a possibility we need to consider. Certain toxins can cause neuropathy, fatigue, and other symptoms that might be mistaken for GBS. Arsenic, for example."

My body stays planted at the bar, but some essential part of me shifts into that other time, as snapshots of Peter's decline parade through my mind—Peter growing thinner, paler, his hands shaking as Sebastian helped him with paperwork. Sebastian always there, always concerned, always ready to take over more responsibilities.

"How do you know all this?" I ask, my voice barely above a whisper.

Lena's fingers drum against the bar's scarred surface. "I did a story on arsenic contamination of groundwater a while back, when I was still doing investigative work. Had to research the symptoms extensively—chronic exposure mimics a lot of other conditions. Fatigue, numbness, muscle weakness, digestive issues." She pauses, watching my face. "The scary part is how easily it can be dismissed as other illnesses, especially if the victim has a medical history that provides cover."

My legs threaten to give out. I grab the edge of the bar, the polished wood cool under my sweating palms. "We need proof," I manage to say, my voice distant to my own ears.

"Yes. We need proof," Lena echoes with assurance. "If we're right about this, it's not just a custody battle or a business takeover—it's murder. And they'll come after you next if you get in their way."

I press my hands to my face, trying to contain everything threatening to break loose inside me—grief, rage, terror.

"This is so much bigger than I thought," I mumble. "I came here thinking I was fighting to get my daughter back, to reclaim my company. But if they killed Peter..."

"Then you're up against people who will stop at

nothing to get what they want." Lena reaches across the bar to grasp my hand, her touch both a comfort and a warning. "Are you sure you want to pursue this? We could focus just on keeping Lucy from Eva, by proving she's unfit."

I lower my hands, meeting my sister's gaze. "If they murdered Peter, they don't deserve anything but prison. I need to know the truth—all of it."

Lena nods, a small, fierce smile tugging at the corner of her mouth. "Then let's find it. I still have contacts, people who owe me favors."

"Detective Adams and Megan?" I ask.

"Among others." Lena's jaw tightens, her eyes flickering between determination and something darker. "They weren't happy about how things went down, but they understood why I did it. Adams especially—he has three kids. They both know they owe me, and they know Sebastian needs to be stopped."

She glances around the quiet bar. "Besides, this place practically runs itself. I can take some time away."

My knees nearly buckle. "Thank you, Lena. After everything—"

She waves away my words. "Save it. This isn't about forgiveness. This is about justice—for you, for Lucy, for Peter. And yeah, maybe a little bit for me too." Her smile turns predatory. "Sebastian Dorsey destroyed my career. I wouldn't mind returning the favor."

14

———————

Later that night, I'm in our study, my meeting with Lena at the bar having sharpened my focus to a razor's edge. If Sebastian had orchestrated Peter's death, I needed proof.

Carol's text echoes in my mind: *Check your old email from last year.*

My fingers hover over the keyboard before I type in my credentials to the company portal. The screen flashes red with a message: "Account not found."

"Of course," I mutter.

Sebastian wouldn't have to worry about leaving any digital footprints when he can simply delete my existence from the company servers. I drum my fingers against the desk, considering my options.

Then it hits me—I often downloaded emails for offline access. I open my email client and switch to the offline storage. A small victory surges through me as dozens of folders appear, organized by project and client.

A yawn, small and stifled, breaches the silence behind

me. I turn to see Lucy standing in the doorway, hair mussed from sleep, clutching Nibbles.

"Hey, sweetheart. What are you doing up?" I soften my voice, pushing away the darkness that's been clouding my thoughts.

"Mommy, can I ask you something?" Lucy twists one of her stuffed rabbit's ears between her fingers.

"Come here." I hold my arms open to her. "What's on your mind?"

She crosses the room, her bare feet padding against the hardwood. She climbs onto my lap, her small body warm against mine.

"Why was Daddy's friend at school today?" Lucy keeps her eyes on Nibbles. "She was watching me at recess."

My skin goes cold. "What friend? Who was watching you?"

"The lady with the pretty scarf." Lucy tugs at her rabbit's ear. "She was by the fence. She waved and blew kisses."

I force my breath to remain steady. Eva. At my baby's school again. The violation feels like broken glass under my skin—not just to my home or marriage, but to the sacred space of my child's life.

"Did you talk to this lady?"

"No. She was outside the fence. I waved back 'cause it's polite."

"Have you seen her before? Do you know her name?"

At this, Lucy's demeanor changes. Her shoulders curve inward, and she stays focused on Nibbles, refusing to meet my eyes. My normally forthcoming child suddenly closed off.

"I'm not supposed to talk about the secret visits." Her voice drops so low I have to lean forward to hear her.

The chill on my skin seeps deeper. "What secret visits, baby?"

Lucy's lower lip trembles. "Am I in trouble?"

"No, sweetheart." I stroke her hair, careful to keep my hand from shaking. "You're not in trouble at all. I just need to understand what happened."

Tears well in her eyes. "The lady said if I told you, you'd be sad because it was a surprise for later."

I breathe through my nose, counting to three before I respond. "It's okay to tell me now. I promise I won't be sad."

"Sometimes when I went to work with Daddy, this lady who worked at the office gave me presents." Lucy looks up at me, her eyes wide and uncertain. "She said she would be my new mommy someday."

The words punch through my defenses like a fist breaking through drywall. Something hot and fierce fills me. I struggle to keep my face neutral as Lucy continues.

"She brought me gummy bears and showed me pictures of her house where I'd have my own special room." Lucy's brow furrows. "But I told her I already have a mommy. That made her look mad, but then she smiled again."

Every maternal instinct screams at me to rage, to demand more details. But I recognize the delicacy of this moment—how Lucy's words could be crucial, how they might be twisted if I react too strongly, and how I don't want to cause my darling girl to be more upset.

"You were right, baby." I manage to keep my voice even. "You do have a mommy who loves you very much."

"Are you mad at the lady?" Lucy asks.

"No, sweetheart, I'm not mad." The lie sticks to my tongue. "I'm just surprised. Did Daddy know about your talks with this lady?"

Lucy shakes her head. "She came when Daddy was in meetings. Said it was our special secret." She frowns. "But Ms. Carter says we're not supposed to keep secrets from parents."

"Ms. Carter is right." I pull Lucy close, breathing in her scent—strawberry shampoo and the faint sweetness of the cookies she had earlier. "You can always tell me anything, no matter what anyone else says."

I walk Lucy back to her room, tuck her butterfly comforter around her shoulders, and sit on the edge of her bed until her breathing grows deep and regular. Then I stand, my legs stiff, and return to the study where I pick up my phone.

Patricia answers on the third ring. "Juliette? It's after ten. Is everything okay?"

"Eva was at Lucy's school today, watching her through the fence." My voice comes out flat. "And Lucy just told me that Eva used to visit her at Peter's office, giving her gifts and telling her she'd be her 'new mommy' someday."

"Jesus Christ." Patricia's voice sharpens, the lateness forgotten. "How long has this been going on?"

"Lucy didn't say exactly, but she mentioned multiple visits." I move to the window, peering out at the darkened street. "What do I do? Can I file for a restraining order? Use this to stop this crazy temporary custody thing?"

"Let's keep to our plan. Document everything Lucy told you—write it down word for word while it's fresh." Patricia's voice is calm, professional. "But Juliette, be careful about questioning her further. If you push too hard, Sebastian's attorneys could claim you're coaching her."

"She was at my daughter's school, Patricia." My voice cracks. "She's been manipulating my child."

"I'm not saying let it go. I'm saying we need to be strategic." Her sigh rustles through the phone. "This is significant, but we need more. Testimony from a six-year-old isn't enough on its own."

When I hang up, I return to my laptop. Time to focus on what I can control.

I search through the archived emails, scrolling past client communications and meeting notices. Then I see it—a company-wide announcement from December of last year:

"SD Title & Escrow welcomes Eva Lerner to our family as our newest associate in Financial Compliance. Eva brings five years of experience in regulatory oversight and will be working closely with Sebastian to ensure our continued excellence in compliance matters."

Attached is a professional headshot of Eva—hair styled differently, wearing subtle makeup and conservative business attire, but unmistakably the same woman who now claims to be Peter's wife. Now I know why she seemed familiar. Not just this email, but she was at the holiday party shortly after she was hired.

I forward the email to Lena with a brief note: "Found something. Confirming Eva was an employee at our company long before Peter's death. Lucy saw her at school today. More to discuss. Can we meet tomorrow?"

I close my laptop and pull out the photo of Peter and Eva together. I study it again, forcing myself to look past the two of them to the details of the background.

And then I see it—in the distance is an island. I know that island. This isn't Cabo, it's California. That's Catalina Island. And there's another arm on the edge of the photo. Peter's on the right, Eva's on the left, but their positions are strange for an intimate pose. I look closer at the disembodied arm. I can just make out a watch. It looks like the one Sebastian wears. A Breitling.

My phone buzzes with a text bearing Lena's response: *Come over after you drop Lucy off at school tomorrow.*

I sit on the edge of my bed, the photo still in my hand. The pieces are falling into place—Eva inserting herself into the company, into Peter's life, into Lucy's world. A long con orchestrated by Sebastian, with my family as the target.

"She thinks she can take my daughter." My voice has an edge, even to my own ears. "Let her try."

Breaking through the fog surrounding me since Peter's death, I feel something beyond grief and confusion. A sharpening clarity. This isn't just about reclaiming what was mine—it's about protecting Lucy from people who see her as nothing more than a pawn in their game.

I wasn't able to protect Peter. But I will protect our daughter, no matter what it takes.

15

W hen Lena opens the door to her apartment above the bar, I'm greeted first by the scent of cinnamon and coffee, then by her living space, transformed into something that suggests comfort surrendered to a desperate search for truth. Her dining table has disappeared beneath scattered papers and empty energy drink cans. The wall behind it blooms with a patchwork of Post-it notes.

"Welcome to command central," she says, ushering me inside. The circles under her eyes match mine. "Get any sleep?"

"Nightmares don't count as sleep." I drop my bag on the couch, taking in the war room she's assembled. "When did you do all this?"

"Been up all night." She presses a warm mug into my hands. The ceramic bears a hairline crack down one side —Lena never throws anything away that can still function. "After your email, my brain wouldn't shut off."

I take a sip of coffee. "All night long, I kept seeing Eva at Lucy's school. Her face, watching..."

"She's worse than we thought." Lena gestures toward the dining table. "Come see what I've found."

I sink into a chair at the table as Lena spreads several copies of documents in front of me.

"I pulled some strings so hard they nearly snapped, but my contact in the records office delivered this morning." She taps a finger against the top page. "Eva Lerner has had at least three different identities in the past decade."

The coffee burns my tongue as I take too large a sip. I gulp it down, then sputter. "Three?"

"First, there's Evelyn Dorsey." Lena slides a birth certificate forward. The woman's face in the attached ID photo is unmistakably Eva, though her hair is darker, styled differently. "Born thirty-eight years ago in Arizona. Then Emily Loring." Another document, another version of Eva with lighter hair and heavier makeup. "And finally, Eva Lerner, created about two years ago."

I line the copies up, side by side. "These look so real."

"That's what makes this so disturbing." Lena tucks a strand of hair behind her ear, revealing a small rose tattoo behind it, the first one she got during her rebellious years. Okay, maybe she's still rebellious. "My contact says the paperwork is flawless. Social security numbers, tax records, everything. This isn't amateur hour."

"What's her pattern? Why keep changing identities?" I trace the date on the birth certificate for Eva Lerner.

Lena's mouth tightens into a thin line. "Each time, she implanted herself into wealthy families. In Phoenix, she was a live-in caregiver for a widower with a young daughter. The man died in his sleep eight months after hiring her—apparent heart attack. In Seattle, she was a private tutor for a finance executive's children when his wife had a mental breakdown and was institutionalized."

A chill spreads across my scalp, down my spine. "And each time?"

"She becomes indispensable first. The reliable outsider who's suddenly essential." Lena's eyes harden. "Then something happens to the existing parent or caretaker. Something that looks natural, or at least plausibly deniable. And suddenly she's positioning herself to benefit."

I press my fingertips against my temples, where pressure builds like a thunderstorm. "So Sebastian brought in his half-sister, created a position for her at our company, and they worked together to—" I can't finish the sentence.

"To set up an inheritance grab, using you and Lucy as pawns." Lena completes my thought. "While Eva worked on getting close to Lucy, Sebastian was working on Peter." She straightens. "Speaking of which, let's see what Peter left behind."

"What do you mean, what Peter left behind?"

Lena beckons me to come with her, out the front door and into the hallway to the neighboring apartment. She opens the door as she raps on the frame before entering. I follow her inside.

The studio apartment smells like instant ramen and energy drinks. Clothes drape over a single chair, and pizza boxes stack beside an unmade futon. A young man hunches over a laptop at a cramped table, his fingers flying across the keyboard with practiced speed.

"This is Malcolm," Lena says. "He can get into systems most people think are locked forever."

Malcolm glances up, eyes magnified behind thick lenses. "Hey." Then back to his screen, muttering something about encryption protocols.

"Malcolm is helping us access Peter's cloud storage," Lena explains. "If Peter documented anything suspicious, that's where we'll find it."

"But his passwords—"

"Passwords are for people who follow the rules." Malcolm doesn't look up. The keys on the laptop click-clack with an irregular rhythm. "Everything leaves digital footprints. Delete doesn't mean gone. It just means hidden."

"Malcolm's close to finding Peter's files," Lena says.

"Give me a minute," he says, as his fingers continue to tap away.

For the next ten minutes, we watch Malcolm work. At one point, he curses under his breath, slams the table with his palm, then dives back in. Lena paces behind him, peering over his shoulder occasionally.

"Almost..." Malcolm mutters, then stops. "Wait. This isn't—" He leans closer to the screen. "Hmm. They've tried to corrupt the backup. Amateur hour." His typing speed doubles.

"What does that mean?" I ask.

"Someone tried to delete your husband's cloud storage. Did a decent job of it, too." A thin smile crosses his face. "But they didn't know about the secondary backup protocol."

A few more minutes of silence, broken only by keyboard clicks and Malcolm's occasional murmur to himself. I sit on the edge of the futon, my foot bouncing on the floor, a nervous rhythm I can't control.

"Got it." Malcolm finally leans back, releasing tension from his shoulders. "Your husband's cloud backup from the past two years."

The screen fills with folders—meticulously organized, labeled with dates and project names. So like Peter that my skin prickles, as if seeing his organizational system is more intimate than seeing his handwriting.

"Start with the most recent," Lena suggests, pulling a chair beside me.

Malcolm navigates to folders from the last few months of Peter's life. One labeled "Financial Discrepancies" catches my eye.

"That one," I say, pointing.

Inside are dozens of spreadsheets, each documenting unusual transactions at the company. Peter had highlighted patterns, added notes, created timelines.

"Look at the dates," I whisper, touching the screen as if I could reach through it to Peter. "He started investigating right when he got sick."

Lena leans forward, her shoulder pressing against mine. "These show systematic fund transfers to and from offshore accounts. Sebastian wasn't just stealing—he was laundering."

"And Peter knew." My voice catches. "Why didn't he tell me?"

We find an email folder where Peter had saved correspondence with Sebastian. Confrontational messages from Peter, followed by Sebastian's reassurances that they would handle it privately, keep it "between partners."

We'll talk Monday after the clients leave. I'm sure there's an explanation for the discrepancies. No need to involve others yet. Get some rest, Peter. You haven't been yourself lately.

After reading a few more emails, Lena says, "Peter wanted hard evidence. And with his medical symptoms, he probably worried people would dismiss him as paranoid or confused. Sebastian was already laying the groundwork for that."

I remember how the doctors referenced Peter's past Guillain-Barré syndrome when diagnosing his new symptoms. How easily his concerns could have been attributed to anxiety or some other neurological issues.

"And then he got worse," I say, my voice barely audible. "Conveniently worse."

Malcolm clicks through to a password-protected folder dated two weeks before Peter's death. He tries one approach, cursing when it fails. Then another method. A progress bar crawls across the screen.

"This is heavily encrypted," he mutters. "Your husband didn't want just anyone finding this."

After the third attempt, the folder unlocks.

"Look at this." Malcolm turns the screen toward me. "FOR JULIETTE" glows in bold letters next to a folder icon.

My mouth goes dry. Peter knew he might not get to tell me himself.

When Malcolm opens the folder, we see it all laid out. Transaction records. Account numbers. Names. Dates. My fingers press against my lips as I see it—a shell company registered to Eva Lerner receiving regular payments from our company accounts.

Lena thanks Malcolm, who promises to upload everything to a new location and send her a link for access. "I'll keep digging through the cloud data. Some of these files look corrupted, but I might be able to recover fragments."

We go back to her apartment.

"He knew," I whisper. My chest tightens until breathing becomes a conscious effort. "Peter figured it out."

Lena squeezes my shoulder, her grip strong enough to anchor me. "This is the connection we needed, Juliette. This proves coordination between Sebastian and Eva."

I pull out my phone, fingers trembling so badly I nearly drop it. "We need to take this to the police. This proves financial fraud, at a minimum."

Lena catches my wrist, her fingers cool against my

pulse point. "Wait. Think this through. If we go to the authorities now, what happens?"

"Sebastian and Eva get arrested for fraud."

"Maybe. Or maybe Sebastian knows people who can buy him time to destroy evidence. And what about Peter's death? Do these financial records prove they had anything to do with it?"

My hand drops. "No." I flop onto her couch.

"We need more," Lena says, her eyes locked on mine as she sits next to me. "The money trail is clear, but if we want to prove they killed Peter—and based on what we've found, I believe they did—we need something concrete that connects them to his death."

I sink deeper into the couch. "If we alert them now, they'll know we're onto them."

"And they might accelerate whatever they're planning with Lucy." The intensity in Lena's eyes makes me flinch. "Right now, they think you're just a grieving widow who's overwhelmed and fighting for Lucy's custody. We need to keep it that way until we have everything."

The hearing from the day before looms in my mind, and now I have only one day until I have to surrender my home and partial custody of Lucy to Eva. The thought of my daughter alone with that woman makes bile rise in my throat.

"So what do we do?" I ask.

Lena stands and begins pacing, her socked feet silent on the wooden floor. "I'll keep digging into Eva's past identities and follow the money trail with Malcolm. You can focus on Peter's medical angle—his records, his medications, anything that could show tampering."

A memory surfaces—Peter sitting beside his mother during our last visit to her nursing home. *"She remembers the oddest things,"* he'd said. *"Sometimes I think she's more present than we realize."*

"I should talk to Margaret," I say suddenly. "Peter's mother."

"Margaret? I thought she has dementia."

"She does, but Peter visited her every week, even when he was sick." I straighten, a new energy coursing through me. "He told me once that he could tell her anything because she wasn't judging him anymore. What if he told her things he wasn't ready to tell anyone else?"

"It's worth trying," Lena says. She checks her watch—a vintage piece our father gave her before he passed away. "But you've got to go today. You don't have much time."

"And Sebastian and Eva have resources," I add, gathering my bag. "Legal teams, money, influence—they've been planning this for a while, and we're playing catch-up."

She grabs my arm as I head for the door. "Juliette—be careful. If they killed Peter, they won't hesitate to eliminate other obstacles."

"I've been careful for too long." My voice strengthens with each word. "They've taken my husband, my company, and now they're trying to take my home and my daughter."

"Just remember our advantage." Lena's expression is fierce, a reminder of the sister who once fought off neighborhood bullies for me. "They think they've already won. Let them keep thinking that."

At the doorway, I pause. The weight of everything we've uncovered presses on me. Peter had been fighting a silent battle against Sebastian's betrayal while his body was failing him. He'd tried to leave me the truth, knowing he might not survive to tell me himself.

"If anything happens to me," I say quietly, "promise you'll protect Lucy."

Lena's eyes meet mine, and in that moment, the years of distance between us vanish. "With my life, Jules. But nothing's going to happen to you. We're ending this. Together."

As I drive toward the nursing home, Peter's final gift—the truth—strengthens my resolve. The fog of grief that's clouded my judgment since his death begins to lift, replaced by clarity.

I check the rearview mirror, watching for any cars that might be following me. No sign of surveillance, but I take an extra turn anyway, doubling back to make sure.

Sebastian and Eva have no idea what's coming. That knowledge fills me with a dark satisfaction I haven't felt since losing Peter.

16

Thistlewood Senior Living appears on the horizon, its elegant stone facade catching the midday light. I ease my foot off the gas, my reflection in the rearview mirror revealing a face transformed—no longer the grieving widow but the hunter, tracking clues to decipher the deception that's unraveling my life. Since leaving Lena's apartment, I've been mentally cataloging everything we've uncovered—Eva's multiple identities, Sebastian's financial crimes, Peter's desperate attempts to document it all.

He knew something was happening and tried to leave breadcrumbs for me to follow. But I missed them. What else had he hidden? What messages had I been too blind to see?

Inside, an artificial citrus scent hangs in the air, a thin veil covering the unmistakable clinical odor beneath. I approach the front desk and sign the visitor log. My pen freezes mid-signature when I spot an entry from yesterday —Eva Lerner, signed with precise, deliberate strokes.

My insides contract as if someone had reached in and wrung them like a dishcloth.

"Mrs. Samson!" The receptionist, Darla, greets me with a wide smile. "It's been a while. Margaret will be so happy to see you."

I return her smile, the muscles in my face stiff with effort. "Has she had many visitors lately?"

"Oh yes, that lovely woman comes by almost every day now. Such a blessing." Darla beams as she points to Eva's name in the log. "Margaret's been much more alert since she started visiting."

I nod as a phantom ice cube slides between my shoulder blades.

"Does Lucy have a birthday coming up?" Darla asks as she hands me a visitor badge. "Margaret's been talking about shopping for a present. Says she wants to get her something special this year."

"Yes." I clip the badge to my blouse, fingers fumbling with the clasp. "She turns seven next month."

"Such a sweet age." She buzzes me through the security doors. "Margaret's in her room. She should be finished with physical therapy by now."

The hallway stretches before me, carpeted in a soft beige that muffles my footsteps. Margaret's room is on the third floor, in the memory care wing where staff check on residents more frequently. Peter had insisted on the best care for his mother, even as her mind began to slip away in fragments.

I knock lightly on her door.

"Come in!" Margaret's voice carries through the wood, still surprisingly strong despite her age.

When I enter the room, a dismal rush floods my veins, leaving my fingertips numb and my thoughts scattering like startled birds taking flight.

Photos. Framed on every surface. Peter and Eva on a

beach, Peter and Eva at what looks like a Christmas party, Peter and Eva smiling in front of a restaurant.

My photos—the ones that used to show Peter with me, with Lucy—have vanished.

Margaret sits in her favorite armchair, a crocheted blanket across her knees despite the warmth of the room. Her silver hair is freshly styled, likely from the salon downstairs. She smiles at me, but there's confusion in her eyes.

"Juliette," she says, a question in my name. "You're early. I thought you weren't coming until tomorrow."

I cross the room and bend to kiss her cheek, her skin like crepe paper. Up close, she smells of talcum and the lavender sachets she still insists on placing in her dresser drawers.

"I wanted to surprise you," I tell her, even though we didn't have plans to see each other. I settle into the chair across from her, my eyes drawn to the photos that surround us like silent ridicules. "How are you feeling?"

"Oh, the same. Doctors say I'm doing well for my age." She waves a dismissive hand, arthritic knuckles prominent. "Eva brought me new photos yesterday. Aren't they lovely?"

The air in my lungs turns to cement. "They certainly are," I manage to say. "I didn't realize you had so many pictures of Eva and Peter together."

Margaret's brow furrows slightly. "Eva says I should keep them where I can see them. To help me remember." She leans forward, lowering her voice conspiratorially. "Sometimes I forget things now. Did you know that?"

I swallow hard, the lump in my throat expanding until I can barely breathe. "Yes, Margaret. I know."

"Would you like to help me with my puzzle? I was just working on it." She gestures toward a card table near the window where a partially completed jigsaw puzzle spreads across the surface—a pastoral scene with rolling hills and a red barn.

"I'd love to help." I follow her to the table, pulling up a second chair. The puzzle appears to be about halfway finished, with the border completed and clusters of pieces forming recognizable sections.

"Eva usually helps me when she visits," Margaret says, settling into her chair and picking up a piece with a fragment of blue sky. "She's very good at finding the right pieces."

I bite the inside of my cheek until I taste blood. Instead of responding, I scan the scattered pieces, looking for corner sections to work on. My hands need something to do while processing the shock of seeing my life erased from every photograph in this room.

"When did you first meet Eva?" I ask, keeping my voice light as I fit two pieces together.

Margaret examines a piece with part of the barn's roof. "Oh, a while ago. I don't remember exactly when. Last spring, I think. Peter brought her to visit. He said she was someone special he wanted me to know."

A puzzle piece slips from my grasp, clattering onto the table. "So, around six months ago? That's when Peter first got sick."

"Was it?" Margaret frowns, her eyes momentarily vacant as she turns a piece between her fingers. "Time gets so confusing these days. But I remember he wanted me to meet her. Said it was important."

"And he introduced her as..." I prompt gently, fitting another piece into place.

"His friend from work, of course." Margaret smiles, successfully connecting a piece to the barn section. "Such a kind girl. She visits me more than anyone." She reaches for another piece. "Peter said I should keep their secret until he could figure out how to tell you about the divorce."

The word steals my breath like a sucker punch. "Divorce?" I stammer, my hand freezing over the puzzle pieces.

"That's what Eva said." Margaret continues working on her section, seemingly unaware of my distress. "That Peter was going to divorce you, but then he got so sick, there wasn't time." Her hands tremble slightly as she tries to force two pieces together that don't fit. "I don't remember if Peter actually said that part. But Eva reminded me."

I gently take the pieces from her before she can damage them, finding their correct positions. "Margaret, did Peter actually tell you he wanted a divorce, or did Eva tell you that?"

She blinks at me, confusion clouding her face as she stares at the puzzle. 'I... I'm not sure anymore. Eva visits so often, and she helps me remember things. My mind plays tricks, you know."

"I know." I hand her a piece that clearly belongs to the barn, giving her something to focus on. "Did Peter ever bring Eva here himself? Did you see them together?"

"Oh, yes." Margaret nods emphatically, then points to one of the photos on a nearby shelf—the same beach scene I found in our study, also cropped to remove Sebastian. "Right here. This is when they went to Cabo together."

She abandons the puzzle piece to reach for a tin on the table. "Would you like some cookies while we work? Eva brought almond ones yesterday. My favorite."

"That sounds lovely," I say.

As Margaret busies herself with opening the tin of cookies, I continue working on the puzzle, my hands needing the structured task while my mind reels.

But I can't ignore the fact that every surface in this room holds evidence of Eva's presence—my wedding photo now shows Eva in a white dress; Lucy's birth announcement shows Eva holding a newborn; our family vacation snapshots have all been manipulated to erase me and insert her instead.

I stand and float over to the nearest frame, picking it up with trembling fingers. The glass is cool against my skin as I trace the outline of Eva's face where mine should be. Small inconsistencies reveal the forgery—shadows falling at impossible angles, lighting that doesn't quite match. I set it down before the urge to smash it overcomes me.

Instead, I snap a picture of the photos with my phone.

Margaret returns to the puzzle, setting the cookie tin between us, suddenly looking tired. "I've been taking new medication," she confides, placing a piece with excessive concentration. "For my nerves. The doctor Eva recommended said it would help with my anxiety about Peter."

"What doctor?" I ask, though I already suspect the answer.

"Dr. Wilson Grant. Such a nice man." She gestures toward her bedroom. "The pills are in there. Eva makes sure I take them properly."

"Would you mind if I looked at them? Just to make sure they're not interfering with your other medications."

Margaret waves permission, and I step into her bedroom. Here too, photos have been changed. On her nightstand, a prescription bottle sits next to a glass of water. I pick it up, reading the label, the medication prescribed by Dr. Wilson Grant. I snap a photo of it with my phone.

My hands shake as I return to the living room. Margaret has forgotten the puzzle and is staring out the window instead, her attention drifting as it often does.

I sit beside her, taking her frail hand in mine. "Margaret, I need to ask you something important." I keep my voice gentle. "Did Peter ever leave anything with you? Something he wanted you to keep safe?"

Her eyes remain on the window. "He was such a good boy. Always prepared."

"Yes, he was." I squeeze her hand lightly. "Did he leave anything for me? Or for Lucy? Perhaps a letter or a package?"

Margaret turns to me, clarity suddenly sharpening her gaze. "He said you might ask someday."

The hairs rise on my arms. "What did he say exactly?"

"He said, 'If Juliette ever comes asking for something I left with you, it means something strange has happened to me.'" She frowns. "Has something strange happened, dear?"

The question stings like salt in an open wound. "Peter passed away, Margaret. Remember? We had the funeral last week."

"Oh." Her face crumples briefly, then smooths out again. "Yes, of course. Eva mentioned that. She's been so good to me since then."

I squeeze her hand again, grounding myself in the present. "Margaret, if Peter left something for me, it's very important that I have it now. Lucy might need it someday."

The mention of her granddaughter sparks recognition. "Lucy! Her birthday is coming. I need to get her a present."

"Yes, her birthday is coming." I lean closer. "Margaret, please try to remember. Did Peter leave an envelope or a package with you? Anything?"

She stares at me blankly for a long moment. I'm about to try another approach when something shifts in her expression.

"In my jewelry box," she says suddenly. "He said only you would know what it meant."

I follow her to the bedroom again, watching as she opens the walnut jewelry box on her dresser. Beneath a tray of costume jewelry, she removes an envelope, plain white without anything written on it.

"He left this," she says, holding it toward me. "A while ago. Said to give it to you if anything strange happened to him." She frowns. "I forgot until now. I get so distracted with grief and Eva's frequent visits."

I take the envelope, feeling its weight—light yet somehow immeasurably heavy. "Thank you, Margaret. This means a lot to me."

"Is it important?" she asks.

"Very important." Suppressing my urge to tear it open right there, I tuck the envelope into my purse. "A gift from Peter."

We work on the puzzle a little longer, making small talk about Lucy's school and Margaret's physical therapy. I promise to bring Lucy to visit soon, though every mention of my daughter makes Margaret glance at the manipulated photos, as if trying to reconcile conflicting memories.

When I stand to leave, Margaret grabs my wrist with surprising strength. "Juliette," she says, eyes suddenly clear, "Peter was afraid at the end. He told me things weren't what they seemed."

My breath catches. "What else did he say?"

But the moment of clarity passes, her expression clouding again. "I don't remember now. But he loved you very much. I'm sure of that."

I bend to hug her, breathing in her familiar scent one more time. "I know he did. And he loved you too. I'll come back soon."

IN THE PARKING LOT, I sit in my car before starting the engine. The envelope from Margaret waits in my purse. I tear it open and pull out a single sheet of paper. Peter's handwriting, as familiar to me as my own face, fills the page:

I hope you never see this, but if you do, the <u>key</u> *to everything is why we hated our accounting class. And remember our first date, how I spilled my beer on you? Love you forever, Peter.*

I read it three times, fingers tracing his words. He underlined "key" once—he must have meant the key I found in our study. We hated our accounting class because of Professor Whitman, who'd been a director at National Trust Bank.

The key must be for a safe deposit box at that bank.

And our first date—I close my eyes, remembering. October 23rd. The box number must be 1023.

A surge of energy courses through me. Whatever Peter hid in that safe deposit box, he made sure only I would understand how to find it. Thank God Margaret didn't accidentally give the envelope to Eva.

I start the car, checking my mirrors before pulling out of the parking space. Only one more day until I'm ordered to surrender my home and partial custody of Lucy to Eva. But now I have a new destination—National Trust Bank—and with it, the promise of whatever evidence Peter managed to hide before he ran out of time.

The envelope sits beside me on the passenger seat as I drive, Peter's final gift illuminating the way forward.

17

———————

National Trust Bank sits at the base of a downtown highrise, its granite columns and glass facade projecting stability and permanence—a stark contrast to everything my life has become. I pull into a parking lot around the corner, choosing a spot near a security camera. I need witnesses, even if they're just digital eyes.

The bank's interior feels intentionally imposing—all marble floors, high ceilings, and hushed conversations. Money speaks in whispers here. I approach the main desk where a young woman with a perfect blonde bun greets me with a practiced smile.

"I need access to a safe deposit box," I say, keeping my voice steady.

"Of course. May I see your ID and box key?"

I produce my driver's license and the key from my purse. "Box 1023," I say, hoping I've interpreted Peter's note correctly.

The woman picks up the key, examining it closely. "Just one moment, please." She turns to her computer, tapping keys with manicured fingernails.

I shift my weight from one foot to the other, counting the seconds. Through the floor-to-ceiling windows, I watch cars driving by on the street, mentally cataloging each one. A red sedan. A black SUV. A delivery truck. Each new vehicle spikes my adrenaline until it passes by.

The woman looks up from her screen, then hands my key and license back to me. "Mrs. Samson, would you mind following me? You'll need to see the manager."

A knot forms in the pit of my stomach. "Is there a problem?" I blurt out before I remember that usually managers are the ones who have access to the vault.

"Not at all." Her smile remains unchanged, professional to the core. "This way, please."

I follow her through the lobby. Financial advisors sit at their desks with clients, their hushed conversations about retirement plans and investment strategies creating a gentle murmur. At the far end, we stop before a glass-walled office. "Anthony Richards, Branch Manager," is displayed on a gleaming brass plaque.

"He'll be with you shortly," the receptionist says, gesturing to a plush chair opposite the empty desk.

Left alone, I take inventory of the office. Diplomas hang on one wall, slightly askew as if recently adjusted. A family photo of Richards with his wife and teenage children sits on the credenza, with everyone wearing matching blue shirts against a beach backdrop. Everything is meticulously arranged, evoking a sense of reliability and trust.

Through the glass walls, I have a clear view of the bank's entrance and teller windows. I watch customers come and go, studying each face. My fingers find the edge of Peter's letter inside my purse.

I hear a voice in the hallway and turn as a man in his early fifties enters. His dark gray suit fits perfectly, his red tie knotted with precision. He offers his hand with a well-honed smile.

"Mrs. Samson, I'm Anthony Richards. I apologize for the wait."

I shake his hand, his grip firm. "Is there an issue with accessing the box?"

He settles into his chair, folding his hands on the desk. "I just need to verify a few things. May I please see your identification and the key again?"

I slide my driver's license across the desk along with the key. Richards examines both, then turns to his computer.

"I understand this box is registered solely in your husband's name," he says, typing on his keyboard. "I'm just confirming that you're authorized to access it."

"I am." My tongue sticks to the roof of my suddenly dry mouth. What if Peter hadn't added me? What if—

"Here we are." He nods, seemingly satisfied. "Yes, you're on the authorized list."

Relief floods through me as I slowly exhale. But before Richards can continue, a young teller appears at the door.

"I'm so sorry to interrupt, Mr. Richards, but we have a situation at the front that requires your attention."

Richards frowns. "Can't Jessica handle it?"

"She asked for you specifically, sir." The teller's eyes dart to me, then back to Richards. "It's regarding the Westbrook account."

"Very well." He rises from his chair. "Mrs. Samson, please excuse me for a moment. This shouldn't take long."

As he leaves, I shift in my seat to maintain my view of the lobby. That's when I see her—Eva Lerner, stepping through the main doors, her camel coat belted tightly around her waist, dark hair swept back in a severe ponytail. Her face is composed, but I recognize the predatory alertness in her movements.

A cold numbness spreads from my center to my finger-tips, leaving me momentarily paralyzed.

She approaches the teller window, speaking to a different employee than the one who helped me. Though I can't hear her words, I recognize the confident tilt of her head, the persuasive gesture of her hands. Why is she here? Did she follow me?

Richards returns, retrieving a set of keys from his desk drawer. "Sorry about that. Now, let's get you to your safe deposit box."

"Thank you." I rise quickly, angling myself so my back is to the lobby. "I appreciate your help."

He leads me toward the vault, away from the main lobby where Eva continues her conversation. As we proceed, he makes some bland comments about new services the bank is offering, which I barely register. I manage a noncommittal "Mm-hmm," glancing over my shoulder. Eva has moved away from the teller window and is now speaking with a woman in a blazer, who must be another manager. The woman's arms are crossed, her posture ungiving.

In front of the vault, Richards pauses to enter a code on a keypad. The heavy metal door swings open with a soft hydraulic hiss, revealing rows of metal boxes embedded in the walls. He leads me to box 1023, inserts his key, then gestures for me to insert mine.

"I'll give you some privacy," he says once the box is open. "There's a viewing room to your right. Just let me know when you're finished."

The metal box slides out smoothly. I carry it to the small room he indicated, closing the door behind me. The quiet is absolute, as if the room has been designed to swallow sound.

My fingers tremble as I lift the lid.

Inside lies a sealed manila envelope marked "Insurance" in Peter's distinctive handwriting. Beside it, a USB drive labeled with the same word. Beneath these items, a stack of medical records bearing Peter's name and Dr. Wilson Grant's signature. On top of everything rests a letter in a sealed envelope with my name written on the front.

I break the seal with unsteady fingers. Peter's handwriting is on the paper inside, with the familiar loops and angles I'd seen on hundreds of grocery lists and birthday cards, but the lines wavered slightly, as if his hand struggled to stay steady. I unfold the pages, my throat tightening:

Juliette, if you're reading this, I fear something has happened to me. Sebastian is not who we thought. He and his half-sister Eva have been planning something I'm only beginning to understand... I'm desperately trying to get irrefutable proof before going to the authorities, but Sebastian's influence is far-reaching. My past GBS diagnosis means any claims of foul play on my part could easily be dismissed as paranoia or mental instability. I have to gather everything quietly, hoping you will find this if I fail.

The words blur together momentarily, swimming on the page like they're underwater. I brace myself against the table, the fluorescent light suddenly harsh and pulsing as I continue reading:

I noticed financial discrepancies several months ago—unaccounted withdrawals, falsified expense reports, money being funneled through shell companies. When I confronted Sebastian privately, he denied everything, but the next day I started experiencing symptoms similar to my old GBS flare-ups. I've been secretly keeping track of everything, which you'll find documented on the thumb drive.

Hopefully I'll have enough evidence to give to the authorities soon, but I'm writing this letter now, in case something happens.

I love you more than I can say. I'm so sorry I didn't protect us better. Trust no one connected to Sebastian.

All my love forever,

Peter

My hands shake so violently that the paper rustles like dry leaves. The small room feels too warm and airless, the walls pressing closer. I taste blood in my mouth where I've bitten the inside of my cheek. Quickly, I take photos of each page with my phone, holding it steady with both hands to ensure the images are clear. The USB drive goes into my pocket, everything else I jam into my purse. Each second feels like borrowed time I don't have.

Leaving the viewing room, I find Richards waiting nearby, checking his watch discreetly.

"All finished?"

"Yes, thank you." I return the empty box, which he locks back into the wall.

A drop of sweat trickles down my back as we exit the vault. I keep my expression neutral while scanning for Eva, praying our paths don't cross. But as we round the corner back toward the lobby, I see her—her back to me, gesturing animatedly at the female manager, who shakes her head firmly.

"I'm sorry, Ms. Lerner, but as I've explained, without proper authorization or the correct key, we simply cannot grant access to any safe deposit box."

"You don't understand," Eva says, her voice carrying across the marble floor. "My husband intended for me to have access to his personal effects. It was his verbal wish before he passed."

The manager remains unmoved. "Our policies are

quite clear. Unless you're listed as an authorized representative or have legal documentation, such as power of attorney, I cannot help you."

I duck my head, letting my hair fall forward to partially shield my face as Richards leads me back toward the exit. We're almost clear when Eva turns, her frustrated gaze sweeping the bank—and landing directly on me.

Recognition flashes in her eyes, followed immediately by calculation. Her lips part slightly, surprise quickly masked by a frosty smile.

I keep walking, my face carefully composed despite the riot inside me. She doesn't know what I found or even if I accessed the box at all. For now, that uncertainty is my only advantage.

"Thank you for your help," I tell Richards as we reach the door, conscious of Eva's eyes tracking my every movement.

"Anytime, Mrs. Samson. Is there anything else you need today?"

"No, that's all." I push through the glass doors into the early afternoon sun, resisting the urge to break into a run.

Once inside my car with the doors locked, I release a ragged breath that fogs the window slightly. My phone is in my hand before I consciously decide to call, my finger automatically finding Lena's number.

"I need to see you right away," I say when she answers. "I have the proof. Peter left evidence."

"Where are you?" Lena's voice is sharp, focused.

"Leaving National Trust Bank. Eva's here too—she tried to access Peter's safe deposit box."

"Did she see you?"

"Yes. Just as I was leaving."

"Come to the bar. Back entrance. I'll make sure no one follows you in."

I start the engine, checking my mirrors obsessively as I pull out of the parking lot. No sign of Eva.

The edges of Peter's documents and letters peek out of my purse. They're not just his last words, but vindication. Proof I'm not crazy. Confirmation that everything I've felt —the wrongness, the manipulation, the sense of being hunted—was real.

18

On the drive to Lena's bar, I check my rearview mirror repeatedly. Is that the same black sedan two cars back? I make a sudden right turn down a side street, holding my breath until I confirm the car continues straight ahead. My shoulders drop a touch, but the knot in my stomach remains.

At the next intersection, I double back, circling the block before continuing toward the bar. I eye my purse on the passenger seat, where the contents of Peter's safe deposit box lie hidden—tangible proof that I'm not paranoid, that the violations inflicted on me exist in cold, hard reality.

I pull into the alley behind Lena's place. The early afternoon light throws dark shapes across the brick walls and dumpsters. She stands in the back doorway, glancing both directions before waving me forward.

"Park behind the dumpster," she says, pointing to a spot invisible from the main road. "No one will see it there."

I squeeze into the tight space and exit clutching my

purse against my chest. The stench of garbage and stale beer hangs in the air.

"Did anyone follow you?" Lena asks.

"I don't think so. I made some random turns and doubled back on myself."

She nods and leads me inside. The back stairwell creaks under our weight as we climb. Chipped paint covers the walls, exposed pipes run alongside us, and decades of must fill my nostrils. At the top, Lena unlocks the back door to her apartment.

Warm light bathes the space. Being here again, I take in more details: books arranged along shelves, leather furniture worn soft with age, exposed brick walls lending a fortress-like solidity to the room. My shoulders drop another inch—no watchful eyes here.

Lena clears folders and papers from her dining table, revealing a dark wooden surface marred with countless glass rings.

"Let's see what you have."

I empty my purse onto the table—the manila envelope, Peter's letters, the thumb drive, and medical records. Possible evidence of my husband's murder lies spread before us.

"Peter really was quite busy," Lena says, staring at the pile.

My fingers stop trembling as I focus on practical matters. "We need copies of everything. Physical and digital backups in different locations."

"I've got a scanner and an external hard drive. But first, let's see what we're dealing with."

I slide the thumb drive toward her. Lena retrieves her laptop from the other room and connects the drive while I open the manila envelope.

"Is Malcolm around?" I ask.

"He's at work."

"So are you two…?"

Lena shakes her head. "Just friends." She falls silent, turning her attention to her laptop.

I sift through the contents of the envelope. Bank statements, company financial records, and what look like surveillance photos. I arrange them in groups as Lena navigates through the files from the thumb drive.

"Look at this," she says, turning the screen toward me. "Seems Peter found evidence of embezzlement earlier this year."

The spreadsheet displays transactions between company accounts and several shell corporations. Red highlights mark suspicious transfers dating back nearly two years, totaling millions. All similar information to what Marcus had found in the cloud, but more detailed.

"You were right about Sebastian all along," I say. My mouth goes dry as the reality sinks in.

Lena opens another document. "There's a dated memo here. Peter confronted Sebastian about this six months ago."

We lean forward together, reading Peter's private notes:

March 15 – Met with S privately re: financial discrepancies. Initial denial, then partial admission when presented with evidence. Claims personal financial trouble, requested discretion. Introduced E as his half-sister who 'needed financial help' and has been working as associate since December. Agreed to repayment plan and oversight measures. Will monitor closely.

My heart pounds as pieces lock into place. "Eva's been part of this from the beginning."

Lena's eyes meet mine across the table, radiating silent frustration.

The memory stings—how I'd dismissed my sister's

concerns and chosen my husband over her. "I'm sorry I didn't believe you."

She closes her eyes, breathes in deeply, relaxing her face. "That's all in the past," she says, though something shadows her expression again briefly.

After a moment, she reaches across and squeezes my hand. "What matters is what we do now. I'm just glad you came to me, to help you through this."

I nod, placing my other hand on her forearm and squeezing back before letting go. We return to Peter's documentation. After that first confrontation, Peter had noted Sebastian's failure to start repayments. The subsequent entries grew increasingly alarmed:

April 10 – No repayment installment received. S claims company cash flow issues require delay. Monitoring accounts closely.

April 22 – Experiencing unexplained fatigue, tingling in extremities. Dr. Grant suggests possible GBS relapse. Timing concerning given confrontation with S.

May 8 – S continues to delay repayment. E increasingly present around my office. Have noticed her particular interest in Lucy, offering to watch her multiple times.

"He connected his health issues to the confrontation," I say, my heart pounding like a fist against my ribs as I flip through the medical records. "These are from when his symptoms first started."

Stark medical terminology lays out the progression—fatigue and numbness becoming muscle weakness and pain. Dr. Wilson Grant's notes consistently reference Peter's teenage bout with Guillain-Barré Syndrome, attributing all symptoms to a rare relapse.

"Wait," Lena says, opening a video file. "Look at this."

Shaky surveillance footage shows Sebastian entering a restaurant, checking his watch before taking a seat. A minute later, a man in a white coat joins him—Dr. Wilson Grant.

"The date stamp shows this was two weeks after Peter's symptoms began," Lena says.

Heat percolates through me. "Who took these videos? Did Peter hire someone?"

"Maybe a private investigator, but there's no mention of one in his notes."

She scrolls through more videos: Eva following me at the mall while I shop with Lucy, Sebastian accessing Peter's office after hours, Eva and Sebastian meeting in a parking garage.

"Peter was building a case," Lena says. "Documenting everything step by step."

I turn to another file from the envelope—lab results dated two weeks before Peter died. My heart stops, then lurches painfully forward.

"Lena," I push the paper toward her, my hand shaking. "These are test results from an independent lab. Peter had his hair and blood tested for toxins."

As she reads the document, her jaw clenches. "Arsenic. Low levels, but consistent with long-term exposure." She looks up, her expression grim. "Classic chronic poisoning —the symptoms mimic neurological disorders."

Reality fractures like thin ice beneath my feet, the proof sending spiderweb cracks through everything I thought I knew about Peter's final months. My stomach churns violently as the full horror of what I'm seeing settles into my bones with sickening clarity.

"They murdered him," I say. The words scrape my throat. "When I was taking care of him, watching him fade away—they were killing him little by little."

Lena covers my hand with hers. "Peter got these results back the day before he collapsed and went to the hospital.

His notes say he was planning to take this to the police that week."

The timing clicks into place. "They must have increased the dose," I say. Bile rises in my throat. "When they realized he suspected something, they needed to silence him."

I push up from my chair and start to pace the apartment. Heat floods my face while my hands turn to ice. "We need to go to the police. Today. They murdered Peter."

"Before we do that, we should think this through," Lena says. "Accusations this serious require ironclad evidence. Besides, they're already working to discredit you, painting you as unstable and unreliable."

"What more do we need? We have the lab tests, the financial records—"

"Tests that they'll explain away by saying the samples were contaminated. Or that maybe he drank contaminated water, ate contaminated food, or something else. Financial records that could be dismissed as accounting errors, or that they've been taken out of context." She holds my gaze. "From what I've found, Sebastian has resources and connections. If we move too quickly with evidence that can be picked apart, we lose our shot."

I lean against the wall, swallowing the bitter taste of frustration. "So what do we do?"

"Call your lawyer first—she needs to know what we're dealing with. I know someone at the medical examiner's office from my reporting days. We should find out if exhuming Peter's body would still show evidence of poisoning."

My stomach turns at the thought of disturbing Peter's remains, but I nod.

"Wait—" Lena has opened a new folder labeled "Eva."

Inside is a collection of background research—previous addresses, employment records, news clippings.

A headline from a small Ohio newspaper jumps out: "Elderly Man's Death Raises Questions; Grandson's Fiancée Under Scrutiny."

The article, dated four years ago, details suspicions around a woman named Elaine Damon. Authorities had briefly investigated her after her fiancé's grandfather died unexpectedly.

Cold dread slithers down my spine as I read on. The elderly man had changed his will to include "Elaine" shortly before his death. Posthumous testing revealed traces of heavy metals in his system. Prosecutors ultimately dropped charges for lack of concrete evidence.

"Eva," I whisper. "Or whatever her real name is."

"He found another case where she's done this before," Lena says.

I stare at the photo accompanying the article. The woman looks similar to Eva, but with auburn hair instead of dark, her features subtly altered with different makeup. Those same predatory eyes stare back at me.

My knees weaken. I drop back into my chair.

"The court has ordered Eva to move into my home tomorrow and take custody of Lucy," I say. A cold hollowness spreads through my chest. "They're forcing me to hand my daughter to a murderer."

"That's not going to happen," Lena says. Her voice hardens with determination. "We'll keep working to build an airtight case to stop her."

19

———————

I glance at my phone and jolt upright. "I need to go. Lucy gets out in twenty minutes."

Lena looks up from the documents. "Is she safe at school?"

A cold wire of tension coils itself around my ribs. "I set up a password system with her teacher and the principal. Anyone picking her up has to know it."

Lena's eyebrows draw together. "Is that enough?"

I meet her eyes, the silence stretching between us as neither of us voices what we're both thinking.

"It has to be, for now." I sling my purse over my shoulder. "We'll have copies of everything by tonight?"

She nods. "I'll handle it. Go get Lucy."

LUCY CHATTERS ABOUT her art project from the backseat as we approach our house The winter sun casts long shadows across the street, and something about the quality of light makes me pause.

"Mommy, can I watch Bluey?"

"Just a minute, sweetie," I say as I pull into our driveway.

A black Escalade is parked at our curb, and a figure sits on our porch—broad shoulders, expensive suit. Sebastian.

The insides of my body seem to hollow out, as if I've missed a step on a staircase. "You can watch one show when we get inside. I need to talk to Mr. Dorsey first."

Her small face scrunches. "From Daddy's work?"

"Yes." I force a smile. "Let's go in through the garage door."

Inside, I settle Lucy with her show, my hands trembling slightly as I navigate to her favorite episode. She curls up on the sofa, clutching Nibbles.

"I'll be right outside on the porch talking to Mr. Dorsey. Stay here, okay?"

She nods, already absorbed in the colorful animation. I press my lips to the crown of her head, inhaling the scent of the school day—crayons, playground dust, and that indefinable sweetness that is purely Lucy.

I don't invite Sebastian in. I step outside. The front door closes firmly behind me. He rises from the wicker chair, smoothing his tailored jacket with manicured hands.

"Juliette." His smile reveals perfect teeth. "You're looking well."

I remain by the door, arms crossed. "What do you want, Sebastian?"

"Direct as always." He gestures to the chairs. "May we sit? I'd like to discuss an amicable resolution to our situation."

I don't move. "Our situation?"

"These legal disputes." He shakes his head, a picture of regret. "They're becoming unnecessarily contentious. I believe we can find common ground that benefits everyone."

"Everyone meaning you and Eva?"

"Everyone, including you, Juliette." He sits back down, crossing one leg over the other. The creak of the wicker chair breaks the silence between us. "I'm offering you a settlement."

Despite myself, I take the chair farthest from him. The cushion is still warm from the afternoon sun. "A settlement?"

Sebastian's smile widens a fraction. "Two million dollars. Cash. Tax-free."

Two million dollars. More money than I've ever seen at once, even during the company's best years. The breeze stirs the potted chrysanthemums beside the porch, but I barely notice their movement.

"In exchange for what, exactly?"

"A clean break." Sebastian leans forward, his voice dropping. A faint whiff of sandalwood cologne reaches me as he leans closer. "You would relinquish all claims to the house, the company..." He pauses, studying my face. "And Lucy."

Time stops, like film caught in a projector, one frame burning brighter and brighter as I focus solely on Sebastian's face. "What did you say?"

"Eva has grown quite attached to Lucy," he continues, his tone smooth as glass. "And as Peter's legal wife, she has strong grounds for full custody, especially given your documented mental health issues."

Blood rushes to my face, hot and violent. "My what?"

"Your hospitalization for postpartum depression is now part of the court record." His expression feigns sympathy.

My heart stutters, a sudden heaviness in my chest. I

straighten, forcing myself to appear composed, but I feel as though the ground beneath me has shifted.

"The records indicate suicidal ideation, Juliette. The judge already found that concerning, otherwise she wouldn't have awarded Eva shared custody. It wouldn't take much to convince her to award full custody, especially considering your recent erratic behavior. You've been awfully distraught since Peter passed away. Heck, even since your divorce and Peter's marriage to Eva."

I bolt out of my chair. "Leave now." The words scrape my throat, raw and jagged.

He spreads his arms in a placating gesture. "This is a generous offer. Two million dollars would let you start fresh. Perhaps somewhere warm?" His smile remains cold, calculating. "You could build a new life, away from painful memories."

"I'll be building my life right here, thanks," I respond, my voice steady.

He glances at the front door, then back at me with a smirk. "You should reconsider. It'll take more than a few re-keyed locks to keep me from what I want, Juliette."

"A life without my daughter?" My voice rises. "You can't possibly think I'd consider that."

Sebastian's posture shifts—almost imperceptibly, but I catch the tightening of his jaw. "I understand your emotional attachment—"

"Emotional attachment? She's my child!"

"—but consider what's best for Lucy. Stability. Continuity. Two parents in a loving home."

"Two parents?" I laugh, the sound harsh in my own ears, like broken glass against metal. "You mean Eva and who? You?"

Something flickers across his face—discomfort? Disgust? It's gone before I can name it.

"Eva will provide everything Lucy needs."

"Like she provided for that elderly man in Ohio? The one who conveniently died after changing his will?"

Sebastian's eyes narrow. "I don't know what you're implying."

"I think you do." I lean forward. "Just like I think you know about the money disappearing from company accounts. Peter certainly knew. He was gathering evidence of your embezzlement."

"Peter's paranoid delusions during his illness are hardly evidence." Sebastian waves a dismissive hand. "His declining health affected his judgment, his memory. He became confused about many things."

"Peter wasn't confused about anything."

"The doctors documented his deteriorating mental state." Sebastian's voice softens with contrived concern. "You were there, Juliette. You saw how he changed toward the end."

I watch him carefully. "When did you first notice his symptoms? The tingling, the fatigue?"

A flash of tension crosses Sebastian's shoulders before he settles back into performative ease. "I believe it was early spring. April, perhaps? He mentioned feeling off during a board meeting."

"And you suggested he see Dr. Grant?"

"Peter thought Dr. Grant took great care of him."

I nod slowly. "And the symptoms just happened to start right after he confronted you about the missing money."

Sebastian sighs heavily. "This conspiracy theory does you no credit, Juliette. Peter died from complications of pneumonia, exacerbated by his Guillain-Barré relapse. It was tragic but natural."

"Natural." The word tastes bitter. "Like poisoning is natural?"

His face remains composed, but his finger taps once against his knee—a tell. He adjusts his expensive watch— the Breitling from the photo—on his wrist, the metallic clink of the band punctuating the silence.

"I've been through Peter's safe deposit box," I say, watching his expression. "He left quite a collection of interesting items."

Sebastian's composure cracks—alarm flashes across his face before he can suppress it. "What box?" His voice sharpens.

"Peter left me everything I need to understand what really happened to him." I hold Sebastian's gaze, unflinching. "I'm not signing anything, I'm not taking any settlement, and I'm certainly not abandoning my daughter to people who murdered my husband."

The polished façade crumbles like dried mud, revealing something harder beneath. Sebastian stands, looming over me. I hold my ground, refusing to be physically dominated despite the racing of my heart.

"Eva gets what Eva wants," he says, his voice dropping to a cold murmur. "She wants to be Lucy's mother. She wants this house. She's prepared for this role in ways you can't imagine."

"Is that a threat?"

"It's reality." He steps closer. Our faces are inches apart. "You have twenty-four hours to reconsider the offer before things become much more difficult for you."

He turns and strides down the porch steps. The wooden boards creak under his weight. I remain frozen, watching as he slides into his Escalade and pulls away from the curb.

As his car disappears around the corner, movement catches my eye—the familiar black sedan with tinted windows parked half a block away. The same one I've glimpsed near Lucy's school. The same one I thought I'd lost on my way to Lena's

They're watching us. Constantly.

I back into the house, double-checking that the door is locked. Through the window, I watch the sedan. It doesn't move. Its presence is the message—we see you, we know where you are, we're always here.

My gaze drifts to Lucy, innocently engrossed in her show. Despite resisting Sebastian, Peter's death still claws at me. Perhaps he was right about one thing—my distress may be skewing my perception. Doubt, a persistent throb, remains.

My phone vibrates in my pocket. Lena.

"Get back safe?" she asks.

I keep my voice low, moving away from the front windows. "Sebastian was waiting here when we got home."

"What did he want?" Alarm sharpens her tone.

"To buy me off. Two million dollars to walk away from everything." My voice catches. "Including Lucy."

Silence on the line stretches for three heartbeats.

"Are you both safe right now?"

I glance again toward the living room where Lucy giggles at something on the TV, blissfully unaware. Her sneakers rest beside the couch, laces tangled into knots I'll have to undo later. "For the moment. But Lena—" I swallow hard. "There's a car outside. They're watching the house."

"Pack a bag," she says without hesitation. "For both of you. You're not staying there tonight."

"Where—"

"Here. My apartment. As far as they know, we haven't spoken in years." The sound of drawers opening carries through the phone. "I'm clearing space now."

"But the court order—"

"Says Eva moves in on Friday. It's Thursday. We have time to figure this out, but not if you're under surveillance."

The shadowy sedan sits like a malevolent guardian at the corner of my street. How long has it been there? What have they seen?

"I'll be ready to leave in fifteen minutes," I say, moving toward Lucy's room to pack her things. "And Lena? Thank you."

"Family protects family," she answers. "Now hurry."

20

Lucy treats our sudden relocation to Lena's apartment like an adventure—camping indoors, she calls it— and falls asleep quickly on the sofa in Lena's spare room amid a nest of pillows. I sit beside her for half an hour, watching the gentle rise and fall of her chest, my hand resting lightly on her back to feel each breath.

I think I managed to lose the black sedan by taking a circuitous route through three different neighborhoods and doubling back twice, but I'm not a professional at this. Every car behind us could have been someone working for them for all I know.

When I finally emerge from the makeshift bedroom, Lena is at her laptop, surrounded by printouts of Peter's documents.

"She asleep?" She glances up, the blue light from the screen casting hollows beneath her cheekbones.

I nod, sinking into the chair across from her. "What time is our appointment tomorrow?"

"Nine-thirty." Lena pushes a mug of tea toward me, the ceramic scraping against the scarred tabletop. "After we drop Lucy at school. Dr. Kumar is doing us a favor—he normally doesn't take consultations like this."

"And you're sure we can trust him?"

"With my life." Lena's voice is firm. "And more importantly, with yours."

Later that night, I lie awake on Lena's lumpy couch, staring at the water stains on the ceiling. Two million dollars. Sebastian's voice echoes in my head, the number flashing behind my eyelids whenever I close them. That's what they think my daughter is worth. That's the price they've calculated to buy my silence, my surrender.

THE STING of antiseptic and industrial cleaner assaults my nostrils as we walk through Northside Medical Center. That universal hospital smell instantly transports me back to Peter's last days. My stomach clenches—I hate how it hurls me back to that room, watching him slip away. But maybe today we'll uncover something, find answers about what really caused his death. We follow a series of color-coded lines on the floor, turning left at the blue intersection, then right at green.

"How do you know this doctor again?" I keep my voice low, though the corridor is empty except for us.

"Dr. Kumar was a source for an investigation I did on pharmaceutical fraud several years ago." Lena's boots squeak against the polished floor. "He's one of the good ones—brilliant and ethical. Too ethical for some of his colleagues' comfort."

We reach a door marked "Toxicology Lab—Authorized Personnel Only." Lena knocks twice, pauses, then once more. The door opens to reveal a man in his fifties with silver-streaked black hair and wire-rimmed glasses.

"Lena." His smile is warm, but his eyes quickly assess us both. "Come in, please."

The lab gleams with an order that feels reassuring—everything in its place, everything clean and controlled. The opposite of my life right now. Dr. Kumar navigates the space with efficiency, leading us to a small conference room where privacy glass shields us from the main laboratory.

"Dr. Kumar, this is my sister, Juliette Samson." Lena makes the introduction as we sit around a small table.

"Mrs. Samson." He nods, his hands resting perfectly still on the tabletop. "Lena explained some of your situation. I understand you have concerns about your husband's death?"

I place Peter's medical file on the table between us. My fingers linger on the folder, nervous about sharing this last piece of Peter I have left.

"My husband was diagnosed with a relapse of Guillain-Barré syndrome earlier this year. He deteriorated rapidly and eventually died from complications of pneumonia."

Dr. Kumar opens the file, his brow furrowing as he scans the pages. "But you suspect something else?"

"We found these independent lab results among my husband's possessions after his death." I push the separate folder toward him. "He apparently had tests done without his doctor's knowledge."

Dr. Kumar's eyebrows rise. He opens the second folder and immediately stiffens. His finger traces the columns of numbers, stopping at one value highlighted in yellow. The silence stretches as he flips through additional pages, comparing them with Peter's medical records. I can hear the soft hum of equipment from the lab beyond, the distant ping of an elevator, the rush of blood in my own ears.

"Mrs. Samson, these levels of arsenic are quite elevated." He looks up, his expression grave. "They suggest long-term exposure."

My breathing becomes deliberate, manual—in, out, in, out. I'd suspected it, but hearing it confirmed turns suspicion into sickening reality. I swallow hard before asking, "Could these levels cause the symptoms my husband experienced?"

"Absolutely. Progressive weakness, sensory changes, hair loss..." He consults the medical chart again. "The gastrointestinal distress noted here, the weight loss, the neurological symptoms—all consistent with chronic arsenic poisoning."

Lena leans forward. "His official diagnosis was a relapse of Guillain-Barré syndrome. Could that have been a misdiagnosis?"

"It would be reasonable to include it in the differential." Dr. Kumar removes his glasses, polishing them with a cloth from his pocket. "Both conditions affect the peripheral nervous system, causing ascending sensory abnormalities, weakness, sometimes paralysis. A doctor would have to specifically test for heavy metals to rule out poisoning, but if they weren't looking for it..."

"They wouldn't find it," I finish.

"What about the pneumonia?" Lena asks. "That's what ultimately killed him, according to the death certificate."

Dr. Kumar nods. "It fits. Someone with significant neurological impairment from arsenic exposure would be at much higher risk for developing pneumonia. The infection would spread more rapidly, and they'd have less physiological reserve to fight it."

My throat closes as if someone has tightened a vise around it. I see Peter again—his hollowed cheeks, the blue tinge to his lips as he gasped for breath through the oxygen mask. All while poison coursed through his veins.

"I don't understand," I force the words past the constriction in my throat, "could his doctor have genuinely mistaken arsenic poisoning for a relapse of his previous condition?"

"It's possible, but..." He hesitates, his fingers tap-tap-tapping a rhythm on the file. "A competent physician would develop a differential diagnosis, a list of other conditions that could cause these symptoms, especially with a deteriorating patient. They'd run tests to rule in or rule out each of the diagnoses until they had a definitive answer. And heavy metal screening isn't uncommon in cases of unexplained neurological symptoms, even with a history GBS, because relapses are pretty rare." He flips through Peter's chart. "Who was his primary physician during this illness?"

"Dr. Wilson Grant."

The change is subtle but unmistakable—a slight widening of the eyes, a momentary stillness. Dr. Kumar carefully replaces his glasses.

"You know him?" Lena asks, catching the same reaction.

"By reputation." Dr. Kumar's shoulders stiffen. "Dr. Grant lost his privileges at this hospital several years ago after a patient died under... questionable circumstances."

"What kind of circumstances?" My pulse quickens as I lean closer, the antiseptic smell of the lab suddenly sharper in my nostrils.

Dr. Kumar presses his lips together, glancing toward the door before lowering his voice. "There were concerns about medication errors. Nothing was proven conclusively, but the review board found sufficient cause to revoke his privileges."

"And yet he's still practicing medicine," Lena says.

"Unfortunately, yes." He frowns, looking again at Peter's chart. "This is troubling."

"There's more," Lena adds. "I've been investigating connections, and Dr. Grant and Sebastian Dorsey—my brother-in-law's business partner—were fraternity brothers in college. They've maintained connections over the years."

Something flickers across Dr. Kumar's features, like a ripple passing over the surface of a pond before it smooths again. "So you suspect Dr. Grant deliberately misdiagnosed your husband to mask the poisoning?"

"It's starting to look that way," Lena says.

I reach into my purse and withdraw a prescription bottle. "This is the medication Peter was taking for neuropathic pain. Gabapentin. It was prescribed by Dr. Grant."

Dr. Kumar accepts the bottle, unscrews the cap, and peers inside at the remaining capsules.

"May I?" He gestures to a magnifying lamp at a nearby workstation.

We follow him as he places one of the capsules under the powerful magnifier. He studies it carefully, turning it with a pair of fine forceps.

"Interesting." He adjusts the magnification and points to the seam where the two halves of the capsule meet. "See this? The edge here shows slight compression marks, and the seam isn't perfectly aligned."

I lean closer, squinting at the tiny imperfections he indicates. The yellow capsule looks normal to my untrained eye, but under his scrutiny, I can just make out the irregularities.

He places another capsule under the light, then a third. "They all show the same pattern. These capsules have been opened and resealed." He carefully separates the two halves of one capsule with his forceps, revealing the powder inside. "And look—the contents aren't uniform. There are different textures and colors mixed together that shouldn't be there."

I lean closer, my heart pounding as I see the tiny imperfections he indicates. "What does that mean?"

"It means someone carefully opened these capsules, added another substance to the original medication, then pressed them back together." Dr. Kumar's voice is grim. "It's actually quite simple if you know what you're doing—and virtually undetectable unless you examine them closely."

My knees buckle. I clutch the counter edge, my fingernails scraping against the cold surface. I'd handed Peter those pills myself. Counted them out. Brought him water. Watched him swallow them, believing I was helping him. All while they were killing him, day by day, dose by dose.

"We need to know for certain," I say, my voice steadier than I feel. "Is there a way to test Peter's body? Could an exhumation prove arsenic poisoning?"

"Arsenic remains in the body long after death, particularly in hair and nails." Dr. Kumar nods. "An exhumation and proper toxicological analysis could provide definitive proof."

Lena places a hand on my shoulder. "That process takes time, Juliette. Legal hurdles, permits. Sebastian and Eva would be alerted immediately."

"We need to tackle this on all fronts," I decide. "The exhumation through legal channels, but also—" I look at the pill bottle. "We need to know who had access to Peter's medication, who could have tampered with it."

Dr. Kumar carefully returns the capsules to the bottle. "I can document my observations for a potential investigation. And I'd recommend having these tested at a forensic laboratory."

He writes down a name and contact information. "This lab specializes in pharmaceutical analysis. They can determine if these capsules contain arsenic."

"How long would that take?" Lena asks.

"A few days for preliminary results." He hesitates. "I should note that I'm being cautious in my assessment. While these findings are highly suspicious and consistent with arsenic poisoning, there are other possible explanations for elevated arsenic levels."

"Such as?" I ask.

"Certain occupational exposures, antique restoration, contaminated water sources, even some alternative medicines can contain arsenic." He sighs. "I'm not saying that's what happened here—the evidence points strongly toward deliberate poisoning—but any investigation will need to rule out other possibilities."

"Thank you, Dr. Kumar." I extend my hand, which he clasps firmly. "Your help means more than I can say."

"I've seen too many cases where the truth is buried." He looks away briefly, a muscle twitching in his cheek. "Particularly when powerful interests are involved. If someone deliberately poisoned your husband, they need to be held accountable—especially if they wear the mantle of the medical profession."

As we leave the hospital, the truth settles over me like a physical weight. Peter hadn't just died—he'd been murdered. Slowly. Methodically. By people we'd trusted with our lives.

And now they want my daughter.

My breath turns into the steady bellows of a glassblower's furnace as we walk to the parking lot, each exhale stoking the fire of my determination until it burns white-hot and unstoppable. Sebastian and Eva may have taken Peter from me, but they won't get Lucy. Not for two million dollars. Not for any price.

21

———————

I drive in silence with Lena. They poisoned my husband —murdered him by tampering with his medication. And now they're trying to take my daughter. We don't have proof yet, but I'll follow this thread through a labyrinth of lies until it leads me to the monster at its center.

"Drop me off at my apartment," Lena says as I merge onto the freeway. "I'll start researching that forensic lab Dr. Kumar recommended and see how quickly we can get those pills tested."

"Before I do, why don't you come with me to see Patricia? Her office isn't far from your place."

"Good idea," Lena replies. "She needs to know everything. Surely this has to be enough to stop Eva from getting custody."

The dashboard clock reads 11:42 a.m. Lucy's day at school is half over. By tonight, according to the court order, Eva is supposed to move into my house and take custody of my daughter. The thought makes me nauseous, as if my body is physically rejecting the idea.

"We're not letting those snakes anywhere near Lucy," Lena says, her jaw set. "Not after this."

PATRICIA'S OFFICE is all glass and clean lines—no mahogany or leather-bound books. She told me she designed it to put clients at ease rather than intimidate them with tradition. Today, its brightness feels almost offensive against my dark thoughts. Carmen, the receptionist, a young man with tortoiseshell glasses, immediately recognizes me.

"Mrs. Samson. Ms. Torres is expecting you." He gestures toward the hallway. "Go right in."

Patricia stands when we enter, straightening the sleeve of her tailored navy suit with a precise tug. The tight line of her mouth tells me she is already strategizing.

"This is Lena, my sister and a former investigative journalist," I say.

After Patricia and Lena exchange greetings, Patricia says, "What have you found out?" She motions us to the chairs across from her desk.

I extract the folders containing Peter's medical records from my bag.

"Peter was poisoned." I say flatly, pushing the documents across her desk. "Arsenic. In the prescription his doctor gave him—the pills were tampered with." I go on to explain everything we found and what we learned from Dr. Kumar.

Lena adds what she'd learned from her previous investigative work related to arsenic contamination, explaining how its symptoms can mimic a GBS relapse, since that's what I'd initially believed Peter suffered from.

Patricia goes utterly still, just as she did when Eva's

lawyer presented the supposedly damaging evidence from my medical history during the hearing. She opens the folders and scans the contents, her fingertip trailing along the lines as she reads.

"Dr. Kumar also pointed out that Dr. Wilson Grant, Peter's physician, lost his hospital privileges years ago after a patient died under suspicious circumstances." I lean forward, my chair creaking. "And Lena discovered that Dr. Grant and Sebastian were fraternity brothers in college. They've maintained connections ever since."

Patricia examines the documents methodically, her glasses perched at the end of her nose. She takes her time, reading thoroughly, occasionally asking Lena and me to clarify things.

"So? What do you think?" I ask after she finishes the last page.

Lena adds, "This has to be enough to stop Eva from getting custody, right?"

Patricia sighs, removing her reading glasses and setting them precisely on her desk blotter. "This is certainly concerning, but Dr. Kumar is right—this isn't conclusive evidence that Peter was poisoned by Eva and Sebastian."

"What do you mean it's not conclusive? Peter had arsenic in his system!" My voice echoes off the glass walls.

"Which could be attributed to other causes, as Dr. Kumar noted." She holds up a hand when I start to protest. "I'm not saying that's what happened. I believe you. But courts require solid evidence, especially for allegations this serious."

I reach into my bag and pull out Peter's notes and financial records from the safe deposit box.

"There's more. Peter discovered Sebastian was embezzling from the company. He documented everything." I spread the papers in front of her like a winning poker hand. "And remember Lena's investigative work years ago? The work that led to our estrangement? She was right all along—Sebastian has a history of financial misconduct at other companies."

Patricia pauses for a long moment, her fingers drumming silently against the glass surface of her desk as she processes the weight of what I've just presented. The afternoon sunlight streaming through her office windows catches the gold frames of her diplomas, casting elongated shadows across the wall behind her. She picks up Peter's handwritten notes, examining his careful documentation with the practiced eye of someone who's spent decades building cases from fragments of evidence.

"This is significant," she says finally, her voice carrying a gravity that makes my pulse quicken with hope. "These financial records show a clear pattern of theft, and your husband's meticulous record-keeping demonstrates he was building a case against Sebastian. Plus, the timeline of this discovery seems to correlate with the onset of his symptoms."

"That's not all." I pull out additional documents Lena has compiled. "Eva has used multiple identities in the past, inserting herself into other families. And there have been suspicious deaths in those cases too."

Patricia takes the documents, her eyes darting across the pages. "Now we're building a case." She presses her intercom. "Carmen, clear my calendar for the afternoon. And see if we can get an emergency hearing scheduled for Monday morning."

She turns back to me. "The documentation of Sebastian's embezzlement creates a clear motive. Combined with Eva's history and the suspicious medical findings, we have enough to make a compelling case to a judge."

The tension wound through me loosens like a guitar

string tuned down, but the momentary relief snaps back as I glance at the time. "But what about tonight? Eva is supposed to move into my house and take custody of Lucy this evening."

Patricia frowns, tapping her pen against the desk in a rapid staccato. "The wheels of justice move slowly, even in emergency situations."

"So there's nothing we can do?" The words scrape my throat raw.

Patricia pauses, folding her hands together. "Do you have somewhere you and Lucy could stay over the weekend? Somewhere safe, until we can get in front of a judge on Monday with this evidence?"

"Yes—we stayed at Lena's apartment last night." I suddenly realize I'd forgotten to tell her about my encounter with Sebastian. "God—I forgot to mention—Sebastian was waiting at my house when I got home yesterday."

Patricia's focus sharpens. "What did he want?"

"He offered me a settlement. Two million dollars if I walk away from everything, including Lucy." The number sounds even more obscene spoken aloud. "Just leave and never come back."

Patricia's head tilts slightly. "That's unusual. If they were confident in their legal position, why offer such a substantial settlement?" A small crease appears between her eyebrows. "And frankly, it sounds like an admission of guilt."

"Of course, I told him off."

"Good." Patricia nods, leaning back. "Since you currently have custody of Lucy, at least until tonight's handover, I think you should keep her over the weekend at Lena's apartment."

"Won't that violate the court order?"

"Yes," she admits. "The court won't be happy about that. But by Monday, when we get in front of a judge with this evidence, it will likely be forgiven. It's a risk, but one I think we need to take."

I bite my lip, watching a cloud pass outside the window. "Won't this just make things worse? Make me look unstable or defiant?"

"It could," Patricia concedes, her voice measured. "But with this evidence, circumstantial though some of it may be, I don't believe any decent judge would allow Eva near Lucy once they see what we've compiled. The risk of temporary disobedience is outweighed by the potential danger to your daughter."

I close my eyes, conjuring Lucy's face—the constellation of freckles across her nose, the gap where her front tooth had fallen out last week. I've already lost Peter. I can't lose her too.

"Okay," I say, opening my eyes with newfound resolve. "I'll pick Lucy up from school and take her back to Lena's. We'll stay there until the hearing on Monday."

"Good." Patricia gathers the documents, sliding them into a folder. "I'll work on the emergency motion this afternoon. And Juliette?" Her expression softens slightly. "Stay vigilant. These people have already shown what they're willing to do."

The weight of her warning settles on my shoulders as I rise to leave. "What about the police? Shouldn't we report what we've found about Peter's death?"

Patricia pauses, her fingers still on the folder. "We will. But right now, our priority is protecting Lucy. Once she's safe, we'll pursue criminal charges. If we go to the police first, it could complicate and delay the custody proceedings."

I nod, gathering my things.

"I'll research forensic labs that can test Peter's pills to prove conclusively that he was poisoned," Lena says.

"Good. That would strengthen our case significantly." Patricia checks her watch. "What time do you pick up Lucy from school?"

I glance at my own watch. "In about forty minutes."

"Perfect timing. Go get your daughter and keep her safe. I'll call you once I have the hearing confirmed for Monday."

As we leave Patricia's office, a strange calm settles over me. The path forward is fraught with risk, but now I feel like I'm fighting back—not just reacting to the chaos around me.

22

———

Two-fifty-four. The bell is about to ring. I step out of my car and join the cluster of waiting parents under the large metal awning near the main doors of Lucy's school, breathing in the familiar scent of playground mulch. Alison stands with two other mothers I recognize, all laughing at something on one of their phones. When she spots me, her smile freezes before stretching wider, her hand rising in an overly enthusiastic wave.

"Juliette! Hey!" She breaks away from the group, her auburn curls swaying as she crosses the pavement toward me. "Didn't expect to see you today. I thought—" She stops herself, a flicker of something—guilt?—crossing her features.

My shoulders clench with the same tension I had when Sebastian denied me access to my company. "Why wouldn't I be picking up Lucy?"

"Oh, I just..." She glances back at the other mothers, who are now watching us with poorly disguised interest. "Nothing, never mind. How are you doing?"

The bell rings before I can answer, saving me from small talk I have no patience for. Children burst through the doors—shouting, laughing, backpacks bouncing, lunch boxes swinging—the familiar after-school explosion that usually brings Lucy running to me, her Bluey keychain jingling on her unicorn backpack as she calls out "Mommy!" I position myself where I always stand, scanning for her face in the crowd.

I watch as classmates from Lucy's grade skip past, some racing to waiting parents, others forming rowdy clusters as they wait for the bus. No Lucy. Minutes stretch on, each second amplifying the hollow feeling inside me. The crowds thin. Still no Lucy.

Ms. Carter, Lucy's teacher, emerges escorting the last few stragglers. She falters mid-stride as she spots me, and my heart drops into my stomach before she even opens her mouth.

"Mrs. Samson." She approaches, lowering her voice to a near-whisper. "I'm sorry, but Lucy isn't here. Her stepmother picked her up early."

I grab the nearest pole to steady myself, suddenly dizzy. "We went through this before. Lucy doesn't have a stepmother."

Ms. Carter's words emerge with the hesitancy of someone testing ice on a frozen lake. "Eva Dorsey? She signed Lucy out around lunchtime for a doctor's appointment."

"What?" The word comes out too loud, drawing stares from nearby parents. "That's impossible. What about the password system? No one can pick up Lucy without using the password I gave you."

Ms. Carter's shoulders stiffen. "Mrs. Samson, Ms. Dorsey had all the proper paperwork, even a court order.

Principal Hoffman reviewed everything, and it all checked out."

"Why didn't you call me? You assured me that no one would be able to pick Lucy up without my authorization."

I become aware of the audience we've attracted. Alison stares, her eyes wide and unblinking. Another mother whispers behind her hand to a friend. No one approaches. No one offers support.

"Perhaps we should continue this inside," Principal Hoffman says as he joins Ms. Carter, his voice low and controlled. "Mrs. Samson, please come to my office."

I follow him through hallways plastered with construction paper artwork and science projects. My heart hammers so violently I can feel it in my fingertips, my throat, behind my eyes. The fluorescent lights overhead seem to pulse with every beat.

Inside his office, with its institutional furniture and framed educational certifications, he gestures for me to sit.

"Mrs. Samson, I understand this is challenging, but we followed all proper protocols. Ms. Dorsey presented the appropriate documentation. She had the court order showing temporary shared custody—"

"That woman is not Lucy's stepmother." I remain standing, my hands gripping the back of the chair so tightly my wedding ring digs into my finger. "She's not related to Lucy at all."

Principal Hoffman's eyebrows lift, his head tilting slightly—the exact expression people wear when talking to someone they think is unstable.

"Mrs. Samson, the paperwork was in order. We verified the court's seal. Ms. Dorsey explained that you're going through a difficult adjustment period—"

"Adjustment period?" My laugh comes out as a cackle.

"My husband died. That woman was never married to him."

Principal Hoffman folds his hands on his desk, the wood grain between us suddenly fascinating to him. "I understand you've been through a lot recently. Divorce is always difficult, even when the parties are amicable."

"Divorce?" Once again, the word crashes into my existence like a freight train derailing in slow motion. "My husband and I were never divorced. Peter died three weeks ago. Look at me—I'm still wearing my wedding ring!" I thrust my hand toward him. The gold band catches the fluorescent light—the same ring Peter slid onto my finger at our wedding, his hands trembling slightly, his eyes damp.

Principal Hoffman's gaze flickers down to my hand then back to my face, a mask of professional sympathy failing to hide the pity beneath. "We have copies of the legal documentation on file, Mrs. Samson. I can show you—"

"They're forged. All of it—forged." The words crack, splitting open to reveal the raw fear beneath. "Please, call the police. Eva Dorsey has kidnapped my daughter."

"Mrs. Samson." Principal Hoffman's voice takes on an edge of authority. "Making accusations of that nature is extremely serious. Ms. Dorsey has legal documentation establishing her right to pick up Lucy. If you believe these documents are fraudulent, that's a matter for the courts, not for us to determine."

I stare at him, reality crashing down around me like broken glass. What will happen if I continue ranting? If I demand police intervention? They'll see a frantic woman making wild accusations against someone with seemingly valid legal documents. Eva will appear calm, collected, concerned about my mental state. With Sebastian's connections, they might have even manipulated police records. And Lucy—my Lucy, with her gap-toothed smile and freckled nose—will be caught in the middle of it all, frightened and confused.

I force air into my lungs, counting the seconds of inhale like my therapist taught me after Lucy was born. One, two, three, four. My hands won't stop shaking as I lower myself into the chair.

"I apologize, Principal Hoffman." The words taste like metal. "You're right. This is... complicated. I need to speak with my lawyer."

Principal Hoffman's shoulders relax, the tight lines around his mouth softening. "That seems wise. Family matters can be so complex, and everyone wants what's best for Lucy."

I nod mechanically, swallowing hard against the sour taste in my mouth. "May I see the documentation Eva provided? Just to understand what we're dealing with legally."

"Of course." He turns to his computer, clicks through several screens, then swivels the monitor toward me. "Here's the scanned copy we have on file."

Except for the court order, all lies. Elaborate, detailed, convincing lies.

"Thank you for showing me this." I control every muscle in my face, refusing to let them twitch or tremble. "I'll need to review this with my attorney."

Principal Hoffman nods sympathetically. "Of course. And Mrs. Samson..." He hesitates, adjusting his tie. "We all want what's best for Lucy. She's a wonderful child. Whatever issues exist between you and Ms. Dorsey, I hope you can resolve them amicably for Lucy's sake."

The patronizing tone, the assumption that this is simply

a contentious divorce rather than a calculated theft of my life, makes my skin crawl. But I offer a thin smile, thank him again, and rise to leave.

As I walk through the hallway toward the exit, past the construction paper cornucopias, past the bench where I tied Lucy's shoe just Monday morning, I see Alison. She's waiting by the water fountain, clearly positioned to intercept me. Her son Luke, who's one grade above Lucy, is chatting with a friend just outside the doors. She reaches out, touching my arm gently.

"Juliette, is everything okay? You seemed upset earlier."

I study her face, searching for signs of complicity.

"Everything's fine." The lie burns my throat as I pull my arm away from her touch. Heat floods my chest with the same rage I felt watching her cozy up to Eva at the luncheon, choosing business connections over our friendship.

Alison's eyes widen with theatrical concern. "Are you sure? Because I thought you knew that Eva was picking up Lucy, but you came here this afternoon and seemed upset when you talked to Ms. Carter, and then I saw you walking away with Principal Hoffman—"

"Since when do you care?" The words slice through her performance. "Two days ago you made it crystal clear that Eva's your new best friend. Something about protecting your interests?"

Her cheeks flush pink. "Juliette, that's not—I was trying to explain the situation from a business perspective. People are talking, and I thought you should know—"

"People are talking." I step closer, my voice dropping to a whisper. "Is that what this is? Are you here fishing for more gossip to share at your next power lunch?"

"That's not fair—"

"Fair?" My laugh comes out sharp and bitter. "Nothing about this is fair, Alison."

I push past her toward the exit, my pulse hammering in my ears. I don't have time for her guilt or her curiosity. Lucy is somewhere with Eva, and every second I waste here is another second my daughter spends with that woman.

23

I careen down the tree-lined streets toward my house, my fingers cramping around the steering wheel, the speedometer needle trembling past forty-five in a thirty zone. Scenarios strobe through my mind like a manic slideshow. Maybe Eva's taken Lucy to our home, where she was supposed to "move in" tonight. Each red light and stop sign feels like a personal betrayal, every dawdling driver an accomplice to Lucy's kidnapping.

I screech into my driveway, tires squealing against the smooth pavement. The house looms before me—deceptively normal with its slate-blue trim and potted chrysanthemums flanking the porch steps. The place where Lucy took her first steps, where Peter and I danced in the kitchen on rainy Sundays, now a fortress I need to breach.

Out of habit, I press the garage door opener clipped to my sun visor. Nothing. I jab it again, harder this time, the plastic resisting my fingertip. Still nothing.

A cold weight sinks from my chest to my gut, like swallowing ice whole. They've already changed the code.

I abandon the car, driver's door still hanging open, and sprint to the front entrance. My keys jangle as my shaking hands pick through them. Office, car, house. I jam the silver key into the lock and twist.

It won't budge.

"No, no, no." I twist harder, the metal biting into my fingers, then yank it out and try again. The key slides in smoothly but refuses to turn, as foreign now as if it belonged to another house entirely.

They've changed the locks too.

I cup my hands against the glass panel on the door, the cool surface fogging with my panicked breath as I peer inside. The foyer sits dim and silent, no sign of movement, no Lucy, no Eva.

"Lucy!" I hammer against the door, the wood vibrating under my fists. "Lucy, sweetie, are you in there? It's Mommy!"

The silence from inside my own home is devouring my hope. Lucy has to be here. She has to be. Because if she's not, then I'm standing at the edge of a cliff with nowhere left to turn, and there's nothing below but darkness.

Mrs. Henderson's house sits just twenty yards away. I bolt across our adjoining lawns, the grass crunching with fallen leaves beneath my feet, and jab her doorbell. After no response, I press it repeatedly in quick succession, the chimes echoing inside. One, two, three, four times. Nothing.

Over my shoulder, I look around the neighborhood. Movement catches my eye—a shadow shifting behind my front door. I spin around, already running.

The door cracks open. A small face peers out.

"Lucy!" Her name rips from my throat.

Her eyes widen when she sees me—confusion, recognition, fear all battling across her features. She opens her mouth, but before any sound emerges, a hand appears from behind, yanking her backward. The door slams shut with the decisive thud of a coffin lid.

I pound on the door with both fists, the impact sending shock waves through my wrists and elbows. "Lucy! Lucy, it's Mommy! Open the door!" My voice fractures, splintering into desperate shards. "Please, baby, open the door!"

"Mommy!" Her muffled cry penetrates the barrier between us, sending electrical currents of adrenaline through my body.

"I'm here, Lucy! I'm right here!" The skin on my hands stings raw as I continue hammering.

"Go to your room, honey. Everything's okay. I'll handle this." Eva's voice filters through the door, calm and controlled—a perfect impersonation of maternal concern.

"That's not your mother!" I scream, slamming my foot against the door now. "Lucy, she's not your mother!"

Behind me, car doors slam with dual metallic cracks. I whirl around to see a police cruiser parked at the curb, blue and red lights pulsing silently. Two officers approach —one male, one female. I recognize them immediately, their faces familiar from my previous attempt to report Sebastian.

"Officers," I gasp. My shoulders loosen for a millisecond before tension claims them again. "Thank God you're here. That woman has taken my daughter. She picked her up from school with falsified documents. She's changed my locks—"

Officer Davis raises her palm to stop my torrent of words. "Ma'am, we received a call about a disturbance at this residence."

Reyes positions himself slightly behind his partner,

hand hovering near the Taser on his belt. "We've responded to this address before, haven't we?"

"Yes! I called you when someone broke into my house, but—"

"But it wasn't actually a break-in, was it?" His eyes narrow slightly. "It seemed to be a civil matter, because there was an issue with ownership of the property."

"Yes, but this is different," I say, my words colliding into each other like cars in a pileup. "My daughter—" I point frantically at the house, my finger trembling in the air. "She has my daughter in there!"

A few neighbors emerge from their homes like ants from a disturbed hill, drawn by the commotion. Mrs. Henderson stands on her porch, arms folded across her chest, lips pressed thin. Other familiar faces appear in doorways and on yards, all watching. I feel their stares burning into me—curious, judgmental, pitying.

The front door opens again, and Eva steps out, the picture of composure and concern in a soft cream sweater that looks achingly familiar—*my* sweater. No Lucy in sight.

"Officers, thank you for coming so quickly." She descends the porch steps, her voice quavering with perfectly calibrated vulnerability. "I didn't want to call, but she keeps showing up, making scenes in front of our neighbors. Lucy is terrified."

"That's a lie!" I lunge toward her, but Officer Reyes steps between us, his bulk suddenly immovable as concrete.

"Ma'am, I need you to calm down," he says, one hand rising in warning.

"This is my house!" My voice scrapes from my throat. "That woman stole my identity, my child—"

"Ma'am, you're becoming agitated," Officer Davis says, her tone hardening to granite. "I need you to take a step back."

Through the front window, I see Lucy peering around the edge of the curtain, her small face pinched with confusion and fear. Our gazes lock through the glass. I see her lips form that sacred word—"Mommy."

"Look! Lucy's in there, she sees me!" I point frantically, hope surging. "Ask her who I am! Just ask her!"

Eva murmurs to the officers, her voice pitched too low for me to hear, but fragments drift my way—"psychiatric evaluation" and "custody arrangement" and "becoming worse."

"You lying bitch!" I try to shove past Officer Reyes, my shoulder colliding with his unyielding arm. "You're filling their heads with lies!"

Officer Davis unclips her handcuffs, the metal catching the sunlight. "Ma'am, I'm going to need you to calm down right now, or we'll have to restrain you."

"She has my daughter!" The words tear from somewhere deep in my chest. Neighbors edge closer, phones raised like weapons, recording my unraveling. Mrs. Henderson whispers to another woman, shaking her head. "Why aren't you listening to me? Why won't anyone listen?"

"That's enough." Officer Davis seizes my arm, spinning me around. "Put your hands behind your back."

Cold metal bites into my wrists before I can process what's happening, the cuffs clicking tighter with each ratchet.

"You're under arrest for disorderly conduct," she recites, the words as impersonal as a recording. "You have the right to remain silent..."

The officer's voice fades to a distant hum as I stare at Eva over my shoulder. She stands on the porch now, arms folded across her chest, eyes gleaming with triumph behind her concerned mask.

"She's lying to you," I say, my voice suddenly clear and deadly calm. "She's not who she says she is."

Officer Davis guides me toward the police car. "Save it for the station, ma'am."

The back door of the cruiser yawns open. With the officer's hand firm on my head, I fold myself into the seat. The smell of vomit, thinly veiled by industrial cleaner, hits me immediately. The world narrows to what I glimpse through the window—Eva talking to Officer Reyes, gesturing dramatically at papers in her hand, playing the role of a concerned, widowed stepmother dealing with an unstable, dangerous woman.

I press my forehead against the cool glass, leaving a smudge, a mark of my existence. "My daughter," I whisper, the words fogging the window. "She has my daughter."

The drive to the station blurs into a kaleidoscope of suburban streets and traffic lights, punctuated by the occasional squawk of the police radio. Inside, the booking officer processes me like machinery—pressing my fingers into ink, positioning my face for the camera flash, cataloging the contents of my pockets into a plastic bin.

The officer, a heavyset woman with eyes hollowed by too many shifts, asks questions I answer automatically, my mouth forming words while my mind remains trapped in that moment when Lucy mouthed "Mommy" through the glass.

Name: Juliette Samson.

Address: The house I no longer have access to.

Phone number: The cell phone now sitting in a plastic bin with my keys.

"One phone call," the officer says, gesturing toward a wall-mounted phone with chipped beige plastic. "Make it count."

I dial Lena's number from memory—thank God she

never changed it—praying she'll answer an unknown call. One ring. Two. The sound drums against my ear.

"Hello?" Her tone is wary, stretched thin.

"Lena, it's me." My voice fractures like glass. "I'm in jail."

"What? Juliette, what happened?"

"They have Lucy. Eva took her from school, and when I went home, they'd changed the locks. The police came and arrested me for disorderly conduct when I tried to get her back." The words tumble out in a desperate cascade. "Lena, she has my daughter."

A heartbeat of silence. Then: "Where are you exactly?"

"County detention center."

"I'll call Patricia and we'll be there as soon as we can. Don't say anything to anyone, okay? We're coming."

The line goes dead with a click. The booking officer leads me to a holding cell—stark concrete walls stained with decades of desperation, a metal bench bolted to the floor, a stainless steel toilet with no privacy screen. I sink onto the bench, handcuffs removed but replaced by the knowledge that I'm trapped here while Eva has my daughter.

Several others share the space—a young woman with mascara charting black rivers down her cheeks, sobbing quietly; an older woman staring at nothing, her eyes fixed on some middle distance that might be the future or the past. None of them look at me. None of them care that reality crumbles like sand beneath a wave, leaving me nothing solid to stand on.

I close my eyes and see Lucy's face at the window again, her small lips forming that hallowed word—"Mommy"—through the glass that once protected us but now keeps us apart. I see Eva in my sweater, in my house, using my things, holding my child.

And for the first time since this nightmare began, despite the rage and fear scorching through my veins, a dangerous clarity crystallizes within me. If the system won't help me—if the police, the school, everyone believes Eva's lies—then I'll have to find another way.

Whatever it takes, I will get my daughter back.

24

The cell's other occupants increase in number during the night: belligerent drunks who eventually pass out snoring, a teenager caught tagging an overpass who sketches invisible designs on the floor with her finger, and a woman caught shoplifting baby formula who weeps silently in the corner for two hours before being processed.

By morning, I'm sagging against the grimy wall, my eyelids sandpaper-rough from a sleepless night. A chill seeps through my thin pants from the holding cell's concrete slab, while weak sunlight taunts me through a high, narrow window near the ceiling. How can I rest when Lucy is in Eva's clutches?

Patricia arrives shortly before noon, the sharp lines of her tailored blazer incongruous against the institutional drabness. She confers with the booking officers, her posture rigid. When she finally approaches my cell, her face remains professionally blank, but her eyes flash with contained fury.

"They're processing your release papers now," she

murmurs, adjusting her stance to block our conversation from the nearest guard. "Lena paid your bail."

"How much?" The question catches on something jagged in my throat.

"Two thousand. Misdemeanor disorderly conduct." Her lips press into a thin line. "We can discuss our legal strategy when we're somewhere less monitored."

The release process stretches interminably—paperwork shuffled between hands, redundant signatures, the ceremonial return of my keys and my phone, more signatures. Patricia maintains her tactical silence until we push through the building's heavy glass doors. The afternoon sun assaults my sleep-deprived eyes, making me squint and duck my head.

Lena waits in her battered Subaru, engine running. When she spots me, she launches herself from the driver's seat and wraps me in a fierce hug. She smells of bar soap and the single cigarette she allows herself in times of stress.

"We're going to fix this," she whispers against my hair, her fingers digging into my shoulder blades.

"Lucy—" My daughter's name cracks between my teeth.

With her hands on my shoulders, Lena holds my gaze. "We'll get her back," she promises with the quiet certainty that's carried her through years of reporting on society's darkest figures. "But first, let's get you somewhere those vultures can't circle."

When we arrive at Lena's apartment, she welcomes Patricia into our makeshift war room. She suggests I clean up as Patricia starts laying documents across the coffee table, since the dining table is already buried under Lena's collected evidence and notes. After the shower, I find everything arranged in precise rows. Settling cross-legged on the floor with my laptop balanced on my knees, I watch Patricia perch awkwardly on the couch before the organized display. Lena circles the room's perimeter, her steady footsteps creating a comforting rhythm.

My fingers freeze mid-keystroke as realization strikes. "The cameras." I straighten, pulse quickening. "I installed nanny cams before everything unraveled. Hidden ones—disguised in the kitchen clock, Lucy's bookshelf dinosaur, and the hallway smoke detector."

Patricia's eyebrows arch. "You installed surveillance equipment in your home?"

"After Sebastian broke in, I changed my locks and set up the cameras. I needed..." I swallow, remembering the night I'd carefully placed each device. "Documentation. If they haven't discovered them, we might be able to see what Eva's doing with Lucy."

My hands tremble slightly as I navigate to the secure cloud server where the cameras upload their footage. The first feed flickers to life, the kitchen camera capturing Eva moving through my space with unsettling confidence. She pulls ingredients she shouldn't know how to find from a cabinet, reaches unerringly for utensils as if she'd arranged them herself. Watching her inhabit my kitchen makes my stomach contract, my skin prickling with the wrongness of it.

"Wait." Lena leans closer, her finger hovering near the screen. "She's talking to someone."

Eva's mouth moves, her face animated as she gestures with a wooden spoon I brought back from a cooking class in Tuscany. The camera angle catches just enough of the doorway to reveal Sebastian entering the frame, dressed in casual weekend clothes. Seeing him in the space where

Peter and I had built our life—where we'd cooked Sunday breakfasts and slow-danced after Lucy had fallen asleep—makes my head spin like I've stood up too fast.

I click to Lucy's bedroom feed. My daughter sits on her bed, hunched over a coloring book I've never seen before. Her usual exuberance is absent, her movements mechanical as she fills in shapes with careful precision. I scan the room, panic mounting.

"Where's Nibbles?" I whisper, searching for the threadbare rabbit Peter gave her on her second birthday. "She never goes anywhere without him. She wouldn't leave him behind willingly."

Before Lena can respond, the feed from Lucy's room disappears, replaced by blank static.

Patricia straightens. "What happened?"

I frantically switch back to the kitchen feed—static. The hallway—static.

"They've cut the feeds." My mouth goes dry. "All of them."

My phone vibrates against the coffee table's surface.

A text message from an unknown number: *We found your cameras. Stop watching or we'll show Lucy what her mother really is.*

I shove the phone toward Lena, who reads it and mutters something that would have made her more colorful sources blush.

"They found the cameras." I turn to Patricia, my body numb. "They're threatening to turn Lucy against me."

Before Patricia can respond, my laptop screen flickers. Windows begin opening without my command—documents, browser history, email accounts.

Lena steps back. "Jesus Christ."

"Someone's accessing my computer remotely." My stomach knots tighter with each file that opens without my command—the carefully documented timeline of Peter's symptoms, the research into Eva's past identities... "They're going through everything I've collected."

"Disconnect it now," Patricia orders, reaching over to slam the laptop closed. "Pull the battery if you can."

Too late. The screen goes black before I can respond. When I reopen it, the computer reboots to an empty desktop. Every file, every folder, every digital breadcrumb I've gathered—erased.

My phone vibrates again. Same unknown number. This time, the message contains images—me outside Dr. Kumar's office, my face tense and drawn; me entering Lena's bar, shoulders hunched; me standing in the police station parking lot with Patricia, looking haggard and unraveled.

A final message appears beneath the photos: *Back off or you'll never see Lucy again.*

The phone slips from my fingers, clattering to the floor.

Patricia retrieves it, her eyes narrowing as she scrolls through the messages.

"They wouldn't resort to threats if they weren't afraid of what you know," Lena says.

I press my palms against my closed eyes, trying to block out the violation that surrounds me. "But how did they find the cameras? How are they tracking every move I make?"

"Classic gaslighting techniques," Patricia says, her voice taking on the precise cadence she uses when entering legal territory. "And they're accumulating felony charges in the process—unauthorized computer access, cyberterrorism, harassment, stolen medical documents."

I look back and forth between them, anchoring myself in their competence. "What's our next move?"

"We have strategic options," Patricia says, setting her tablet on the coffee table and tapping it thoughtfully. "Option one: we report the cybercrime and harassment to police cybercrime division. This creates an official record of their intimidation tactics."

"After yesterday, would any officer believe me?" I rub my wrists where the memory of handcuffs lingers.

"Digital crimes are handled by different agencies," Patricia explains, her voice taking on its usual methodical tone. "And electronic evidence is much harder to dispute. There's a digital record, timestamps, metadata—it's difficult for them to deny what happened. But," she cautions, "filing a report will definitely put them on notice that we're taking this seriously."

"Or," Lena interjects, "we shift to a counterintelligence approach. Change communication methods, use burner phones, gather evidence they can't track."

I stand abruptly, needing movement to process the violation crawling under my skin. "If they found the cameras, they've been searching my house. They've gone through Lucy's room, her personal space." My stomach clenches at the thought of Eva pawing through Lucy's things, studying her routines, learning all the small details that make up our private world. "What else have they discovered? What other preparations have they made?"

Silence settles over the apartment as we each contemplate the invisible web tightening around us.

Finally, I say, "Patricia, how can we present the harassment and camera tampering? That has to violate the custody arrangement."

Patricia nods, her fingers flying across her tablet screen. "I'll add this to our evidence for Monday's hearing. But Juliette," she looks up, her expression grave, "they'll frame your arrest as the culmination of erratic behavior—exactly the narrative they need to convince a judge that Lucy needs 'stability' with Eva."

"Let them try." My voice comes out fiercely, a tone I

barely recognize. "Lena, does Malcolm understand this kind of digital invasion? Is he someone who can help secure our communications?"

"He sure can," Lena says with confidence.

A spark ignites inside me, raw and electric, so different from the cold metal of the handcuffs that had bitten into my wrists. Not quite hope—that feels too fragile for this— but something sturdier, something with teeth.

"Call him. I need to know what they've taken and how to stop them from taking more."

NIGHT PRESSES against Lena's windows, the city lights forming constellations beyond the glass. Patricia left hours ago to prepare motions, promising to meet in the morning with legal updates. Malcolm has taken my devices, assuring me he will salvage what he can and fortify them against further intrusions. Lena drove me to the impound lot, bailing out my car just as she'd bailed me out.

I lay on the couch, with no ability to see Lucy through the cameras, no way for me to fall asleep, the sleep I desperately need after a night in jail, and Lucy's absence manifesting as a physical ache inside me. So I sneak out of Lena's apartment after she's gone downstairs to tend her bar on the busiest night of the week.

Now I sit in darkness half a block from my house, engine off, watching the warm glow emanating from Lucy's bedroom window. The curtains are drawn, but shadows move across them—her bedtime routine in progress. The silhouette that bends to adjust something on the bed is too tall, too angular to be my daughter. Eva, in my place, reading stories I should be reading, her voice filling the space where mine should be. My fingers curl around the steering wheel until the tendons strain.

My phone illuminates the darkened car interior. A text from Patricia: *Eva has filed a countermotion for the emergency hearing, seeking immediate full custody on grounds that you've demonstrated "unstable and paranoid behavior."*

My vision tunnels, Patricia's words blurring as my brain processes the devastating implications. Through the windshield, I watch Lucy's bedroom light switch off, that corner of the house—my house—falling into darkness.

The rules of engagement have fundamentally changed. This isn't just about reclaiming my property or proving my identity anymore. The stakes have escalated to something far more primal—my psychological credibility, my fundamental right to mother my child.

A new front has opened in this peculiar war. They aren't just trying to steal my life anymore. They are trying to erase me from it completely, beginning with severing my connection to Lucy.

I start the car, its quiet rumble matching the determined pulse in my veins. Tomorrow will bring preparations for Monday's hearing. Tomorrow we will find whatever evidence remains for us to construct our defense.

But tonight, I will drive back to Lena's apartment and force my body to rest. I will lie in darkness and remember every detail of Lucy's face, every inflection in her voice, storing them like ammunition. Because Eva has just made her most dangerous move yet, and I won't face the battle for my daughter with the handicap of exhaustion.

25

———

Last night's fragments of sleep left me with nothing but snapshots of Lucy's confused face and Eva's calculating smile. My eyes burn, and my third cup of coffee sits half-empty in front of me, doing little to clear the fog in my mind, as I strategize with Patricia in her office.

"Judge Harriet Simmons will be hearing our case tomorrow," she says, reviewing notes on her tablet. "She's known for being sympathetic to mothers, particularly in cases without clear evidence of abuse."

"So we're going before a different judge?" I ask, trying to keep the anxiety from creeping into my voice.

"Yes," Patricia says, setting down her tablet and leaning back in her leather chair. "Emergency hearings are assigned based on who is on call for the week to preside over these types of cases. It's completely standard procedure, though I know it feels unsettling when you're already dealing with so much uncertainty."

She reaches for her coffee mug, taking a measured sip before continuing. "Frankly, Judge Kemp's ruling last week was rather unexpected, so it will be advantageous to have a fresh judicial perspective on this matter. And Judge Simmons has twenty-three years on the bench, most of it in family court. She's seen every variation of custody dispute imaginable, which works in our favor. She won't be easily swayed by theatrical performances or manipulative tactics."

"And our evidence?" I ask as I grip the armrests of my chair. "Will she understand the complexity of what we've uncovered? The timeline of Eva's deception, the financial fraud, the poisoning—it's so much to process."

"It's significant." Patricia picks up her tablet again, scrolling through documents, her manicured fingernails tapping decisively against the screen. "Eva's previous identities, Sebastian's fraudulent behavior with the company, and the labs showing Peter's arsenic poisoning create a compelling narrative. Unless they have something substantial to counter with, I believe we should fare well."

"What about my arrest?" The words taste bitter. "It was obviously a setup—the police arrived too quickly. Eva must have called them before I even got there."

Patricia closes her tablet, meeting my eyes directly. "We'll need to address that head-on. It's a minor misdemeanor that occurred during obvious emotional distress following the violation of your home—"

"And the kidnapping of my child!"

"Precisely. From your perspective, your child was unlawfully taken."

"What do you mean, 'from my perspective'?"

"They'll undoubtedly cite the existing court order."

"But the terms were that Eva was supposed to take custody of Lucy at 5:00 p.m. Instead, she abducted her from school."

"And we shall present these material facts to the court

during the proceedings. As for the arrest, contextually, it's explainable and ultimately insignificant compared to the documented pattern of deception we've uncovered." Patricia squeezes my arm. "We have the truth on our side, Juliette. That counts for something."

If only I believed that were enough. The truth hasn't protected me so far.

～

THE NEXT MORNING, the courtroom swallows us into its cavernous belly. My footsteps echo against floors scuffed to a dull sheen by decades of desperate petitioners. High above, crown molding frames acoustic ceiling tiles stained yellow with age.

We take our seats at the plaintiff's table. Patricia arranges our evidence in precise stacks, each document protected in a clear folder, each tab color-coded for efficient reference. The quiet rustle of papers mingles with the anxious whispers of others waiting their turn before the court.

The heavy oak door at the rear of the courtroom groans open. My breath catches in my throat, shoulders drawing up as Eva glides in wearing a modest navy dress with understated pearl earrings. Every element of her appearance seems premeditated—the hemline hitting just below the knee, the sensible one-inch heels, the minimal makeup projecting a maternal glow. She's wearing the costume of the perfect mother and doing it well.

Karla Winters joins her, moving with predatory grace in her sleek black pantsuit. And beside her walks a woman I don't recognize, carrying a leather portfolio embossed with the crest of an academic institution. The portfolio looks new, barely creased—as if purchased for this specific performance.

"That's not good," Patricia murmurs, catching my questioning glance. "Dr. Elizabeth Mercer. She's a child psychologist. Why would they have—"

The bailiff's voice cuts through the murmured conversations. "All rise for the Honorable Judge Raymond Morris."

Patricia's hand freezes mid-gesture. A tiny muscle jumps in her jaw as an older man with steel-gray hair and wire-rimmed glasses takes the bench. Cold dread pools in my stomach, thick and heavy as mercury.

"Who is he?" I whisper as we sit, the wood creaking beneath us.

Patricia's face remains professionally neutral, but her voice tightens. "Different judicial philosophy entirely. He's typically assigned to corporate law cases, not family court."

The proceedings begin with impersonal efficiency. Judge Morris reviews the case files, his expression impassive. When he speaks, his voice carries the dry, dispassionate tone of someone who values spreadsheets over human connection.

"I see we have an emergency petition and cross-motion filed before us today." Judge Morris adjusts his glasses, the gesture automatic. His fingers drum once against the mahogany bench before stilling completely. "It appears this particular matter has been brought before the court twice now in less than a week's time—an unusual frequency that suggests either genuine urgency or tactical maneuvering."

His pale eyes sweep across the courtroom with clinical detachment, lingering briefly on Eva before settling on our table. The weight of his gaze feels like ice water trickling down my spine.

"Ms. Torres," he continues, his voice carrying the same dispassionate efficiency he might use to approve a corporate merger, "you may present your client's case first. I trust you'll be succinct given the expedited nature of these proceedings."

Patricia rises, her composure unwavering despite the unexpected judicial substitution. She outlines our evidence methodically—Eva's false identities, the financial irregularities at SD Title & Escrow, the labs indicating Peter had been poisoned with arsenic. The fluorescent lights buzz overhead, casting harsh shadows that deepen the lines of concentration on her face.

"Your Honor, these documented patterns reveal a coordinated effort to disenfranchise my client of her property, her identity, and now, most egregiously, her child. We request immediate restoration of full custody to Juliette Samson, the child's biological mother, and a restraining order against Eva Lerner."

The judge's expression remains unchanged, his pen making occasional notes. The scratch of nib against paper seems unnaturally loud in the waiting silence. When he looks up from his notes, his pale eyes fix on Patricia with the same expression he might use to examine a questionable line item in a budget report.

"That's quite a set of accusations, Ms. Torres, particularly the assertion that Mr. Samson was poisoned." His voice carries no inflection, no hint of the gravity such words should command. "Do you have concrete evidence to support such a serious claim, or are we dealing with speculation born of grief?"

Patricia straightens, her hand moving to the stack of medical documents. "Your Honor, we have independent toxicology analysis showing elevated arsenic levels in the deceased's system, tampered medication capsules, and a statement from Dr. Rajeev Kumar regarding—"

"Independent analysis." Judge Morris interrupts, the words clipped and precise. "Not court-ordered autopsy results. Not official coroner findings."

My pulse skips like a scratched record. The way he emphasizes the word "independent" makes it sound like something dirty, unreliable.

"We're requesting exhumation and official forensic examination to confirm—"

"Ms. Torres." His voice cuts through the air like a blade. "This court deals in established facts, not fishing expeditions disguised as emergency hearings."

He turns to Karla Winters. "Your response, Counselor?"

Karla rises, her movements fluid and well-executed. "Your Honor, Ms. Lerner has established a stable, nurturing environment for her stepdaughter during a period when Ms. Samson has demonstrated increasingly erratic and concerning behavior."

She gestures to the professional beside her. "Dr. Mercer conducted an emergency evaluation of Lucy Samson Friday afternoon and found significant concerns about the child's emotional state that directly correlate with Ms. Samson's recent actions."

"Objection!" Patricia's voice cuts through the courtroom. "We received no notification of any psychological evaluation. This constitutes ambush evidence, Your Honor. I move to exclude Dr. Mercer's testimony as it violates discovery rules."

Judge Morris barely glances up. "Given the emergency nature of these proceedings and the child's welfare being paramount, I'll allow Dr. Mercer's testimony. Overruled."

Patricia's shoulders stiffen, the only indication of her surprise. She scribbles a note on her yellow legal pad: *Challenge Mercer's credentials - 1 hr eval insufficient.* The pen presses so hard I can see the impressions carving valleys into the paper beneath.

Karla approaches the bench with a USB drive. "Your Honor, we've discovered evidence of Ms. Samson's invasive surveillance of the property in question. Rather than simply expressing concerns about Ms. Lerner's care, she installed hidden cameras throughout the residence without court approval or notification."

My heart misfires like a broken engine, sputtering and stalling as a video appears on the courtroom monitor. The footage shows me instructing Lucy in our living room, my face earnest as I kneel down to her level. I recognize the moment instantly—Lucy's favorite unicorn pajamas, the small chocolate smudge on her cheek that I'd missed when washing her face. The audio has been enhanced, isolating my words with devastating clarity.

"Remember, sweetheart, be careful what you say to Eva. Some things should just stay between us, okay?"

The context has been deliberately stripped away—every moment showing my desperate attempt to protect Lucy from manipulation carefully edited out—leaving only the fragments that show the opposite, casting *me* as the manipulator. My teeth sink into my bottom lip hard enough to taste iron.

"Ms. Samson has engaged in a pattern of behavior designed to undermine Lucy's relationship with her stepmother," Karla continues. "Dr. Mercer, could you please share your professional observations?"

The psychologist approaches the stand, her credentials establishing her as the director of a prominent child development center. Her testimony flows with practiced precision, each syllable landing with the hollow rhythm of memorized conclusions.

"Lucy exhibits signs of anxiety and confusion consistent with a child caught in conflicting narratives about family structure. When asked about her home life, she expressed uncertainty about 'which story' she was supposed to tell, showing coaching behavior from Ms. Samson."

Beneath the table, I twist my wedding ring, the circular motion a futile attempt to unscrew the tension coiling in my gut. One hour. This stranger spent one hour with my daughter and now presumes to understand Lucy's mind better than I do. Of course Lucy is confused by this whole situation. Hell, I'm confused too. But as I've learned over the last couple of weeks, that's completely by design.

Patricia's objection regarding the psychologist's limited time with Lucy is promptly overruled, Judge Morris dismissing it with a flick of his wrist as if swatting away an annoying fly.

Karla asks Dr. Mercer a few more questions before concluding, but I can already feel the damage settling into my bones like a chill. *This is it. They're painting me as the villain in my own daughter's story.*

During cross-examination, Patricia asks, "Dr. Mercer, how many custody disputes have you provided expert testimony for in your career?" *Please let there be something here. Some crack in their perfect narrative.*

Dr. Mercer shifts in her seat, her confident demeanor flickering. "Well, I specialize in general child development—"

"That's not what I asked. How many custody cases specifically?"

"I... this would be my first formal custody evaluation."

Patricia's eyebrows lift slightly. "And you feel qualified to make definitive conclusions about Lucy's psychological state after a single sixty-minute session?"

"Your Honor," Karla interjects, rising from her chair. "This line of questioning—"

Judge Morris waves his hand dismissively. "Ms. Torres, I've already ruled on the admissibility of Dr. Mercer's testimony. The court recognizes her expertise in child psychology as sufficient for these proceedings."

Patricia's jaw tightens, but she presses forward. "Dr. Mercer, isn't it standard practice to conduct multiple sessions before drawing conclusions about a child's mental state?"

"Objection," Karla calls out. "Asked and answered."

"Sustained. Move on, Ms. Torres."

Patricia's hands clench at her sides. "Your Honor, this issue hasn't actually been addressed. One hour is insufficient to—"

"Ms. Torres." Judge Morris's voice carries a warning edge. "Actually, I *have* addressed this matter. The witness's qualifications and methodology have been established to the court's satisfaction."

The weight of defeat settles on my shoulders as Patricia's determined advocacy shifts to reluctant acceptance—Judge Morris has made clear he won't entertain further challenges to Dr. Mercer's rushed evaluation or problematic methodology.

"No further questions for this witness, Your Honor," Patricia says with professional resignation, her voice crisp but controlled, tension visible in her shoulders as she clicks her pen once before setting it down with deliberate precision.

Judge Morris nods curtly, his attention already shifting away. "Dr. Mercer, you are dismissed. Thank you for your testimony."

But Patricia isn't done yet. She rises, her voice cutting through the courtroom with renewed purpose. "Your Honor, Dr. Mercer's testimony emphasized the importance of providing Lucy with a stable, consistent environment.

However, the court must examine what genuine stability means in this context."

She circles back to the documentation she previously presented of Eva's multiple identities, including birth certificates showing various names for the same birth date, newspaper clippings mentioning an "Evelyn Dorsey" in connection with a family in Oregon, and social media posts showing Eva's face with different names.

"Your Honor, the evidence clearly demonstrates that 'Eva Lerner' has assumed multiple identities over the years, infiltrating families before—"

Karla interrupts. "Objection, Your Honor. Counsel is making unsubstantiated claims about my client. There's no definitive proof these individuals are the same person, and the quality of these documents is questionable at best."

Judge Morris nods. "Sustained. Ms. Torres, please limit your assertions to verified facts."

Patricia goes over the financial evidence again, documents showing irregular transfers and account manipulations at SD Title & Escrow following Peter's death. The papers make a soft shuffling sound as she presents them, the noise mingling with the squeak of someone's chair and the distant sound of a door closing somewhere else in the building.

"The alleged 'irregularities' amount to minor discrepancies in expense reports, easily explained by clerical errors, not intentional fraud," Karla counters. "Furthermore, it is highly suspicious that these documents, conveniently supporting Ms. Samson's claims, have originated from an untraceable source. Lastly, these have nothing to do with Ms. Lerner."

"Those documents," Patricia states, her voice calm and steady, "were provided to my client from a USB drive left to her by her late husband, Peter Samson, in the event that something happened to him. Additionally, Eva Lerner and Sebastian Dorsey—"

Karla scoffs, a brittle, dismissive sound. "Given that Ms. Samson's sister was fired from her journalism job for fabricating sources while supposedly investigating Mr. Dorsey, this suggests a retaliatory motive for these conveniently discovered 'documents.'"

Judge Morris waves a hand, cutting through the escalating tension. "Counselors, we're getting off course. This emergency hearing was scheduled to determine the custody status for the minor child, Lucy Samson. These arguments regarding a third party not involved in this custody determination are irrelevant." His gaze sweeps over us, cold and impersonal. "We'll focus on the child's well-being. Dr. Mercer's report clearly indicates that Ms. Samson's behavior is creating a hostile and unstable environment. Ms. Torres, unless you have compelling evidence to refute these findings, I'm inclined to grant Ms. Lerner temporary full custody pending further investigation."

My stomach lurches. The room tilts, the faces blurring around me. *Temporary full custody.* The words echo in my ears, hollow and terrifying. I open my mouth to speak, to protest, but no sound comes out. Patricia places a reassuring hand on my arm, her grip firm.

Her jaw muscles work briefly before she responds. "Your Honor, all of these issues—the false identities, the financial irregularities, the rushed psychological evaluation —they're part of a larger pattern." She points to the lab results showing arsenic in Peter's system. "These results strongly suggest Peter Samson was being poisoned in the months leading to his death, which was misattributed to complications from Guillain-Barré syndrome resulting in pneumonia."

Karla appears almost bored, examining her perfect

manicure. "Mr. Samson was an avid restorer of antique furniture, a hobby documented in numerous social media posts. Exposure to arsenic from old paint and wood treatments is well-established in such activities."

Each piece of evidence we offer is methodically countered, reinterpreted, or dismissed as circumstantial. The ground beneath our case shifts with every exchange, like trying to build on quicksand. A headache begins to throb at my temples, keeping time with my racing heart.

Karla's voice then takes on a tone of synthetic concern, the kind reserved for discussing particularly tragic cases. "Your Honor, I must also address Ms. Samson's arrest for disorderly conduct this past Friday when she refused to comply with officers in front of Ms. Lerner's residence, further traumatizing young Lucy."

The words hit me like a baseball bat to the ribs, doubling me over. *Ms. Lerner's residence.*

That's *my* house. *My* home.

I grip the edge of the table, my knuckles white as I start to push myself up from the chair.

Patricia's hand clamps down on my forearm, her fingers digging into my skin with surprising strength. She pulls me back down into my seat, her voice barely a whisper but sharp as glass. "Don't. This will only make things worse."

The injustice burns in my throat like acid. Every fiber of my being wants to scream the truth, to tear down their carefully constructed lies, but I force myself to remain seated. The courtroom feels smaller now, the walls pressing closer with each heartbeat.

Patricia rises smoothly, her composure unshaken despite the landmine Karla just detonated. "Your Honor, while it's true that Ms. Samson was arrested, the circumstances are entirely understandable given that Ms. Lerner had essentially kidnapped Lucy from her elementary school."

She pauses, allowing the weight of that word—*kidnapped*—to settle over the courtroom. "According to the custody arrangement, Ms. Lerner was supposed to arrive at the domicile at 5:00 p.m. to take residence and custody of Lucy. Instead, Ms. Lerner circumvented the proper channels and tricked the administration at the school into releasing the child to her custody hours earlier."

Karla doesn't miss a beat, her response smooth. "The early pickup was necessary to accommodate Dr. Mercer's evaluation, which had been arranged for that afternoon. Ms. Samson had agreed to these arrangements in advance."

My body moves before my mind can stop it, my chair legs scraping against the floor as I start to rise again. The blood pounds in my ears, drowning out everything except the need to speak, to fight back against these fabrications. Patricia's hand finds my arm once more, her grip firmer this time, and I sink back into my seat like a marionette with cut strings.

"Your Honor," Patricia says, her voice cutting through the tension, "I need a moment to confer with my client."

Judge Morris nods curtly, his expression suggesting this is yet another delay in what should be a straightforward proceeding.

Patricia leans close, her breath warm against my ear. "What is she talking about? These arrangements?"

"None of this is true," I whisper, my voice hoarse with barely contained frustration. "I never agreed to any evaluation. I never received any notification about changing the pickup time. This is the first I'm hearing about any of this."

Patricia's eyes flash with something—anger, determination, maybe both. She straightens, addressing the judge with renewed conviction. "Your Honor, my client never received any notification from Ms. Lerner regarding these alleged arrangements. There was no communication about Dr. Mercer's evaluation or any change to the custody transition schedule."

Karla moves with the easy confidence of someone playing a winning hand. "Your Honor, we have clear evidence of their communication regarding these arrangements."

She approaches the bench with a manila folder, extracting what appears to be printed screenshots. "These are copies of the text message exchange between Ms. Lerner and Ms. Samson confirming the appointment with Dr. Mercer and the adjusted pickup time."

The subterfuge cuts deeper than a knife. Text messages I never sent, conversations I never had, all presented as gospel truth in this sterile courtroom. My mouth opens, words forming on my tongue, but Patricia is already moving.

"Objection, Your Honor," she says, her voice sharp and clear. "As opposing counsel has repeatedly stated regarding our evidence, we have no way to verify the authenticity of these text messages. Digital communications can be easily falsified, and without proper chain of custody documentation or forensic verification, these alleged messages hold no more weight than any other unsubstantiated claim."

"So noted," Judge Morris says.

"One last thing, Your Honor," Karla says, her voice taking on a note of regret, "we hesitated to introduce this evidence given its sensitive nature, but Ms. Samson's mental health history directly impacts Lucy's wellbeing."

She produces a sealed folder. "These are medical records showing Ms. Samson sought treatment for intrusive thoughts about harming herself and Lucy in the past year. This is in addition to the medical records we'd previously presented to the court regarding Ms. Samson's treatment for postpartum depression."

Air solidifies in my lungs. A high-pitched ringing fills my ears as memory collides with this grotesque distortion. They'd used my postpartum anxiety—the responsible steps I'd taken to ensure my daughter's safety—twisted into a weapon against me before. Sure, I'd suffered typical new-mother worries—fears of dropping her, of not hearing her cry—standard concerns I'd been assured were not unusual. But now these people have woven an entirely new narrative, one that suggests my struggles never ended—that I'm still drowning in the same dark waters that once threatened to pull me under. The implication hangs in the courtroom air like poison: that the woman who once sought help responsibly is now a continuing danger, her mental health deteriorating rather than improving with proper treatment.

Patricia rises immediately, the scrape of her chair against the floor jolting me back to the present. "Objection, Your Honor! Counsel is introducing what appears to be medical documentation without proper foundation or chain of custody. We haven't had the opportunity to authenticate these records or verify their source, and given the serious nature of these proceedings, I request time to examine these documents before they're admitted into evidence.

"Ms. Winters?" Judge Morris prompts.

"These records were released with proper authorization by Mr. Peter Samson before his death, as part of estate planning that included contingencies for his daughter's care." Karla's lie flows smoothly from her lips. "They were legitimately in Ms. Lerner's possession as the child's stepmother."

Judge Morris turns to us. "Ms. Torres, your client will have the opportunity to review these records," he states, his tone suggesting this generous allowance should satisfy any reasonable objection. "However, I'd like to hear what Ms. Winters has to say regarding their contents."

The casual dismissal hits like a slap. Patricia's posture straightens, her voice cutting through the courtroom with surgical precision. "Your Honor, without the opportunity to verify the validity of these records first, anything Ms. Winters says about their contents may prejudice the court against my client based on potentially fabricated evidence."

The judge's pale eyes narrow behind his wire-rimmed glasses, the first crack in his judicial composure. A muscle in his jaw tightens as he leans forward slightly, his displeasure radiating across the bench like heat from a furnace.

"Objection noted, Ms. Torres."

The words carry a warning that settles in my stomach like lead. His tone suggests Patricia has crossed some invisible line, pushed too hard against procedures he'd rather not examine too closely.

Karla stands with renewed confidence, the manila folder clutched in her manicured hands like a weapon she's eager to wield. She strides to the bench to present it to the judge.

"These are fake," I whisper.

Patricia responds, her breath warm against my ear. "I believe you. Unfortunately, it seems the damage has already been done."

As Karla continues detailing my supposed mental instability, she dramatically circles back to my recent arrest for disorderly conduct as "further evidence of escalating behavior patterns incompatible with primary custody."

A vise tightens around my chest. Everything we've

presented has been neutralized, while manufactured falsehoods against me pile higher by the minute.

Judge Morris clears his throat. "I've reviewed the evidence presented by both sides in this matter," he says, his tone unchanged from the beginning of the hearing. "While Ms. Torres has presented concerns that merit further investigation, they remain insufficiently substantiated at this time for the current hearing. The documentation provided could potentially be defamatory without sufficient context, and while I'll allow it to be filed, it carries minimal weight in today's determination."

The judicial language hits me like a punch to the gut. Behind the polite phrasing lies the unmistakable message: everything we've presented means nothing.

"Concerning the immediate matter of custody, evidence has been presented indicating genuine concerns about Ms. Samson's current stability and judgment. Given the paramount importance of providing the child with a consistent, secure environment during this investigation period, I am granting temporary full custody to Ms. Lerner pending comprehensive psychological evaluations of all parties involved."

Each word falls like a hammer blow. Full custody to Eva. My daughter, entirely in the hands of the woman who has methodically dismantled my life. The taste of defeat is metallic and bitter.

"Ms. Samson will be permitted supervised visitation once weekly, to be conducted at the family services center with a court-appointed supervisor present, after an initial evaluation by Dr. Mercer. This arrangement will continue until full psychological assessments can establish a recommended permanent custody arrangement."

Patricia immediately begins noting objections for the record, but the words blur together. Through a haze of disbelief, I watch Eva's face. Her expression maintains appropriate solemnity, but her eyes meet mine in a moment of unmistakable satisfaction. The corner of her mouth twitches upward for just a fraction of a second—so brief only someone watching for it would notice.

The gavel strikes. The sharp crack echoes in my hollow chest, finalizing the decision that has just severed me from my daughter.

As we gather our now-useless evidence, Patricia clutches my arm with unexpected strength. "There's an unseen hand at work here, Juliette," she whispers, her voice tight with controlled anger. "A very powerful one. This was decided before we walked in."

26

———————

The courthouse doors swing shut behind us with the finality of a prison cell. Patricia's arm supports me as we descend the stone steps, my legs wooden, my mind still reeling from the judge's ruling.

Full custody to Eva.

The words refuse to settle, drifting through my mind like debris floating in the air after an explosion.

"Let's reset," Patricia says, her voice low. "We knew this was a possibility, but I still expected some basic adherence to legal precedent." Her fingers tighten on my arm in silent support. "This changes our strategy, not our goal."

I nod numbly, unable to form words. My chest cramps, each breath shallow and insufficient, as though my body is forgetting how to function.

Lucy in Eva's care—entirely in Eva's care—with me reduced to once-weekly supervised visits like some dangerous criminal.

"The judge also ordered you to collect your personal belongings from your house today," Patricia continues as we reach her car. "A court officer will supervise. We'll go now, while the order is fresh."

Turning to face her, I swallow hard. "I'll see Lucy?"

Patricia's eyes soften with sympathy that makes my stomach sink. "If she's home, yes. But it's Monday—isn't she at school?"

I offer a ghost of a response, feeling disconnected from my own body, as if watching myself from a distance. "They've had her since Friday," I whisper. "What are they telling her? Does she wonder why I haven't come home?"

Patricia drives my car. The twenty-minute ride passes in silence, my head pressed against the cool window, watching familiar streets blur into smears of color. My neighborhood approaches—manicured lawns, elegant facades, the carefully maintained illusion of safety and normalcy that I once believed in.

Her phone buzzes with a text. She glances down, then says, "A court officer will meet us there. Name's Booth."

I barely register her words as she turns onto my street. The house comes into view—my house, Peter's house, Lucy's home. The freshly painted shutters, the flower beds I'd tended, the basketball hoop Peter installed when Lucy started showing interest. All of it still looks like mine, which makes the reality that much harder to bear.

A plainclothes officer waits in an unmarked car at the curb. He steps out as we park—mid-forties, with close-cropped hair and the rigid posture of former military. His eyes assess us quickly, professionally, revealing nothing of his thoughts.

"Ms. Samson? Officer Booth." He extends a hand that I shake mechanically. "I'll be overseeing the collection of your personal items pursuant to Judge Morris's order."

"Thank you for coming on such short notice," Patricia says, her tone shifting to cautious professional courtesy.

"Just doing my job, ma'am." He gestures toward the house. "Shall we?"

Eva is waiting at the door. The scent of home hits me as we step inside. Lemon furniture polish. The lingering smell of coffee. The faint trace of Lucy's strawberry shampoo.

I glance instinctively toward the staircase, for a fleeting moment hoping to see Lucy bounding down to greet me, though I know she won't be there.

Eva steps back, wiping her hands on a dish towel—my dish towel, the one with embroidered lemons that Peter's aunt gave us as a housewarming gift. She's traded her professional court attire for a simple blouse and jeans, her dark hair pulled back in a casual ponytail. The picture of domestic comfort in my home.

"Juliette." Her voice holds manufactured sympathy. "I didn't expect you so soon."

I swallow back words bitter as unripe persimmons, their astringency coating my tongue as Officer Booth clears his throat. "Ms. Lerner, we're here to collect Ms. Samson's personal effects as ordered by Judge Morris."

Eva's smile spreads across her face like frost forming on a window, beautiful but deadly cold. "Of course. I've already gathered some boxes for your convenience, Juliette." She gestures toward a stack of flattened moving boxes leaning against the wall—the same brand we'd used when moving in, ones she must have discovered in the garage.

"I'd like to gather things myself," I say, my voice scraping out of my throat.

"That's perfectly reasonable," Officer Booth says before Eva can respond. "The court order grants Ms. Samson one hour to collect clothing, toiletries, and personal effects not subject to property disputes."

Eva's smile tightens almost imperceptibly. "Of course. Please make yourself at home."

Her words hit me hard. Make yourself at home? This is *my* home. She's taken my daughter, while I'm being exiled. My jaw clenches so hard I fear my teeth might crack.

I move through the foyer into the living room, Patricia close behind me. The first subtle changes register immediately—the family photos on the mantel have been rearranged. A picture of Lucy and me at the beach last summer has been moved from its central position to the far edge, while a new photo of Lucy with Eva, framed in silver, has appeared in its place.

A cold front moves through my bones. "She's already changing things."

Patricia squeezes my arm. "Focus on what you need. We have limited time."

I nod and head for the stairs, but my gaze catches on the refrigerator as we pass through the kitchen. Lucy's artwork—her weekly kindergarten masterpieces that I've faithfully displayed—has been culled. The drawing of our family—Lucy, Peter, and me beneath a rainbow—is gone, replaced by a new drawing of a house with two stick figures.

I stop, staring at the drawing. Two figures—not three. My hand reaches out, fingertips brushing the paper. Despite everything, Lucy's distinctive style shines through —the swirls she adds to her sun, the particular way she draws clouds like cotton balls. Something inside me loosens fractionally. They can take me from this house, but they can't erase what Lucy and I share.

Eva follows a few paces behind, her footsteps light on the hardwood floors. "Lucy's been so creative lately," she comments, as if we're two friends discussing a shared child. "She's been drawing every night before bed."

I don't respond. Instead, I climb the stairs and walk to my bedroom—our bedroom, mine and Peter's. The door stands slightly ajar. I push it open, and the room that has been my sanctuary feels simultaneously familiar and alien. The bed is made with precision, sharp corners on my lavender sheets. But the pillows have been rearranged, and Peter's reading lamp is gone from his nightstand.

"I'll need suitcases from the closet," I say to no one in particular, moving toward the walk-in.

When I slide the door open, another wave of disorientation hits me. My clothes remain, but they've been compressed to one side, the hangers closer together than I keep them. The empty space beside them looms with implication.

"I've cleared some space for my things," Eva says from the doorway. "I hope you don't mind. The judge said to make accommodations for Lucy's needs, and having me close seemed best for her adjustment."

The casual cruelty of her words—her presumption of sleeping in my bed, in my room—sends a cold shudder through me. I pull down a large suitcase from the overhead shelf, letting it hit the floor with more force than necessary.

"You'll need to limit what you take today," Officer Booth notes, consulting a document. "The order only allows for reasonable personal effects."

I nod mutely and begin selecting clothes—jeans, sweaters, blouses, undergarments. Each item I place in the suitcase represents another piece of my life being excised from this house. Patricia helps silently, her expression grim as she folds my clothes with brisk efficiency.

In the bathroom, more changes await. My toiletries have been pushed to one side of the vanity. New bottles—

Eva's shampoo, her face wash, her moisturizer—now occupy the space where Peter's things once stood. I sweep my items into a toiletry bag without looking too closely at the labels that have replaced mine.

As I gather my medications from the medicine cabinet, Eva leans against the doorframe.

"Lucy had a nightmare last night," she says conversationally. "She was calling for you."

My hands freeze on my orange prescription bottle. "What did you tell her?"

"That you needed some time away to feel better." Eva's voice drips with artificial concern. "I thought it best not to upset her with the details of the court proceedings."

Officer Booth clears his throat. "Ms. Lerner, I'd appreciate it if you'd give Ms Samson some privacy while she collects her belongings."

Eva inclines her head in acquiescence and steps back, but she's already wormed her way into my head. The image of Lucy crying out for me in the night burrows into my chest like a barbed hook.

I pick up the bottle of Ambien, a thread from my private life that Eva has pulled, unraveling the careful tapestry I'd woven to protect Lucy from worry. In Eva's hands, knowledge of these pills—prescribed during Peter's final weeks when sleep became as elusive as hope—will transform from mercy into evidence of maternal negligence. Heat crawls up my neck as I carefully place the medication in my bag, fighting to keep my movements measured while imagining how she'll twist this story: a mother too drugged to hear her child's needs in the night.

After I finish in the bathroom, I move to Lucy's room, pausing at the threshold. Her space remains largely unchanged—the same purple butterfly bedspread, her beloved stuffed rabbit propped against her pillow, the same glow-in-the-dark stars on her ceiling. But there are subtle differences—new books on her nightstand that I don't recognize, a different arrangement of her toys.

I enter slowly, running my fingers on the edge of her dresser. The photo of Lucy and me at her fifth birthday party still sits on top, but it's been shifted to make room for a small potted plant—a succulent in a ceramic pot painted with butterflies.

"I thought her room could use some greenery," Eva comments from the hallway. "Lucy helped pick it out yesterday."

Yesterday. While I was at Patricia's office, preparing for a rigged court hearing, Eva was taking my daughter shopping, creating new memories to replace the ones we'd shared.

I open Lucy's dresser drawer, intending to check that her favorite pajamas are still there—the ones with the unicorns she insists on wearing until they're practically threadbare—but Patricia's hand on my arm stops me.

"Juliette," she murmurs, "the order doesn't allow you to take Lucy's things."

Reality crashes back, and I withdraw my hand as if burned. Of course. I'm not here to check on Lucy's welfare. I'm here to remove myself from her life.

I go downstairs to our study next, where Peter and I used to work when we brought projects home. The door is closed—unusual, as we always left it open in case Lucy needed us.

I turn the knob, but Eva steps forward. "I'm afraid the study is off-limits," she says. "The judge specifically mentioned that business materials are under dispute and should remain untouched."

Officer Booth consults his paperwork again. "Ms.

Lerner is correct. The order excludes access to financial documents, business materials, and disputed property."

"But my personal papers—" I begin.

"Will remain secure until property matters are resolved," Eva finishes, her voice smooth as polished stone.

My heart rate accelerates. The filing cabinet in the office contains the backup copies of Peter's financial records—documents I'd specifically left at home.

"There are items in there that have nothing to do with the business," I insist, turning to Officer Booth. "Family photos, personal correspondence—"

"Perhaps you could specify which items you need, and I can retrieve them for you?" Eva offers, her generosity a transparent ploy to maintain control.

"That won't be necessary," Patricia intervenes, her tone professional but firm. "We'll note in our filing that Ms. Samson was denied access to personal, non-business related items. The court can address this at the next hearing."

I want to argue, but Patricia's warning look stops me. This isn't the battle to fight with a court officer present.

We move back into the living room, and I collect a few more personal items—the small wooden music box my grandmother left me, a framed photo of my parents, the handmade quilt from my great aunt that normally lives in the guest room. Each item gets wrapped in newsprint and placed in a box Patricia has assembled.

As I reach for a leather-bound volume of poetry Peter gave me on our first anniversary, I notice something else missing in the small drawer in the side table where I'd hidden one of Lena's USB drives with copies of our evidence.

"Did you move the contents of this drawer?" I ask Eva, working to keep my voice neutral.

Eva's eyebrows lift slightly. "I tidied up a bit. Just some old receipts and a few odds and ends. I put them in a box in the hallway closet."

My pulse quickens as I try to read her face. Does she know what was on that drive? Has she found it, or merely moved it unaware?

"I'd like to see that box," I say.

"Of course." Eva's smile is serene as she retrieves a cardboard storage box from the closet. "Here you are."

I rifle through the contents—old birthday cards, warranties for appliances, receipts from home repairs. No USB drive. I search more frantically, papers spilling onto the floor.

"Is something missing?" Eva asks, watching me with calculated concern.

"You know exactly what's missing," I snap, standing up so quickly that my vision dims momentarily. "You're erasing me from this house—from Lucy's life. Moving photos, replacing my things with yours. You're probably telling Lucy I've abandoned her—"

"Ms. Samson." Officer Booth's voice cuts through my rising anger. "I need to remind you that the court order specifies civil conduct during this process."

Eva steps back, a perfect portrait of wounded innocence. "I'm only trying to make this transition easier for Lucy. I would never try to replace you."

"Bullshit." The word explodes from me before I can stop it. "That's exactly what you're doing. You've wanted my life since the moment you met Peter, and now you're taking it piece by piece—"

"Juliette." Patricia's hand clamps on my arm, her grip unexpectedly strong. "That's enough."

Officer Booth steps between us. "I think we should finish gathering your items promptly, Ms. Samson."

I'm trembling, my breath coming in short gasps. In the silence that follows my outburst, I glimpse another of Lucy's drawings partially visible behind a picture frame on the bookshelf—this one showing a playground with colorful swings.

The playground. Lucy's school.

A sudden calm washes over me, cooling the rage. I won't find what I need here—not with Eva watching my every move, categorizing my reactions for her next court filing. But I can see Lucy. I can at least see my daughter.

"I'm sorry," I say, the words tasting like ash. "You're right, Officer Booth. Let's finish this quickly."

Patricia helps me gather the remaining items while Eva watches, her arms folded across her chest. When we finally load the last box into my car, the sun sits high overhead, bathing everything in harsh clarity. The house—my house —gleams white in the midday light, the windows reflecting nothing but empty brightness.

"Are you okay?" Patricia asks as I pull away from the curb.

"No," I answer honestly. "But I know what I need to do next."

"Juliette..." her voice holds a note of warning.

"I'm not going to do anything stupid," I tell her, as she watches me with that lawyer-calibrated skepticism. "I just need to get back to Lena's. Being with my sister helps."

Patricia sighs, unconvinced but unwilling to push. "Promise me you won't violate the custody order. Eva's just waiting for you to give her ammunition."

27

———————

I park down the street from the school, positioning my car where the playground is visible but I'm partially obscured by a large oak tree. Through the chain-link fence, I see the jungle gym where Lucy once dangled upside down, while Peter made faces, her laughter floating across the yard. That was before. Before my husband died. Before an interloper stole everything from me.

My reflection catches in the rearview mirror. I don't need the clichéd inventory of my appearance to know I'm a shadow of myself. The woman who used to exchange recipes with the other mothers, who brought homemade cookies to PTA meetings, seems like someone I once knew but can no longer reach.

My phone vibrates. Lena's message appears: "Where are you? Patricia called."

I silence the phone without responding. How could I explain this moment of desperation? This need to see Lucy that overrides legal advice, common sense, self-preservation?

The school bell rings, its distant peal sending my pulse

into my throat. Children spill from the building in a chaotic rainbow of motion and noise. I scan for Lucy's signature bouncing stride, the way she used to race into the schoolyard as if recess might disappear if she didn't hurry.

Then I see her.

Lucy emerges holding Eva's hand. My breath stops—physically stops—as if someone has gripped my lungs. Lucy's hair is woven into a French braid much more elaborate than the simple ponytail I used to do for her. She wears a purple cardigan over a white dress I've never seen before. But it's not her clothes that make me lean forward, eyes straining. It's how she moves.

The Lucy I know races everywhere, feet barely touching the ground. This child beside Eva moves with careful, measured steps, as if someone has adjusted her volume to the lowest setting. Each footfall seems deliberate, hesitant. My maternal instinct stretches across the distance between us like a piano wire pulled too tight, vibrating with discordant warning notes.

Eva leads Lucy toward a cluster of women standing near the fence—Jennifer, Melissa, Alison. Women who used to text me about carpools and birthday gifts. Women I considered friends.

They gather around Eva like she's the center of the solar system. Jennifer throws her head back, laughing at something Eva says, her hand touching Eva's arm with easy familiarity. The casual betrayal doesn't surprise me, yet it still bites deep. Eva has infiltrated my social circle with the precision of a surgeon, excising me and grafting herself in my place.

Her beige sweater and jeans project calculated warmth, her hair falling in soft waves that seem to defy gravity. She's elevated suburban motherhood into a curated Instagram feed, while mine remained an unfiltered family album with dog-eared corners. Of course she has. She's been ghost-following my life, learning which filters to apply to appear more authentic than the original.

Lucy tugs Eva's sleeve and hands her a piece of paper. Every part of me strains to see what she's drawn. Eva examines it with exaggerated interest, her face softening into the exact expression I've made hundreds of times when Lucy presented me with her artwork. She opens her purse—the tan leather tote Peter gave me for Christmas, with the small coffee stain on the inner lining that only I should know about—and slides the drawing inside with a performance of reverence that makes bile rise in my throat.

She's not just taking my place; she's becoming me. Recreating gestures and expressions she must have observed during those months of surveillance, feeding them back to my daughter in a grotesque forgery of motherhood.

Movement flickers at the edge of my vision. Alison has spotted me. Our eyes connect across the schoolyard for one electric moment before she deliberately turns away, her spine stiffening. She leans into Jennifer, whispering something. Jennifer's gaze follows hers, finding my car, then quickly pivots away.

Eva sees their reaction, turning slowly until her eyes lock onto my car. I fight the instinct to duck down, to hide like a criminal. Instead, I straighten my spine and meet her gaze directly through the windshield.

She doesn't scowl or alert a teacher. Instead, her lips curve upward in a smile that contains no warmth—only pity, as if I'm some pathetic creature worthy of indifference rather than fear. The expression cuts deeper than rage ever could. She bends down and whispers into Lucy's ear.

Lucy looks up, searching until she finds my car. For a

breathless moment, sunshine breaks across her face, eyes widening with recognition. Her small hand starts to rise in a wave.

Time suspends in that fraction of a second—her fingers lifting, her lips parting, the beginning of that sacred word forming in her mouth. My entire being hangs on that incomplete gesture.

Then Eva's mouth is at her ear again, her hand clamping onto Lucy's shoulder. Lucy's arm drops like a broken wing. Her face—so briefly alight—shutters closed. She turns away, Eva gripping her hand tighter.

Something ruptures inside me. Not my heart—something deeper, more primitive. The place where motherhood lives. Tears well without warning, turning the playground into a smeared watercolor. The distance between us expands, becomes infinite.

Every cell in my body screams to run to her, to cross that playground and snatch her away. To hold her close and whisper, "I'm here, I never left, I never would." To tell her in words a six-year-old might grasp that bad people are keeping us apart, and I'm fighting my way back to her.

But Patricia's warnings echo in my head—approaching Lucy now would only cement the separation. I'd become exactly what they've painted me as: unstable, dangerous, a mother who can't follow court orders supposedly meant to protect her child.

I press my forehead against the steering wheel, with something between a sob and a scream trapped in my throat. The choice splits me in two—the mother who needs to hold her child versus the woman who must wait, must play this horrific game by their rules to win her back.

When I look up again, rubbing swollen eyes with my sleeve, Eva is leading Lucy toward the parking lot. They're heading for a white SUV—identical to the one I drove until last year, right down to the "Women in Real Estate" bumper sticker. Another piece of my life perfectly replicated.

As they walk, Lucy does something odd. She checks over her shoulder toward Eva, then quickly drops something from her palm, using her foot to nudge it against the sidewalk edge. Eva, preoccupied with waving goodbye to the other mothers as they help the teachers escort the children back inside, doesn't notice.

They climb into the SUV and drive away. I stare at the spot where Lucy dropped something, curiosity overcoming caution. After they disappear around the corner, I exit my car and cross the street, scanning the empty playground for any remaining parents or watchful teachers.

The area has cleared, children returning to classes, parents dispersed. I approach the spot where Lucy stood, my eyes searching the ground.

There, nestled against a tuft of grass, lies a small folded paper. I snatch it up, fingers trembling as I carefully unfold it.

A paper heart. Made from what appears to be the corner of a math worksheet, the crease slightly uneven, folded by small, determined hands. Inside, written in Lucy's unmistakable six-year-old handwriting: "I MISS MOMMY."

A sound escapes me—not quite a sob, not quite a laugh. I press the paper heart against my breastbone, feeling its edges imprint on my skin through my shirt. Lucy remembers. Despite Eva's manipulations, despite whatever confusion and lies swirl around her, my daughter remembers our private language. The folded hearts we used to leave for each other—tucked into lunchboxes, hidden under pillows, always containing messages only meant for us.

This tiny scrap of paper is proof of what Eva can't replicate, can't steal, can't destroy with all her meticulous copying. The genuine bond between Lucy and me still exists, a secret frequency Eva can't jam or intercept.

I refold the heart with careful fingers and place it in my wallet, behind my driver's license where it will stay close. As I walk back to my car, something crystallizes within me, sharp and clear as diamond. I've been playing defense, dutifully following rules in a game that was rigged from the start. Eva and Sebastian are rewriting reality itself, and Lucy is caught between worlds, sending out a desperate signal.

A renewed sense of purpose guides my drive to Lena's apartment. This isn't about reclaiming possessions or repairing my reputation anymore. My daughter is asking for rescue, and God help anyone who stands in my way.

LENA OPENS the door before I knock, relief washing over her face.

"There you are," she says, exhaling sharply. "Patricia's left three voicemails. I was about to check the hospital and the bottom of every wine bottle in town."

I move past her into the apartment, where every surface is layered with papers and folders.

"I saw Lucy," I announce, pulling the paper heart from my wallet. "And she saw me. Eva is working overtime to turn her against me, but she's failing."

Lena takes the paper heart, her eyes widening as she reads Lucy's message. "Holy shit," she whispers, with something like pride flickering in her expression. "Your kid's got guts."

"She's asking for help," I say, sinking onto the couch.

"We need to accelerate everything. My daughter needs me now, not six months from now after we've jumped through every legal hoop."

"What are you suggesting?" Lena asks, her expression both wary and intrigued.

I close my eyes briefly, seeing Lucy's subdued form walking beside Eva, her aborted wave, her secret message. When I open them again, I feel the last remnants of the woman I was fall away like shed skin.

"I'm saying it's time to take a page from their play-book," I reply, holding up Lucy's paper heart. "They're counting on me to keep being the good girl, to follow procedure while they manipulate the system." My fingers close around the heart. "But my daughter needs her mother, not a martyr."

Something beyond grief or rage fills me—a cold, clear purpose that feels like stepping into focus after months of blur. Eva and Sebastian built their strategy on the assumption that I would remain who I've always been—trusting, rule-abiding, predictable.

They have no idea who I'm becoming.

28

———————

Lena stares at the paper heart in my hand, her eyes darkening with resolve.

"Let me call Malcolm," she says, pulling her phone from her pocket. "He's been digging into Sebastian's financials. We might have something."

While she speaks in hushed tones by the window, I spread the paper heart on the coffee table, smoothing its creases with my fingertip. Lucy's handwriting—wobbly capital letters pressing hard into the paper—speaks volumes. My daughter isn't just sending love; she's sending a distress signal.

"He's coming over," Lena says, ending the call. "Says he's found something that might help us understand what Sebastian's been doing with the company finances."

"How long?"

"Ten minutes." Lena studies my face. "You okay? Going to the school was risky."

"I had to see her," I say, the image of Lucy's subdued movements haunting me. "She's different, Lena. Like someone's turned down her volume."

"Kids are resilient," Lena says, squeezing my shoulder. "And Lucy's smart. That paper heart proves she knows something isn't right."

A knock at the door interrupts us. Lena checks her watch, frowning. "That's fast, even for Malcolm."

She opens the door to reveal Patricia clutching her leather portfolio. Her expression balances concern with professional restraint.

"I've been trying to reach you," she says, stepping inside without waiting for an invitation. Her gaze lands on me. "You haven't returned my calls."

"I went to see Lucy," I admit. "From a distance. I didn't approach her."

Patricia's lips tighten. "Juliette, we've discussed this. Any contact—"

"No contact occurred," Lena interjects. "My sister kept a legal distance. And look what Lucy managed to leave for her."

I hand Patricia the paper heart. Her professional veneer softens as she reads the message inside.

"This is compelling," she says, returning it carefully. "But Judge Morris has made his position clear. He sees Eva as the stable caregiver right now."

"How?" I demand, heat rising inside me. "She's living in my house, wearing my clothes, driving a car identical to mine. She's literally stolen my identity!"

"Which the judge views as continuity for Lucy during a difficult transition," Patricia says, setting her portfolio on the table. "Remember, Morris sees this as a squabble between two women who both care for Lucy. He doesn't grasp the manipulation behind Eva's actions."

"Then we need to make him understand," I say, pacing the small living room. My hands tremble as I gesture toward the window. "Lucy doesn't want to be with her. She's asking for help."

Another knock interrupts us. This time, Lena opens the door to Malcolm, who enters with his laptop bag slung over his shoulder. He nods to me, then registers Patricia's presence with surprise.

"Full house," he says, setting his laptop on the table. "Good timing, actually. I've found something you all should see."

While Malcolm sets everything up, Patricia leans forward. "Let me update you on where we stand legally. Another emergency hearing is scheduled for Wednesday. Judge Morris has agreed to review the case based on our claim that material facts were misrepresented, but I want to manage expectations. He's shown a clear preference for Eva's narrative."

"Which is complete fiction," I say, wrapping my arms around myself.

"Got it," Malcolm says, his laptop screen illuminating his face. "Check this out."

We gather around as he pulls up financial records and bank statements.

"Sebastian's been quietly moving money out of the company for years," he says, pointing to highlighted transactions. "Small amounts, spread across multiple accounts, but it adds up to millions over time."

"We knew he was embezzling," Lena says. "Peter suspected it before he died."

"It's not just embezzlement," Malcolm says, opening another window. "The money funnels through shell companies before landing in offshore accounts linked to a trust benefiting both Sebastian and Eva Lerner—or as she's listed on the account, Evelyn Dorsey."

"Unfortunately, this isn't anything new," I say.

"But there's more," Malcolm says, his eyes scanning another document. "Eva—or Evelyn—has a pattern. She's done this before."

"Lena's found this out before—" I say, but an email notification chimes.

Malcolm clicks it open, his eyebrows lifting as he reads.

The room goes quiet. I can hear my own heartbeat in my ears.

"What is it?" Lena asks, voicing the question we're all thinking.

He looks up, his expression grave yet somehow energized. "My contact just sent over police reports from Chicago and Denver." He turns the laptop toward us. "Evelyn Dorsey has been investigated twice for similar schemes—insinuating herself into families, fabricating relationships, attempting to take over someone's life."

Patricia leans forward, suddenly alert. "Charges?"

"Dropped both times," Malcolm says, scrolling through the attached files. "The families withdrew complaints after significant emotional distress. But the pattern is identical— she targets families with young children, creates elaborate backstories, and uses her connection to Sebastian for financial leverage."

Patricia's eyes narrow as she studies the screen. "This is substantial. Email me those files immediately."

"Already done," Malcolm says, tapping his keyboard.

Hope lifts inside me, but Patricia's expression remains guarded.

"This is valuable, but we need to be strategic," she says. "Judge Morris has already dismissed evidence of Sebastian's financial misconduct as irrelevant to Lucy's custody arrangement."

"How is it irrelevant?" I ask, my voice rising. "They're

criminals working together! How can the judge ignore this?"

"Because Eva presented herself as Peter's grieving partner who only wants what's best for Lucy," Patricia says. "And you've been painted as unstable after the confrontation at your house."

The memory flashes through my mind in vivid, painful detail. The cold metal bite of handcuffs against my wrists. The humiliating stares from neighbors. The suffocating helplessness as the police officer guided me toward the cruiser, her hands firm on my shoulders. The crushing weight in my chest as my world disintegrated, piece by piece, while they drove me away from my home—away from Lucy.

"The judge doesn't see the connection," Patricia continues. "He's viewing Eva's custody claim separately from Sebastian's business dealings."

"They're not separate," Lena insists. "It's all one scheme."

"We know that," Patricia says. "But Judge Morris is unmoved by our previous attempts to demonstrate the connection."

I sink onto the couch. "So it doesn't matter what we find. The judge won't listen."

"I didn't say that," Patricia says. "I said we need a new approach. Morris sees Eva as a stabilizing presence in Lucy's life and you as potentially volatile. We need to shift that perception."

Lena crosses her arms. "How? By letting them have even more time with Lucy? While they poison her mind with who knows what?"

Patricia's phone buzzes. She checks it, then looks up with renewed focus. "I have an idea. What if we petition for temporary custody to be granted to Lena instead?"

I blink. "Lena?"

"She's Lucy's aunt—a blood relative," Patricia says. "The courts typically favor family connections. If we argue that Lena provides a stable environment while allowing continued contact with both you and Eva, pending a full investigation of all parties..."

"I'll do it," Lena says immediately. "In a heartbeat."

The suggestion hangs in the air, tempting but incomplete. I stare at Lucy's paper heart in my hand, remembering her subdued movements in the schoolyard.

"It's not enough," I say finally. "Lena seeking custody might help eventually, but Lucy needs help now. She's asking for it." I hold up the paper heart. "There has to be another way to make someone see what's happening."

Malcolm clears his throat. "What about Detective Adams?"

"Who is he?" Patricia asks.

"A source I had when I was investigating Sebastian's financial issues before," Lena says.

"He's already suspicious of Sebastian's testimony," Malcolm says. "If we bring him this new financial evidence, plus the pattern of Eva's previous identity theft attempts, it could push the investigation in a new direction."

"Would that affect custody?" I ask, watching Patricia's face.

She taps her fingers against the table, thinking. "If Adams investigates Eva, it raises questions about her fitness as a guardian. The court would have to take another look at custody."

"So the judge isn't willing to see the truth if it's only us bringing him evidence," I say. "We need law enforcement to validate our concerns."

Lena nods slowly. "I should reach out to Detective

Adams. Since he already had questions about Sebastian's dealings in the past, this might be exactly what he needs to dig deeper."

"If we can show Adams what we have, he might uncover something that could change the tide," Patricia says, her caution giving way to something like optimism.

"Can we do both?" I ask, looking at Patricia. "Prepare a motion for Lena to seek temporary custody while simultaneously bringing all this to Detective Adams?"

Patricia's lips curve in a rare smile. "Absolutely. A two-pronged approach gives us better odds."

"Then let's do it," I say, standing up with renewed purpose.

The room seems to sharpen around me. Malcolm begins organizing his files while Patricia pulls legal forms from her portfolio. Lena squeezes my arm, her eyes bright.

"We'll get her back," she says softly.

I nod, caressing Lucy's paper heart with my fingers. Something new breaks through the grief and rage—hope. Small but real, sparked by Lucy's secret message and the evidence piling up in our favor.

We gather our materials quickly, preparing for Lena to meet Detective Adams. Before she leaves, I pull Patricia aside.

"This approach—you really think it could work?"

"It's our best strategy," she says. "Lena seeking custody introduces a third option the court hadn't considered, while Adams might uncover evidence that forces a reevaluation of Eva's claims."

I picture Lucy with Lena while this mess untangles itself—safe with family who loves her, away from Eva's manipulations.

"Let's do it," I say.

29

I wake to pale sunlight stretching across Lena's living room floor, our evidence against Eva and Sebastian stacked neatly on the coffee table beside me. My body aches from another night on the couch, but for once, exhaustion takes a backseat to possibility. Today, Patricia presents our case to Judge Morris again. Today, things might finally change.

The clock reads 7:14 a.m. Patricia has convinced the judge to allow her to meet with him at 8:00. She insisted on going alone—"Judges respond better to measured legal arguments than emotional pleas," she'd explained yesterday while organizing our files—but promised to call the moment she finished.

I shower in record time, scrubbing hard enough to leave my skin pink. The water washes away the night's sweat but does nothing for the acid churning in my stomach. Lucy's paper heart sits on the bathroom counter, reminding me of what's at stake.

When I emerge, Lena is in the kitchen brewing coffee, still in pajama bottoms and an old t-shirt.

"Did you sleep at all?" she asks, handing me a steaming mug.

I wrap my fingers around the ceramic, drawing warmth from it. "A few hours. You?"

"On and off." She leans against the counter. "What time will Patricia call?"

"Her meeting's at eight. She should be done by nine, depending on how it goes."

Lena's mouth tightens at the corners, her eyes flicking down to her coffee.

"What?" I ask.

"Nothing." She shakes her head. "Just nervous. This judge hasn't exactly been on our side."

"This evidence is different," I say, trying to convince myself as much as her. "Eva's pattern in other cities, the arrest records. It's not just our word against hers anymore."

Lena nods. "You're right. And if Patricia can get temporary custody assigned to me while they investigate..."

"Then Lucy is safe with family." I grip my mug tighter, the edge digging into my palm. "And I can at least see her every day."

The next hour stretches like taffy. I check my phone every few minutes, though I know it's too early for news. I organize our evidence files. I look at my phone again. By 8:30, my skin feels too tight for my body.

"I'm going to wait outside the courthouse," I say, grabbing my jacket.

Lena looks up from her laptop. "Patricia said to wait for her call."

"I won't go inside. I just need to be there when she comes out." To read her face before she has time to compose it for me.

Lena sighs but doesn't argue. "Text me the second you hear anything."

"I will."

The courthouse dominates downtown—stone columns and broad steps designed to make ordinary citizens feel small. I park a block away and walk the rest, each click of my heels against concrete setting the rhythm of my ragged breathing.

I find a bench across the street with a clear view of the main entrance. The morning air carries a hint of autumn, crisp against my face. Business people hurry up and down the steps. Attorneys huddle together, briefcases clutched to their chests. A normal day for everyone else.

My phone buzzes at 9:17. Patricia.

"I'm outside," I tell her. "Just across the street."

"Stay there. I'm coming to you." Her voice is flat, drained of inflection in that careful way people speak when delivering bad news.

I scan the courthouse entrance and spot her, a slim figure in a charcoal suit, descending with measured steps. Her shoulders are pulled back too rigidly, her chin lifted too high.

Patricia crosses the street, her face a professional mask. She sits beside me on the bench, setting her portfolio between us like a barrier.

"What happened?" My voice comes out thin, reedy.

She takes a deep breath. "It's not good, Juliette."

"He didn't accept the evidence?"

"He refused to hear the motion. But that's not all." Patricia opens her portfolio and removes a document. "This was waiting for me when I arrived."

I take the paper. My fingers tremble against the official letterhead where bold letters spell out "TEMPORARY RESTRAINING ORDER."

"A restraining order?" I whisper. "Against me?"

"Karla filed it yesterday afternoon. Judge Morris

granted it immediately." Patricia speaks in that detached attorney voice, the one that distances her from the human wreckage of legal proceedings. "You're barred from coming within 500 feet of Eva, Lucy, your house, or Lucy's school."

My lungs contract, refusing to fill. "That's not possible. I haven't done anything."

"According to the petition, you've been stalking Eva. Following her car, watching the house, sitting outside Lucy's school." Patricia pulls out more papers. "Karla Winters presented these as evidence."

Photographs. Me in my car parked down the street from my own house. Me watching Lucy on the playground from across the street. Me in front of Lucy's school yesterday.

Bile rises in my throat as understanding dawns. "They've been tracking me. Documenting my movements when I tried to see my own daughter."

"There's more." Patricia hesitates. "Someone's been sending threatening emails to Eva from your old account, the one registered to your home internet. And your phone number appears on her caller ID with late-night hang-ups."

"That's impossible! I haven't sent any emails or made any calls!"

"I believe you," Patricia says. "But the evidence is compelling. The timing of these alleged incidents coincides perfectly with your actual movements."

I grip the bench edge hard enough to feel splinters press against my palm. "They planned this. They knew I'd try to see Lucy and they created a paper trail to use against me."

"The sophistication is... concerning," Patricia admits. "These aren't amateur tactics."

"What about our evidence? Eva's past identities, the police reports from Chicago and Denver?"

Patricia's mouth tightens. "Judge Morris dismissed it all as 'irrelevant to the immediate safety concerns.' He said there's no definitive evidence proving Eva is the same person from those cases."

"But the photos, the pattern—"

"Circumstantial, according to Morris." She closes her portfolio with a decisive snap. "And there's one more thing. He's doubled down on the psychiatric evaluation order. Before he'll even consider lifting the restraining order, you'll need to complete a full psychological assessment."

My mind becomes a kaleidoscope that someone has just shaken violently, all the colorful fragments of my life tumbling into an entirely new pattern that I don't recognize. Each new barrier erected between Lucy and me, each legal maneuver orchestrated to paint me as unstable, dangerous.

"What about Lena?" I ask, dreading the answer. "What about temporary custody?"

Patricia shakes her head. "Morris learned about the restraining order Sebastian had against Lena years ago. He shut down that suggestion immediately."

"Of course he did." Bitterness coats my words. "They've thought of everything."

My phone rings. Lena's name flashes on the screen.

"What's happening?" she demands when I answer, her voice tight with tension.

"It's bad," I say. "Really bad. Eva got a restraining order against me. The judge dismissed all our evidence."

"Fuck," Lena exhales. "That's not the only thing. Detective Adams just called me."

Something in her voice makes me sit up straighter. "What did he say?"

"He's been removed from duty, Juliette." Lena's voice cracks with raw fury. "Pending an Internal Affairs investigation—immediately after he tried to present our evidence about Peter's murder."

"What? Why?"

"He said there was 'pressure from above,' Juliette. Political interference." Her voice rises, trembling with rage and disbelief. "They silenced him as soon as he even hinted at foul play."

Patricia watches my face, reading the new disaster in my expression.

"That's not possible," I whisper. "They can't just remove a detective for doing his job."

"They did. And Adams said to be careful. He thinks Sebastian has reach we haven't even begun to understand."

The world swirls around me, the pedestrians walking past blurring into meaningless shapes. Sebastian's influence extends beyond Eva, beyond my house, beyond the company he stole. He has connections in the police department, in the courts.

"I'll be there soon," I tell Lena, ending the call.

Patricia studies me.

"What now?" I ask.

The question hangs between us. What now, indeed? With a restraining order barring me from Lucy, a judge who won't hear our evidence, and our police contact neutralized, what options remain?

"The psychological evaluation," Patricia says into my silence. "If you complete it—"

"It's rigged," I interrupt. "You know that."

"Probably," she concedes. "But refusing will only strengthen their narrative that you're unstable. It's the only path left to maintain any legal access to Lucy."

I stand abruptly, needing to move, to think. "And if I

focus instead on exposing Sebastian and Eva? On proving Peter's murder?"

"Without law enforcement or judicial support?" Patricia sighs. "You'd be working completely outside the system, Juliette. That's dangerous territory."

"More dangerous than letting my daughter remain with the people who killed her father?"

Patricia doesn't answer. She doesn't need to. We both know I've reached the point where traditional legal avenues have failed me completely.

I pace the sidewalk in front of the bench, my mind racing. Every official door is closing. Every system designed to protect the innocent has been corrupted or circumvented.

"What would happen if we took this to the media?" I ask suddenly.

Patricia's eyebrows lift. "The media?"

"Lena has contacts from her journalism days. What if we bring all our evidence to them? Let the court of public opinion hear what Judge Morris refuses to consider?"

"It's risky," Patricia warns. "Going public could backfire spectacularly. It could seem like you're trying to litigate in the press because you can't win in court."

"Or it could force transparency where backroom deals have silenced the truth."

I stop pacing, my decision made. I won't abandon the legal path entirely—that would only play into their hands. But I won't rely on it exclusively either.

"I'll do the psychiatric evaluation," I tell Patricia. "I'll jump through every hoop they set up. But simultaneously, we're taking this to someone who can't be bought or intimidated."

"Who?"

"Megan Rhodes. She's Lena's former colleague at the

Tribune. Award-winning investigative journalist. If anyone can expose what Sebastian and Eva are doing, it's her."

Patricia considers this, her legal mind weighing risks and benefits. "It's unorthodox. But then, this entire situation is unprecedented."

"So I have your blessing?"

"My blessing?" A wry smile touches her lips. "No. My understanding, perhaps. And my continued representation, regardless of which path you choose."

"Thank you." I squeeze her hand, unexpected emotion tightening my throat.

"Don't thank me yet." She stands, straightening her suit jacket. "Schedule that evaluation today. The sooner you complete that requirement, the sooner we can petition for revised visitation."

As Patricia walks back toward the courthouse, my phone buzzes with a text from an unknown number. I open it, expecting spam.

Instead, my heart stops.

Miss you, Mommy. Jenny's sister let me use her phone to text you.

Lucy. My Lucy, finding a way to reach me despite everything.

A second message appears:

Eva keeps asking about Daddy's special hiding places. Says he left something for her. What does that mean?

My hands shake so badly I nearly drop the phone. Eva is still searching. She knows Peter hid something—evidence, perhaps. Proof of what she and Sebastian have done.

Peter, who knew he was dying. Peter, who suspected this betrayal before any of us.

I stare at my daughter's message, tears blurring the screen. This small act of rebellion from my six-year-old has accomplished what all our legal maneuvering couldn't: it has given me hope. Lucy hasn't forgotten me. She's fighting in her own way.

And now I know Eva is looking for something—something she's afraid of.

I send a quick reply—*I love you so much, be brave, Mommy's coming soon*—then delete the conversation, erasing any evidence from my phone.

Standing on the courthouse sidewalk, even with this restraining order in hand, I feel something shift inside me. The grief and shock that have defined me since Peter's death forms into something harder, sharper. More dangerous.

They've blocked every official avenue. They've turned the system against me. They've stolen my home, my reputation, my child.

But they've made a critical mistake. They've left me nothing to lose.

30

———

Eva is searching for something Peter hid. Something important enough that it might be the evidence we need—carefully hidden by my husband before he died.

But what?

Lena and I prepare meticulously to meet with Megan. The county library parking lot has exactly four cars when we arrive. Perfect. My psychological evaluation is tomorrow morning—likely a carefully laid trap—but today we create our insurance policy.

"Are you sure she'll show?" I pull my collar tighter as the wind cuts through my jacket.

Lena checks her watch. "Megan's obsessive about punctuality."

I study the library's brick façade, noting the single security camera above the main entrance. We chose this meeting place with purpose—minimal surveillance, no connection to either of us, no digital footprint.

"There," Lena says.

A blue Mazda pulls in, parking deliberately away from the other vehicles. A compact woman emerges—silver-streaked hair cropped short, shoulders squared against the wind. She carries a worn leather messenger bag and scans the lot before her gaze finds us.

We enter separately. No greetings, no acknowledgments. The study room Lena reserved under a false name waits at the back of the building—beige walls, rectangular table, four chairs, motivational reading posters that have faded from years beneath the fluorescent lights.

I close the blinds while Lena checks for cameras.

"You still haven't learned to trust a public space," Megan says, watching Lena.

"Some habits keep you alive."

Megan sets her bag on the table and turns to me. "You must be Juliette."

"Thank you for coming." I shake her hand. "I know this isn't without risk."

"Lena mentioned Sebastian Dorsey." Her mouth tightens. "That name alone was enough to get me here, though I should warn you—he's not someone I'm eager to cross paths with again."

Lena sits across from her. "You remember what happened."

"Hard to forget when your reporting partner gets destroyed." The warmth leaves Megan's voice. "Why would I stick my neck out again?"

"Because this time we have evidence," I say, placing our folder between us. "Real evidence."

Megan doesn't touch it. "What kind of evidence?"

"Identity theft in multiple states, fraudulent custody proceedings, embezzlement from our company," I tap the folder. "And my husband's murder."

Her eyebrows lift slightly. "Murder? That's quite an accusation."

"My husband, Peter Samson, was Sebastian's business

partner. The death certificate says complications from pneumonia. The truth is arsenic poisoning."

"By Sebastian?"

"Him or his half-sister, Eva Lerner. She's infiltrated my home and used the legal system to abduct my daughter."

Megan finally reaches for the folder. "You're claiming Sebastian Dorsey and his sister murdered your husband, stole your child, and are now what—living your life?"

My voice fractures like ice on a thawing lake, each word cracking under pressure. "I know how it sounds."

She opens the folder. For the next ten minutes, the only sounds are the rustle of paper and the scratch of her pen across a small notebook. Her handwriting is tiny, compressed, nearly indecipherable from across the table.

"Compelling," she said, looking up. "The identity changes are particularly interesting—classic pattern for a confidence woman." She taps the photos. "And the financial trail raises serious questions."

Hope rises in my chest. "So, you'll write the story?"

She holds up one hand. "I didn't say that. This suggests wrongdoing, but doesn't prove it." She points to the medical reports. "You've shown me that exposure to arsenic matches his symptoms. But you haven't connected them to poisoning him."

"He took gabapentin for nerve pain. The capsules could be opened and refilled."

"Can you prove she did it?"

"We sent the medication bottle to a forensic lab for analysis based on Dr. Kumar's initial findings," Lena says. "But it's going to take a while to get the results."

"As expected," Megan says. "Which judge granted Eva custody?"

"Judge Raymond Morris," Lena replies. "Somehow he's got to be under Sebastian and Eva's influence. And I shared all of this with Detective Adams—you remember him?"

Megan nods.

"Right after he started digging around, he was suddenly pulled from duty. Internal Affairs is investigating him for some trumped-up complaint about a case he was on when he was still a patrol officer."

Megan closes her notebook and shakes her head. "That's troubling. Very troubling. But without direct evidence linking Eva to the poisoning, this story is too risky. I need something concrete that can't be explained away."

I twist my wedding ring. "So you won't help us."

"I didn't say that." Megan taps her pen against the table. "Something about this case feels familiar." She picks up her notebook and flips through it, scanning older pages. "About six months ago, I investigated a case involving falsified prescriptions. There was a doctor named Wilson Grant—"

"Wilson Grant was Peter's doctor," I say. "He's the specialist Sebastian recommended."

Megan stops mid-page-turn. "That cannot be coincidence." She continues flipping through her notes. "My story was about doctors writing unnecessary prescriptions for controlled substances. There were hints of something more complex—wealthy patients getting unusual medications, possible insurance fraud. My editor killed the story after pressure from 'influential people.'"

"This has to be related to Sebastian," Lena says.

"I never confirmed who, specifically. But the timing fits. If Sebastian was planning to harm your husband, he'd want to protect Dr. Grant from scrutiny."

I tug at my collar as the walls of the small room seem to inch closer. "Do you still have your research?"

"Everything." A small smile. "I learned from Lena's

mistake. I keep copies where the newspaper can't touch them."

Lena leans forward. "If Dr. Grant falsified prescriptions, and he was Peter's doctor during his decline——"

"He could be the missing link," I finish. "The one who administered the poison, or helped cover it up."

Megan nods. "Worth investigating. But, again, we still need concrete evidence connecting one of them to the poisoning itself."

I close my eyes. My head throbs. What haven't we considered? What might Peter have left behind?

Lucy's text resurfaces in my mind: *Eva keeps asking about Daddy's special hiding places. Says he left something for her.*

"Eva's been searching for something Peter hid," I say. "What if it's proof of how they killed him? He was investigating right before he died—he'd just gotten those lab results back."

Megan snaps her notebook shut. "This is what I need. If we find something showing them tampering with his medication, plus whatever evidence Peter compiled against Sebastian, I can run the story."

"Will your editor allow it?" Lena asks.

"I've built up enough capital since your time. And if he balks, I have other outlets." Megan's eyes narrow. "But I need something solid first."

"I'll find it," I say.

"While you search, I'll dig deeper into Dr. Grant and these falsified prescriptions. If we can prove he knowingly prescribed medication that facilitated murder—"

"He might flip on Sebastian to save himself," Lena says.

"Exactly."

A plan takes shape between us—imperfect but concrete.

"How long will this take?" I brush hair from my eyes

with trembling fingers. "Lucy is with them now. Every day—"

"I understand the urgency," Megan said. "But rushing gives us half-results. Give me a few days on Dr. Grant. You focus on finding whatever it is that Eva's looking for."

We agree to meet Thursday, exchanging burner phone numbers. As we prepare to leave separately, Megan touches my arm.

"Juliette, be careful. If Sebastian has the influence we suspect, he's watching you. And people who poison others rarely show restraint when cornered."

I think of Lucy's small face, her trusting eyes. "That might not be a luxury I have. Not while she's with them."

We exit in five-minute intervals—Megan first, then Lena, me last. The library has filled with afternoon students. I blend with them, another anonymous face.

In the parking lot, I spot it immediately—the sedan with tinted windows across the street. The same one I've noticed for days now. They're not even trying to be subtle anymore.

I slide into my car, my hands cold against the steering wheel. My phone buzzes with a calendar reminder: *Psychological Evaluation—9:00 a.m. Tomorrow.*

The trap they've laid, baited with access to Lucy. I'll walk into it deliberately, knowing exactly what Sebastian intends, while Megan investigates and we search for Peter's hidden evidence.

I start the car. The sedan doesn't move immediately— they want me to know I'm being followed. Another of Sebastian's tactics.

Let them watch. Let them think I'm defeated. They've only ever seen fragments of me—Peter's grieving widow, a desperate mother. They've never bothered to see the woman who built a business from nothing, who crawled back from the edge when depression nearly claimed her.

The sedan pulls out behind me, staying at a discreet distance. I drive exactly at the speed limit, broadcasting harmless compliance.

As I drive, my mind sorts through every conversation with Peter, every offhand comment about hiding important documents, every possible place he might have secreted the evidence that could destroy the people who killed him.

I'll find whatever it is Eva is searching for. Because Lucy needs me, and I can't fail her.

31

The next morning, I arrive fifteen minutes early for my appointment at the designated nondescript medical building. The parking lot is filling up, with only a few spaces left that aren't reserved for staff. In the glass doors, my reflection stares back—a woman wearing my clothes with eyes that belong to someone harder, someone who's been forced to grow armor.

The receptionist directs me to a waiting area with muted beige walls and outdated magazines arranged in perfect rows on a glass coffee table. The air smells of artificial potpourri, a scent that seems designed to mask the anxiety that permeates the space.

When the inner office door opens at precisely 9:00, I rise to my feet.

"Ms. Samson? I'm Dr. Mercer. Please come in."

My pulse spikes, a cold rush flooding my veins. The woman standing before me is the same child psychologist who interviewed Lucy and testified against me. The shock of Eva being awarded full custody must have clouded my mind—I hadn't even registered that I would be seen by the same woman from the other day. Her dark bob frames her face perfectly, not a strand out of place. Her smile stretches her lips, but her eyes study me like data points on a chart. She wears dark slacks with a cream blouse beneath a tailored jacket, projecting authority and professional distance.

"You were in court," I say, not moving from my spot. "You evaluated my daughter and served as a witness against me."

Her smile stays frozen for a moment before she speaks. "Yes, I did work with Lucy. I wasn't attempting to take sides. That's why you're here today, to maintain consistency, since I've already assessed your daughter. The court decided my background makes me uniquely qualified for this evaluation."

Uniquely qualified—an elegant euphemism for "already biased against me."

"I see."

"Please, come in." She steps aside, gesturing to her office.

The space is meticulously arranged—diplomas and certifications in matching frames, two leather chairs angled toward each other with a small table between them and a bin full of toys nearby. A box of tissues sits within easy reach, positioned for the emotional breakdowns she undoubtedly expects. The room itself feels like a stage set, designed to extract certain responses.

"Water?" She indicates a mini-fridge off to the side.

"No, thank you."

We settle into our respective chairs. Dr. Mercer opens a leather portfolio, uncaps an expensive pen that gleams under the recessed lighting, and looks up with professional detachment.

"Before we begin, I want to emphasize that my role is

to provide an objective assessment. Everything you share will be included in my report to the court regarding your psychological fitness for custody."

The warning pulses between us: watch what you say. Everything is ammunition.

"I understand."

She begins with standard background questions—childhood, education, work history. I answer truthfully but carefully, watching her pen move across the page, documenting every word, every hesitation, every shift in my tone.

"Let's discuss your relationship with Peter."

For twenty minutes, I describe our marriage, his illness, his death. Throughout, Dr. Mercer's expression remains neutral, but her questions grow increasingly pointed, like a blade being slowly twisted.

"Did you ever feel Peter wasn't being completely honest with you?"

I recognize the hook in her question, the careful placement of her verbal snare. "Like any couple, we had areas where communication could have been better."

"Specifically regarding his relationship with Ms. Lerner?"

"I had no knowledge of Eva Lerner until after Peter's death."

Her pen pauses mid-stroke. "That must have been quite a shock."

"Learning that my husband had supposedly divorced me and remarried? Finding a stranger claiming to be my daughter's legal guardian? Yes, it was."

Dr. Mercer shifts in her chair, her eyes narrowing slightly as though focusing a lens. "Do you often feel people are conspiring against you, Ms. Samson?"

"I don't walk around suspecting everyone I meet. I

have concrete reasons to be concerned about specific people, based on what they've done."

She notes something in her portfolio, her pen scratching across the paper. "What about anger? Have you ever felt unable to control your anger around Lucy?"

"No." My answer comes out sharper than intended, and I see her make another note. I moderate my tone. "I'm protective of my daughter, but I've never had issues controlling my emotions with her."

"Even during your period of postpartum depression?"

My chest tightens, the muscles cramping around my lungs. "My postpartum depression was properly treated and resolved years ago."

"But it was severe enough to require hospitalization."

Not a question. A statement of fact pulled from medical records that should have been private. I force myself to breathe evenly, imagining Eva and Sebastian getting those records somehow, passing them to her.

"Brief hospitalization, yes. For three days, when Lucy was two months old."

"During which time you expressed thoughts of harming yourself."

"I had intrusive thoughts that frightened me, which is why I sought help. The treatment was successful."

"Successful, that is, until recently."

"Despite the information presented in court, I've had no other instances where I required treatment for my mental health."

"I see," she says. "No need for *any* treatment? What about prescriptions?"

"As I said, I haven't had any issues recently." But then I remember the prescription for Ambien, that Eva undoubtedly saw in my medicine cabinet when she stole Lucy and kicked me out of my house. "However, I did get a prescription for pills to help me sleep. I was having a little trouble when Peter got sick, you know, toward the end."

Dr. Mercer nods, her pen moving continuously. "And you believe your husband was murdered despite the official finding of death from pneumonia. Can you explain that belief?"

Each question connects to the previous one like building blocks, and I can see the structure taking shape— a carefully engineered portrait of a paranoid, unstable mother unfit for custody.

"Peter's medical records show symptoms consistent with arsenic poisoning. This isn't a belief—it's a medical assessment based on evidence."

"Evidence that hasn't convinced the authorities."

"Evidence that was presented to a police detective before he was suddenly removed from the case and placed under investigation himself."

She raises an eyebrow. "You believe this detective was also targeted by this conspiracy?"

"I believe Sebastian Dorsey has considerable influence." I keep my voice level, aware of how each inflection will be interpreted.

Dr. Mercer sets down her pen and reaches for a manila folder on the side table. "Ms. Samson, I'd like to show you something."

She removes several photographs and lays them on the table between us. Lucy's face smiles up at me from each one—Lucy in a park with Eva, Lucy opening presents, Lucy baking cookies with Eva in our kitchen.

"These were taken this week," Dr. Mercer explains. "How do they make you feel?"

My throat tightens into a painful knot. I haven't seen my daughter in person since Friday. In these photos, she appears happy, well-cared for, her smile bright as she looks up at Eva.

"I'm glad Lucy appears to be physically well." My voice emerges hoarse, scraped raw by emotion. "I miss her terribly."

"She seems to have adjusted quite well to living with Ms. Lerner."

I pick up one of the photos—Lucy in an outfit I've never seen before, reaching up toward Eva, whose face is cropped just out of frame. The image is carefully composed to showcase Lucy's apparent happiness.

But something isn't right.

I examine the picture more closely. Lucy's left forearm is visible, extended toward the camera. My fingertips go numb against the glossy photo paper. The room's flowery scent suddenly seems suffocating as I stare at the mark— dark and oval, perfectly positioned on my daughter's forearm where her skin has always been unmarked.

Lucy has no birthmarks on her arms. Not a single one.

I glance at the other photos, blood rushing in my ears. The same mark appears in two others, identical in size and placement. Photos she claims are of my daughter.

My pulse hammers against my ribs as a realization dawns. Someone has doctored these images—most likely pasting Lucy's face onto another child's body. I feel dizzy with the implications, but force my breathing to remain steady, my face to betray nothing.

Dr. Mercer watches me intently. "Is something wrong, Ms. Samson?"

I set the photo down carefully, my fingers trembling slightly despite my effort to appear calm. "Dr. Mercer, I'd like to note for the record that I have concerns about these photographs."

"Concerns?"

I point to the mark on Lucy's arm. "My daughter doesn't have this birthmark. She never has. These photos have been altered."

Her expression remains frozen, but her eyes betray her—a millisecond widening, then a tightening at the corners that speaks of irritation.

"That's a serious accusation."

"It's an observable fact that you can verify by examining Lucy yourself. Additionally, I'm concerned about your impartiality in this evaluation, given your prior testimony in favor of Ms. Lerner."

Dr. Mercer's professional veneer cracks slightly. She gathers the photos quickly, her movements brusque and efficient, returning them to the folder.

"I think we've covered enough ground for today, Ms. Samson."

"We still have twenty minutes scheduled."

"Your defensiveness and accusations of photograph manipulation suggest paranoid tendencies that warrant further assessment." She closes her portfolio with a snap that echoes in the quiet room. "I'll be noting in my report that you exhibit signs of persecutory ideation and an inability to acknowledge your daughter's apparent well-being in her current placement."

The injustice burns inside me, but I keep my voice steady. "I'd like to request a copy of those photographs for my attorney."

"You'll receive all appropriate materials through legal channels. This session is concluded."

She stands, effectively dismissing me. I unfold from my chair and rise with deliberate care, my eyes locked on hers.

"Thank you for your time, Dr. Mercer," I manage to say with as much civility as I can muster. "I look forward to reviewing the complete transcript of today's evaluation with my attorney."

In the hallway, my composed facade nearly crumbles. My breath comes in short gasps that I struggle to control. I walk briskly to my car, sliding into the driver's seat before pulling out my phone with shaking fingers.

"Patricia? It's Juliette." My voice wavers with a mixture of rage and relief. "As expected, the evaluation was a complete setup. She showed me doctored photos of Lucy—with a birthmark my daughter doesn't have. They weren't even subtle about it."

Patricia's voice is grim. "I'm not surprised, but the altered photos give us something tangible. Document everything while it's fresh—every question, every response, the entire sequence with the photos. I'll draft another emergency motion this afternoon."

As I end the call, my phone buzzes with a text message from an unknown number:

meet me this afternoon -C

It's followed by an address for a coffee shop out in the suburbs.

Carol.

My former assistant is reaching out again, despite the risks.

I start my car, scanning the parking lot for surveillance. The sedan with tinted windows is absent today, but I feel watched nonetheless. Sebastian and Eva have orchestrated an elaborate trap with Dr. Mercer, but they've revealed just how desperate they are. And I know from building a business from nothing that desperate people don't just make mistakes—they overreach. They get sloppy. They leave evidence.

Evidence I will use to get my daughter back.

32

———————

I slip into the coffee shop twenty minutes early, scanning for threats before settling at a corner table that offers clear sightlines to both the entrance and parking lot. Half the tables sit empty in the cozy space, where exposed brick walls and mismatched furniture create an atmosphere worlds away from Sebastian and Eva's polished, sterile taste. Perfect for this meeting—anonymous yet public enough to provide some safety.

My phone buzzes with a text from Patricia: *Submitted another emergency motion. Judge will review tomorrow morning.*

I tuck my phone away and order a black coffee I don't want, just to have something to occupy my restless hands. Every chime of the door sends tension crackling through my muscles. The psych evaluation with Dr. Mercer this morning has stripped away my defenses, leaving wounds that still throb. Those doctored photos of another child with the birthmark haunt me—their clumsy execution revealing both their desperation and their confidence that no one will challenge them.

At five after one, Carol Matthews slips through the

door. Her normally immaculate bun has come partially undone, with wisps of hair framing a face marked by exhaustion. Dark shadows pool beneath her eyes as she scans the room, her shoulders hunched forward like someone expecting an attack. When she spots me, her expression softens as if she's recognizing a fellow survivor.

I stand as she approaches, caught in that awkward moment of not knowing the appropriate greeting. We settle for a simple nod as she slides into the chair across from me.

"Thank you for coming," she whispers, her gaze darting toward the entrance. "I can't stay long."

"I appreciate the risk you're taking."

Carol unwinds her scarf with trembling fingers. "Sebastian's been asking questions about where I go during lunch breaks."

"Is he following you?"

"I don't think so. I took an unusual route to get here and doubled back twice." She pulls off her gloves, finger by finger, a methodical process that seems to calm her. "Probably excessive, but after what I've seen..."

A waitress approaches, her cheerfulness jarring against our tension. "Can I get you anything?"

Carol orders herbal tea, her posture remaining rigid until the waitress retreats beyond earshot.

"I should have come to you sooner." She rubs her palms against her thighs in a nervous rhythm. "I've known something was wrong for a while."

I lean forward. "Tell me about it."

Her gaze drops to the wooden tabletop, tracing a pattern in the grain. "At first, it was just little things. Financial records that didn't reconcile. Sebastian working late, shredding documents that should have been archived." She swallows hard enough that I can see the movement in her throat. "I told myself it wasn't my place to question. That I was imagining connections that weren't there."

"But you weren't."

"No." The word cracks between us. "Then I found invoices for services we never provided. Payments to shell companies. Sebastian caught me looking once and said it was a special project for Peter. I believed him because... what else could I do?"

The waitress returns with Carol's tea. Carol wraps her hands around the mug, the steam rising between us like a fragile barrier. She waits until we're alone again before continuing.

"I've been scared," she continues, her voice barely audible over the coffee shop's ambient noise. "You didn't see what Sebastian did to people who questioned him. Remember Maria from accounting? The one who 'moved to Arizona'?"

"She found problems in the books?"

Carol nods, her eyes fixed on something distant. "Sebastian made sure she couldn't get work anywhere in the industry. He planted drugs in her desk, called in an anonymous tip, then offered to drop charges if she resigned quietly and signed an NDA. Last I heard, she's folding sweaters at the mall and living with her parents."

"Why didn't you tell Peter?" I ask, dreading the answer I suspect is coming.

Carol's eyes flicker with discomfort. She takes a sip of tea, flinching as it scalds her tongue.

"This is the hard part," she admits. "I thought Peter knew. That he was... involved."

"Involved how?"

"With Eva." The words tumble out, as if she's been holding them back too long. "There were meetings on his calendar with her initials. Calls he took in private. Sometimes he'd leave early and say he had a doctor's appointment, but his actual medical appointments were all on the shared calendar."

My stomach twists, acid burning the back of my throat. "You thought they were having an affair."

"It seemed obvious. But now..." She sets down her mug with deliberate care. "Looking back, all the suggestions about an affair came from either Sebastian or Eva. Comments they'd drop. Things they'd imply."

"And Peter? How was he acting?"

"Normal. Affectionate when you'd visit." She frowns, the crease between her brows deepening. "That's what never made sense. He didn't act like someone cheating. He acted like a man who missed his wife. But I figured maybe I was misreading everything."

"Then Peter died."

Carol nods, blinking rapidly. "And everything happened with such calculated precision. The reading of the will. You being pushed out. Lucy..." Her voice falters. "When I heard about Lucy, I couldn't remain silent. An innocent child being taken from her mother—I couldn't be complicit in that."

The coffee shop door opens, and Carol jerks in her seat, her grip tightening around her mug. She exhales only when an elderly couple shuffles in, arguing good-naturedly about whether they should split a muffin.

"Sebastian's turned me into someone I don't recognize," she confesses. "Jumping at shadows, second-guessing every word. But I'd never forgive myself if I didn't try to help Lucy. And you."

"Do you have evidence of Sebastian's financial misconduct?"

"Some. Not everything." Her hesitation is palpable.

"But I have something else. Something I think matters more."

From her purse, she extracts a small thumb drive, placing it on the table between us. My fingers twitch toward it, but I force myself to wait, to let her tell the story at her own pace.

"Peter left this," she explains. "Hidden in a book in his office with a note addressed to you. The note said Eva and Sebastian were monitoring everything he did, so he was distributing evidence in different locations."

"When did you find this?"

"The day after the funeral. Sebastian had me boxing up Peter's personal items." Her voice softens. "The note said Peter didn't know what order you'd find things in, but he suspected Eva was planning something, so he installed a camera in his office."

My pulse thuds in my ears, blood rushing so fast I feel lightheaded. "What's on it?"

"Security footage. From the camera he installed. It wasn't connected to the company network." She pushes the drive closer to me. "I watched it. There's a clip that shows Eva searching through his desk when he wasn't there. And another—" her voice drops to barely above a whisper "—where she opens his medication bottle and does something to the contents."

Time stills. The clatter of dishes, murmur of conversations, and hiss of the espresso machine fade to background static as the implications hit me. My lungs seem to forget how to draw breath, and a cold numbness spreads from my core outward.

"She tampered with his medication," I say.

Carol nods, tears glistening in her eyes. "Sure looks like it. I should have come forward sooner. But I was terrified.

Sebastian has connections everywhere. Police, judges, doctors."

My fingers close around the thumb drive. Hard evidence. Not just of financial crimes, but of murder. Of the systematic destruction of my family. The small plastic rectangle feels impossibly heavy in my palm.

"What should we do with this?" Carol asks. "Go to the police?"

The question hangs between us as I weigh our options. The police seem compromised, based on what happened to Adams. But the custody case is immediate—Lucy is with Eva right now. Every second she spends with her father's killer tears at me.

"Can you file a whistleblower report with the district attorney about the financial crimes? I don't trust the police right now, so go over their heads. And I'll take this to my lawyer for the custody case. This evidence of Eva tampering with Peter's medication should help us get Lucy back."

Something tentative dawns in Carol's expression. "You think it will work?"

"It has to." I slip the drive into my pocket, the edges pressing against my leg like a promise. "This is the missing piece. Visual confirmation that ties Eva directly to Peter's death."

Carol checks her watch and pales. "I need to get back. I told Sebastian I was dropping off files at Verdant Realty."

"Alison's office?" The mention of her real estate firm triggers a connection. "Has Sebastian been working with Alison Cole?"

"She's been handling property acquisitions for some of those shell companies I mentioned. I don't think she realizes what she's involved in."

Alison's sudden coldness crystallizes into something

comprehensible. Her avoidance, her discomfort. She's just another strand in Sebastian's web.

As we prepare to leave, Carol's phone rings. She startles so violently she nearly knocks over her tea, fumbling to answer.

"Yes?" Her voice transforms, sliding into professional neutrality like a mask. "No, Sebastian. Traffic was worse than expected." She swallows, a flicker of fear crossing her face. "Yes, I dropped the files off at Verdant like you asked. I'm heading back now."

She ends the call, her hands trembling.

"He's watching me," she whispers. "He's always watching."

I reach across the table and squeeze her hand. "You're doing the right thing. Thank you for your courage."

"I just want this to be over." She stands, rewrapping her scarf with deliberate movements. "Good luck, Juliette. For Lucy's sake."

I watch her leave, counting to thirty before following. In my car, I sit with my hand pressed against my pocket, feeling the outline of the thumb drive—evidence that Peter tried to protect us, even as they were killing him.

I start the engine and rub my hands together while I wait for the heater to kick in. Something ignites in my core, not the wild bonfire of rage I've known, but the steady burn of purpose and relentlessness. Now I feel something beyond anger and fear.

Hope.

But hope is dangerous. Because if Sebastian and Eva discover what Carol has given me before I can use it, they won't just come after me—they'll destroy her too.

33

———————

Back at Lena's apartment, I stare at my laptop, my blood turning to ice as I watch the video again. Eva in Peter's office, opening a desk drawer, taking out Peter's prescription bottle.

"She's not just a con artist," I whisper, my voice shaking. "She's a murderer."

Lena leans closer, her face tense. "And she has Lucy."

Certainty crashes over me like a wave against rocks—relentless and impossible to stop. My daughter is living with the woman who killed her father.

"It's almost six," I say, checking my phone. "They'll be having dinner now."

I grab my keys, already moving toward the door. Lena catches my arm.

"Jules, there's a restraining order. If you go there—"

"I don't care." The words come out with absolute certainty. "Did you see how methodical she was? How rehearsed? I'm sure this wasn't her first time."

The image of Lucy eating food prepared by Eva flashes through my mind. My stomach lurches.

"What if she's already started?" My voice breaks. "What if she's already giving Lucy something? Maybe that's why she looked different at school—more subdued, moving slower."

Lena's eyes widen. "You think she'd hurt Lucy?"

"I don't know what she's capable of anymore." I clutch my keys tighter. "But I'm not waiting for a court to decide if my evidence is good enough. Not when Lucy could be in danger right now."

Lena grabs her jacket. "I'm coming with you."

We rush down to my car. My hands shake so badly I drop the keys twice before managing to start the engine.

"What's the plan?" Lena asks as I pull onto the street.

"Get Lucy out. That's it." I press harder on the accelerator. "I'll deal with the consequences later."

"The police will come."

"Let them." The yellow lines beneath my tires disappear like seconds being devoured—time I can't afford to lose. "By then I'll have Lucy, and they'll have to physically take her from my arms."

The familiar streets blur past. All I can think about is Lucy with that woman, that awful woman.

"I'm coming, baby," I whisper. "Mommy's coming."

Rules, courts, restraining orders—none of it matters anymore. My daughter's life is at stake, and I'm done playing this game that's been rigged against me from the start.

I KILL the headlights as we turn onto my street, coasting the last hundred yards before stopping three houses down from mine.

"No lights on," Lena whispers, leaning forward in her seat.

A weary but familiar sensation spreads through me—the same feeling I had the night Peter was rushed to the hospital. "Something's wrong. We need to get inside. Now."

We approach through the shadows of the oak trees that line the yard. The house I once loved now looms before us, dark and unwelcoming. Lena produces a small pouch from her jacket pocket and removes two thin metal tools.

"Where did you learn to pick locks?" I ask, watching the empty street over my shoulder.

"Investigative journalism isn't always about knocking on the front door," she murmurs, working the tools into the deadbolt. "Some stories require alternative methods of entry."

The lock clicks open with a soft sound that triggers something primal in me—the sound of access to my child.

"Stay behind me," Lena whispers, pushing the door open with her elbow.

We step into the entryway, and I'm immediately hit by the wrongness of it all. There have been even more changes since I was here last. Eva's perfume—vanilla and something medicinal—has replaced the citrus scents I once used. New throw pillows adorn the couch. A strange vase sits on the entryway table where Lucy's school photos should be.

"Lucy?" I call out, unable to contain myself any longer. "Baby, it's Mommy!"

My voice echoes through the empty rooms. No response.

"Check upstairs," Lena says, already moving toward the kitchen. "I'll look down here."

I take the stairs two at a time, my pulse pounding in my ears. The hallway stretches before me, family photos still hanging on the walls—though I notice with rising rage that pictures of Peter and me have been removed, replaced with new frames holding photos of Eva with Lucy.

Lucy's bedroom door stands half-open. I push it wide and flick on the light.

The bed is empty, covers thrown back as if she's left in a hurry. Her backpack—her purple unicorn one with the rainbow zipper pulls and the Bluey keychain—is missing from its hook. The stuffed rabbit she's slept with since she was two is gone from her pillow.

"Lucy?" I call again, my voice cracking. I check the closet, the bathroom, even under the bed, though I already know. They're gone.

I rush back downstairs, my throat tightening with each step. "She's not here! Her bag is gone, and—"

"Juliette." Lena's voice stops me cold. "You need to see this."

She stands in the kitchen, opposite the island from me, holding a wrinkled piece of paper.

"What is it?" I ask, crossing to her side.

"Look." She shows me the crumpled paper. "I found this in the trash."

I stare at an airline confirmation page. Two tickets to Buenos Aires, Argentina. Departing tomorrow at 6:00 a.m. Passenger names: Eva and Lucy Samson.

The air thickens into amber, trapping me in this suffocating moment while she and my daughter are slipping away. "They're leaving the country in less than twelve hours."

"They're making a run for it," Lena says. "Sebastian must've gotten spooked when he realized Carol was gathering evidence."

I rub my temples, trying to think clearly. "Where would

Eva take Lucy this late if they're flying out at 6:00 a.m? A hotel near the airport?"

"Maybe, or—"

A crash from down the hallway freezes us both. We stand motionless, listening. Another creak, this one closer to our study.

"Someone's here," I whisper.

Lena motions for me to stay put while she edges toward the hallway. She peers around the corner, then beckons me to follow. "The office door is open."

We creep down the hallway, the house unnervingly silent except for our breathing and the occasional soft creak of the floorboards under our feet. Light spills from the office into the hallway—a faint glow, like someone using a flashlight.

When we reach the doorway, papers blanket the floor like fresh snow. A pen holder rocks back and forth atop an overturned drawer. No one is there. The cup must have just tipped from its precarious perch. The desk lies toppled, filing cabinet drawers hang open, their contents strewn about. I clamp my hand over my mouth as my eyes fix on the crooked painting—and the empty safe exposed behind it.

"They're destroying evidence," Lena whispers, her phone raised to document the chaos.

"Or searching for something," I add, stepping carefully through the destruction. "They must know about the video."

I kneel beside a pile of documents, rifling through them. Most are meaningless—old utility bills, insurance paperwork—but a few catch my eye. Our joint account statements. Incorporation documents for Samson Title & Escrow, the original name of our company before Sebastian came along.

As I reach for another stack, my phone rings loudly in the silence. I scramble to see who it is, a jolt of panic shooting through me.

The screen shows an incoming call: Sebastian Dorsey.

Lena and I exchange a look of silent dismay. She nods once, mouthing "Answer it" while raising her own phone, ready to record my end of the conversation.

I take a deep breath and accept the call, putting it on speaker.

"Hello, Sebastian." My voice comes out steadier than I expected.

"The game is over, Juliette." Sebastian's voice fills the ransacked office. Gone is the charming business partner who consoled me at Peter's funeral. "By the time you figure out where they are, they'll be gone. Eva finally gets her perfect life, I get the company, and you'll be institutionalized—exactly what you deserve."

Heat floods my face, but I swallow back the rage. Information is what I need now, not the satisfaction of screaming at him.

"Why do you hate us so much?" I ask, gesturing to Lena to call the police. She nods, backing into the hallway with her phone. "Peter trusted you. We welcomed you into our company."

Sebastian's laugh cuts through the speaker like shattered glass. "Your company? Peter always called it 'our company'—his and yours. I was just the hired help who actually built it into something while you played house. Eva and I deserve everything we're taking."

His arrogance loosens his tongue. I press further, keeping my voice deliberately steady.

"Where is Lucy?"

"Somewhere you'll never find her." Pride swells in his

voice. "We're tying up loose ends tonight. By morning, there will be nothing left for you to fight for."

"You can't just disappear with my daughter."

"We already have the new passports and documentation. Eva and Lucy will be gone by dawn, and you'll never see either of them again." He pauses, and I picture his smug expression. But I hear something in the background. Something familiar.

"It won't work, Sebastian," I say, straightening my spine. "We know how you did it. We know how you and Eva killed Peter."

The silence that follows stretches so long I wonder if he's hung up.

Finally, he says, "What are you talking about?" His voice has lost its cocky edge.

"Peter had evidence, direct evidence showing exactly how she poisoned him. It's already with the district attorney."

His breathing changes, becoming rapid and shallow. I've caught him off-guard. And then I remember where I've heard that sound in the background before, that familiar sound I know.

"You're bluffing," he says, uncertainty creeping into his voice.

I stand taller, feeling the power between us shift. "I suggest you start thinking about which one of you is going to flip on the other first. My money's on Eva. She seems the type to save herself."

"You bitch—"

I hang up on him and look up at Lena, electricity coursing through my veins.

"The lake house," I say. "That's where they are."

"How do you know?"

"The wind chimes. I heard them in the background."

Lena is already on her phone again. "I'm calling Detective Adams."

I stand amid the ruins of our study, surrounded by the scattered remnants of our life together. Finally, I'm no longer reacting to their attacks—I'm hunting them. I've spent weeks being erased, replaced, and gaslit while they dismantled my life piece by piece. But no more.

"Let's go," I say, already moving toward the door. "We have to get Lucy."

Lena catches my arm, the phone still at her ear. "He told us to stay put. Let him handle this."

"I need to go, Lena. I have to get my daughter."

She studies my face for a moment, then nods.

The night feels charged with possibility now. Sebastian's carefully constructed plan is unraveling thread by thread.

They tried to steal my identity, my future, my daughter. But they made one critical mistake.

They underestimated how far a mother will go to save her child.

34

———

The distance between me and my daughter shrinks with each mile marker, my resolve hardening into something desperate and unstoppable as I drive. The car's speedometer nudges eighty, but it's not enough—not when every passing second is a reminder that part of me is missing. Lucy. My Lucy. Taken away by them.

Lena's been texting from the passenger seat the whole time. "Adams says the sheriff is sending two deputies, but we'll beat them by at least twenty minutes."

I make a sharp turn, my tires squealing against the asphalt. The lake suddenly materializes between the trees, moonlight creating silver gashes across its black surface. On any other night, I might have found it beautiful. Tonight, it's just another barrier between me and my daughter.

As we come up to a dirt road nearly swallowed by overgrown brush, I slow down. "Sebastian's cabin is at the end."

Killing the headlights, I swing onto the rough path. The car bounces violently over exposed roots, each jolt sending pain through my clenched jaw. As a large, dark structure emerges ahead, I stop the car.

A sleek black SUV—Sebastian's Escalade with the custom grille he'd once bragged about—sits in the gravel driveway. My pulse hammers in my temples at the confirmation. They're here.

"We go the rest of the way on foot."

We ease the doors shut, the soft clicks unnaturally loud in the oppressive silence. No crickets, no night birds—just the occasional creak of branches overhead, as if the forest itself is tense with anticipation.

The damp soil gives beneath my shoes as we skirt the tree line. One dim light glows from a downstairs window, painting a yellow rectangle on the ground outside.

Lena checks her phone. "Signal's gone. The deputies should be fifteen minutes out." She hesitates. "Jules, maybe we should—"

"We can't wait." The words slip out sharply, filed to a point by fear.

I press against the rough wood siding and inch toward the lit window, cracked open just enough to let in a breeze. Pine resin sticks to my palms. Each breath I draw smells of evergreen and lake water, mingling with the acrid tang of my own sweat.

I raise myself just enough to peer through the opening. I freeze, my lungs seizing mid-breath.

Eva moves around the living room with calculated efficiency, folding clothes and stuffing them into a large suitcase. On a leather couch across the room sits Lucy, her small body curled into a defensive ball. Her arms clutch the faded ears of her stuffed rabbit. Her gaze flicks between Eva and the staircase, pupils dilated. She bites down on her lower lip, the flesh whitening under the pressure.

"She's terrified," I whisper. My daughter's shoulders bunch tight against her ears, her toes curling inside mismatched socks—one pink, one purple—as she presses deeper into the couch cushions.

Lena whispers, "Jules, we should wait for—"

A door slams inside, cutting Lena off. Sebastian strides into view, phone pressed against his ear, face twisted, jaw clenched, nostrils flaring.

"I don't care what it takes!" His voice cuts through the opening in the window like a blade. "The transfer needs to happen now. Tonight."

Eva approaches him, arms crossed defensively. "Is it done? Can we leave?"

Sebastian holds up one hand to silence her, still focused on his call. "No, that's not acceptable. I need confirmation within the hour."

"Sebastian!" Eva's voice rises sharply. "We need to go."

He ends his call with a violent jab at the screen. "They're getting suspicious about the timing. The money's stuck in limbo."

"Then we leave without it," Eva insists. "We have enough. Lucy's what matters."

Sebastian glares at her. "This isn't about the girl. It never was. This is about the thirty million dollars that I've spent years setting up."

Lucy draws her knees closer, trying to make herself smaller. My hands tremble so violently I nearly drop my phone as I pull it out, desperate for a signal. Nothing.

"Still no reception," I hiss, shaking the useless device.

"Me neither," Lena confirms. "We need to get closer to the road."

I glance back through the window. Eva kneels before Lucy now, stroking her hair. My daughter flinches at the touch, a barely perceptible recoil that sends rage coursing through me, hot as fever.

"We can't leave," I say. "Look at her."

Through the glass, Eva rises and leads Lucy toward the stairs. Sebastian watches them go, running a hand through his hair, tugging at it in frustration.

"I'll go back to the car, try to get a signal and guide the cops in," Lena suggests. "You stay here and keep watch."

Before I can respond, Sebastian walks to a desk in the corner and yanks open a drawer. My stomach drops as he pulls out a handgun. He checks it with trained efficiency—magazine, chamber, safety—before tucking it into the waistband of his pants. Then he follows Eva and Lucy up the stairs.

My blood transforms into a thousand tiny shards, each one scraping against my veins like broken glass in a tornado. "He's armed."

Lena's face goes ashen in the moonlight. "Jules, if he's got a gun—"

"That's my daughter." The words scrape my throat raw. "If they're planning to run, they'll take her out another exit. We'll lose them."

"The police will be here soon."

"Soon isn't good enough." I scan the cabin, spotting the back door off the kitchen. "You wait for the deputies. Guide them in. I'm going after Lucy."

"Juliette, don't—"

I'm already moving, staying low as I circle around to the rear of the cabin. The back door—a sliding glass door leading to a deck overlooking the lake—is my target. I remember Sebastian complaining about the lock, how the latch never quite caught. Three hundred dollars to replace, he'd said. Too much for a door nobody would ever try to break into.

My feet make no sound on the wooden deck. Splinters catch at my jeans as I crouch, pressing my palm against the glass. Inside, the kitchen stands dark and empty, granite countertops gleaming dully in the ambient light. I push gently. The door sticks, then gives with a soft scrape that sounds deafening to my ears. I freeze, but raised voices from upstairs mask the noise.

"We need to leave now!" Eva's voice tumbles down the stairs. "The pilot's waiting!"

"It's over!" Sebastian shouts back. "We take the money and go now, without the girl!"

Eva's response comes as a shriek that prickles the skin at the nape of my neck. "No! Lucy comes with us! That's the whole point!"

I slip inside, easing the door closed behind me. Takeout containers on the counter release the sharp tang of sesame and soy into my nostrils. I slide off my shoes and move toward the staircase on the balls of my feet.

35

———————

The staircase stretches before me, its wooden steps the only path to my daughter. But each step might announce my presence. Carefully, I place my right foot forward, testing the first one. It groans—softer than a whisper, but enough to make me pause.

I hold my breath.

Upstairs, the argument intensifies. I take another step, then another, keeping my weight against the wall where the wood is less likely to protest.

Their voices become clearer with each careful step. Sebastian speaks with cold precision. Eva pleads with desperate insistence. Lucy is trapped with them.

"The helicopter isn't waiting all night," Eva says, her words muffled but discernible.

"The account transfers are more important than your fixation on the child."

"She's not just a child," Eva says. "She's mine now."

Those words—"she's mine now"—steal the warmth from my body, leaving my fingertips numb. I quicken my pace, no longer worried about small sounds. Their argument has grown loud enough to mask my approach.

At the top landing, I press against the wall, my pulse pounding in my throat. The hallway stretches to either side of me—dark except for a strip of light escaping from beneath the closed door to the right, and a door to the left, standing slightly ajar. Through the crack, I see my daughter sitting small and alone on the edge of a bed, still clutching Nibbles.

She looks up. Our eyes meet.

Her face transforms—shock, recognition, hope—each emotion chasing the next. Her mouth forms a silent "Mommy."

I press my finger to my lips, begging for continued silence. Lucy nods, the seriousness in her eyes breaking my heart. She remembers our games of spy and hide-and-seek, but this isn't pretend.

I inch forward on the carpet runner. Ten feet separate me from my daughter. Then eight. Five.

Lucy shifts on the bed, her small body leaning toward me like a plant seeking sunlight. Her elbow bumps the nightstand. A glass of water wobbles, then tips.

The crash of breaking glass stops everything—the argument, my breathing, time.

"Lucy?" Eva's voice slices through the silence. "What was that?"

The door at the other end of the hallway opens as I dive for the bathroom opposite Lucy's room, leaving the door open just enough to see through.

Eva appears in the hallway, her face arranged into an expression of concern. She approaches Lucy's room and peers inside.

"What happened?"

"I knocked over the glass," Lucy whimpers.

"Okay," Eva says, her words barely masking her underlying frustration. "We'll just clean it up." She steps into the hallway and moves toward the bathroom.

I slip into the bathtub and get behind the shower curtain just as Eva opens the door wider, reaches in, and grabs the hand towel from the rack by the sink.

"We're leaving in a minute, sweetheart," she says, her voice sugary but hollow. "We're going on an adventure, just like I promised."

Lucy stares back at her, unblinking. Her fingers work nervously at Nibble's ear.

Eva glances over her shoulder before returning to the other bedroom, pulling the door nearly closed. Through the gap, I hear her speaking to Sebastian.

"I don't care about your problems. Lucy and I are leaving, with or without you."

I edge out of the bathtub, toward the hallway, measuring the distance to Lucy's room. Three quick steps and she'll be in my arms. But Sebastian's voice, dropping to something dark and sinister, keeps me rooted.

"You don't leave until I say so. This was my plan from the beginning. You were just the tool."

A sharp sound—palm against flesh—followed by Eva's muffled cry of pain.

"Remember who's in charge," Sebastian continues, calm and methodical. "Finish packing while I get the car ready."

The door opens, and heavy footsteps approach. I slip back into the bathroom shadows as Sebastian appears outside the door, straightening his cuffs while checking on Lucy. Light catches the gun in his waistband as he turns toward the landing.

His footsteps fade down the stairwell. I hesitate, torn between moving now or waiting until he leaves the house entirely. Eva could scream and alert him, but with each passing second, my chances of rescuing my daughter diminish, allowing them to escape with Lucy—or worse.

My window is now.

I move silently across the hall and into Lucy's room. Her eyes widen as I get closer, and then she's in my arms, her small body trembling against mine. I bury my face in her hair, breathing in strawberry shampoo mixed with something floral and unfamiliar—Eva's perfume. My stomach tightens. I hold Lucy closer.

"Let's go," I whisper in her ear. "Stay very quiet."

She nods against my shoulder. I stand, taking her hand, and we start toward the door.

"Mommy," Lucy whispers, tugging at my fingers. "Mommy Eva has been crying a lot. She said Daddy Sebastian is mean to her too."

My steps falter. Mommy Eva. Daddy Sebastian. The words burrow into my chest, hollowing me out. They've been reconstructing our family with themselves at the center, with Lucy—my Lucy—caught in their fabrication.

The floor creaks at the end of the hallway. Eva stands in the bedroom doorway, a half-packed suitcase forgotten in her hands. Her eyes lock with mine, widening in panic as she takes in the sight of Lucy's hand firmly clasped in my own.

The facade crumbles, revealing raw desperation beneath. She drops the suitcase with a thud. Her features harden, transforming from pretend mother into tactical adversary before my eyes.

"Lucy," she whispers, the word cracking like glass, her fingers clawing at the doorframe as her carefully constructed world splinters.

36

"Lucy," Eva says again, her voice hardening as she takes a deliberate step forward. "Get away from her."

I shift my weight, positioning myself between them, pushing Lucy behind me to shield her. The hallway suddenly feels too narrow, the walls pressing inward, the distance to the stairs stretching into miles.

"You're not taking her," Eva says, her voice trembling as she creeps closer to us, past the stairway landing. "She's mine now. I've done everything to become the perfect mother for her."

Her conviction isn't just unsettling—it's terrifying in its completeness. Her eyes gleam with something beyond delusion—a possessive certainty that makes my skin crawl.

"The authorities are on their way, Eva," I say, keeping my voice steady even as my pulse thunders in my throat. "It's over."

Eva's face contorts, a flash of panic quickly submerged beneath indignation. "You don't understand what I've sacrificed," she says, her words sharp and venomous.

"Sebastian promised me a family. He promised I could have yours, that I could be you."

Lucy's small fingers dig into the back of my leg. I can feel her trembling, hear the catch in her breath. I keep my eyes locked on Eva, watching for any sudden movements, aware she now blocks the stairs, our escape route.

"All this time," I say, "you wanted to replace me?"

"Replace you?" Eva laughs, a brittle sound that hangs unnaturally in the air. "I became better than you. I learned everything about you. How you take your coffee. The way you fold laundry. Which stories Lucy likes at bedtime." She punctuates each revelation with a step forward. "I perfected you."

I match her movement, stepping backward, guiding Lucy with me. "Peter never loved you," I say. "He never would have betrayed us."

Something dark passes over Eva's features. "Peter wasn't supposed to die so quickly. I was just supposed to meet Lucy, become her friend. Then Peter found out about the money..."

Horror floods my veins. Every suspicion Lena and I had pieced together over sleepless nights now confirmed in a few careless words. Words that stab like daggers—each casual revelation wrenching the knife deeper.

"Eva!" Sebastian's voice thunders from downstairs. "Get down here now! Someone's coming up the drive!"

Eva's eyes widen with panic. For a split second, indecision flickers across her face—caught between Sebastian's command and her obsession with Lucy.

Her expression shifts, calculation replacing desperation. In that moment, I see her choice solidify. She lunges—not at me, but past me, reaching for Lucy with desperate fingers.

"She's mine!" Eva roars, her voice rising to a desperate pitch as she clutches Lucy's wrist.

Lucy screams, the sound piercing straight through my heart, ripping open a rift exposing my deepest maternal horror. My mouth goes dry as Eva yanks her forward, away from my protective grasp. My daughter's wide eyes find mine—terrified, pleading—and something primal awakens inside me.

The narrow hallway leaves little room to maneuver, and Sebastian is still downstairs, armed.

While struggling to hold on to Lucy, I raise my voice, ensuring it will carry down the stairs: "Sebastian told me everything, Eva. How he's been using you. How he plans to leave you behind once he has the money. How it was your idea to poison Peter."

Eva freezes, her grip on Lucy momentarily slackening. "What? That's not—"

Heavy footsteps pound up the stairs. Sebastian appears at the top landing, his face contorted with fury. "Shut up!" The words explode from him, echoing off the walls as he charges forward, his eyes burning with murderous intent.

In the momentary chaos, Eva's attention wavers between Sebastian's fury and my accusation. Lucy wrenches free from her loosened grasp and flings herself toward me. I catch her, spinning her behind me with one swift motion.

"Eva says you manipulated her," I continue. "That she's a victim, and you planned Peter's death. That you showed her how to swap his pills in his office."

Sebastian's jaw clenches, veins bulging at his temples as his carefully constructed facade crumbles. He spins toward Eva. "What the hell did you tell her?"

Her eyes dart between us. "Nothing! She's lying to turn us against each other!"

"Then how does she know about the pills?" Sebastian says, his lip curling, his attention fully on Eva now.

I continue backing away, one hand behind me guiding Lucy, my eyes never leaving the confrontation unfolding before us.

"You promised we'd be a family," Eva says, her voice rising. "You said once we had the money—"

"You idiot," Sebastian says. "You became obsessed with playing house instead of focusing on the money! Did you really think I'd waste half the fortune on you?"

I've reached the end of the hallway. Through the window, blue lights flash against the trees. The deputies have arrived.

"Just like all the other families," I say, throwing one last verbal grenade. "Sebastian uses you to get close to them, then discards you when he's done."

He lunges at Eva, grabbing her by the shoulders, slamming her against the wall. "What did you tell her? What else does she know?"

I pull Lucy forward and angle her toward the narrow gap behind Sebastian's hulking frame. "Go, honey. Run down and out the door."

Eva scratches at Sebastian's hands, her features twisting as tears streak down her cheeks. "You used me," she chokes out. "You promised Lucy could be my daughter!"

His shoulder drives into her chest, pinning her against the wall as his face darkens to crimson. His hand drops to his waistband, fingers closing around cold metal. "This is your fault! You got hooked on playing mommy!"

I hunch over, pressing against the wall as I try to push past him toward the staircase where Lucy disappeared.

Eva's nails rake across Sebastian's face as she thrashes against his grip, her voice climbing to a frantic pitch when her eyes lock onto the gun in his hand.

"Sebastian, please! I did everything you asked! I can still make this work—"

Her words dissolve into panicked gasps as she claws at his grip. In her desperation, she reaches out wildly, her fingers grasping at my arm as I try to slip past them.

Sebastian snarls and throws his full weight forward, slamming Eva back against the wall with brutal force. Her head hits the plaster with a sickening thud, and she crumples, momentarily stunned.

The impact gives me the opening I need. I scrape past Sebastian's bulk, my shoulder brushing against the opposite wall as I duck low and bolt toward the staircase.

Lucy is halfway down, her small hands gripping the banister as she takes the steps two at a time. Her stuffed rabbit bounces against her with each hurried leap.

"Keep going, baby!" I call out, my voice echoing off the walls as I race after her.

Behind us, Eva's renewed screams mix with Sebastian's furious curses, their struggle continuing with even more violence.

Just as I reach Lucy, gunfire explodes through the air. I stumble, instinctively covering her ears as a scream follows, then the dull thump of a body falling.

Another shot rips through the silence. I flinch, pulling Lucy closer to me as we continue our descent. Then nothing but eerie silence fills the house.

I clutch Lucy tightly against me as we burst through the front door into the cool night air. The flash of police lights illuminates the driveway.

"Help!" I shout, my voice cracking with desperation. "Over here!"

A flashlight beam cuts through the darkness. Crunching footsteps rush toward us as a deputy approaches, with static bursting from the radio clipped to his belt. Two more officers sprint past, their weapons gleaming as they converge on the house.

My legs trembling from exhaustion and adrenaline, I kneel down on the gravel driveway. Gathering Lucy into my arms, I pull her close, feeling her warm breath against my neck in quick, frightened puffs. Her rapid heartbeat pounds against my chest, mirroring my own frantic rhythm. Nibbles remains clutched in her tiny fist, pressed between us like a talisman.

She's safe. The realization hits me in waves, each one stronger and more overwhelming than the last. My daughter is alive, unhurt, breathing in my arms. The terror that had consumed me for what felt like hours begins to ebb, replaced by a flood of relief so intense it makes me sway. I can feel her heartbeat gradually slowing as the immediate danger passes, her breathing becoming less ragged as she finds comfort in my embrace.

"Mommy," she whispers, her voice small and uncertain. "Is it over?"

I hold her face between my palms, looking into eyes so like her father's. "Yes, sweetheart," I say as more police swarm around us, securing the scene. "They can't hurt us anymore."

37

My hands have finally stopped shaking since our escape from Sebastian's lake house. The fluorescent lights of the police station still cast their harsh shadows across its institutional walls, but somehow the sterile brightness feels less oppressive now. I settle back into a vinyl-covered chair, which gives a soft squeak beneath me, my body heavy with the kind of bone-deep exhaustion that comes only after surviving the unthinkable.

Across from me, Lucy's small form is curled on a faded couch, her knees drawn up toward her chest in that instinctive way children seek comfort. Her breathing is steady and even now, a rhythmic sound that anchors me to this moment of relative safety. The rise and fall of her narrow shoulders beneath her pink sweater—still wrinkled from our ordeal—creates a hypnotic pattern that soothes my frayed nerves.

Nibbles lies trapped beneath her protective arm, his familiar brown fur matted in places from her fierce grip during those terrifying hours. His frayed ear, worn soft from years of bedtime snuggles, presses against her flushed cheek. Even in sleep, she hasn't loosened her hold on him, as if some part of her mind understands that letting go might mean losing the last piece of normality in a world that has revealed its capacity for unimaginable horror.

It's been four hours since the incident at the lake house. After the paramedics cleared us at the scene, we were escorted straight to the sheriff's department, where one of the deputies took our statements with Detective Adams helping out. Even with his ongoing internal affairs investigation, he'd come running when Lena called, persuading his lieutenant to let him assist on the case. When questioning Lucy, he'd knelt down to meet her eyes, his voice softening to a gentle cadence.

I move to the couch and brush a strand of hair from my daughter's forehead. Her face in sleep looks exactly as it always has—innocent, untouched. But beneath her peaceful expression, I've caught moments when her eyes would flutter in a disturbing dream, her small hand tightening around her stuffed rabbit. I will need to find her help, someone who specializes in childhood trauma—definitely not Dr. Mercer—who can guide her through the darkness Eva and Sebastian have forced into her young life.

A sound from the doorway draws my attention to where Detective Adams stands, a steaming mug of coffee in each hand. He enters with measured steps, placing one cup in front of my chair without a sound and easing into the other chair to avoid waking Lucy.

"How is she?" he asks.

"Finally sleeping." I glance at Lucy, watching the steady rise and fall of her small chest.

The warmth from the mug seeps into my icy fingers, grounding me. "I just wish I could have protected her from all of this," I murmur.

"You know, what you were up against isn't garden-variety manipulation," Adams says, his voice low enough not to disturb Lucy. "Eva and Sebastian used sophisticated tactics—the same ones we see in organized crime and complex fraud."

He takes a sip of his coffee, his eyes softening momentarily before returning to their professional calm. "I have some updates."

My stomach knots. "Sebastian?"

"He's been booked, and Eva Lerner is in surgery. Sebastian shot her in the chest."

My breath catches, an unexpected pang of sympathy cutting through my hatred.

"Is she going to survive?"

"The doctors are optimistic." Adams leans forward. "But there's more, Mrs. Samson. When the paramedics were treating her, she thought she was dying. So she started talking. Confessing."

The coffee trembles in my hand, ripples spreading across its dark surface. "What did she say?"

"She confirmed everything you suspected." Adams keeps his voice low, glancing at Lucy. "She admitted to poisoning your husband at Sebastian's direction. She also revealed she's been in and out of psychiatric facilities since she was a teenager, and Sebastian's been exploiting her instability for years."

I set my cup down to hide the shaking. "So now we have proof Peter was murdered."

"Yes." Adams withdraws a small notebook. "Her confession, the video of her tampering with his medications, the lab report—it all fits."

I grip the edge of the chair. "It definitely was poison, not his condition returning."

"That's right. Sebastian arranged for your husband to

be treated by someone he could influence—Dr. Wilson Grant. He deliberately misdiagnosed the symptoms as a relapse of his previous Guillain-Barré syndrome."

I think of Peter in those final weeks—his hands shaking so badly he couldn't hold a fork, the confusion in his eyes when he couldn't remember our anniversary. The pain that made him cry out in the night. All from deliberate poisoning.

Adams continues, "Sebastian embezzled from your company for years. When your husband began noticing financial discrepancies, Sebastian accelerated their plan." He turns a page in his notebook. "They needed both you and Peter out of the way, and Eva's... fixation on Lucy provided the opportunity."

I wrap my arms around myself, suddenly chilled despite the overheated room. "How far did this go?"

Adams looks up from his notes, his expression grave. "We're still determining the full extent." He reaches for a folder beside him, the papers rustling in the quiet room. "At Sebastian's lake house, we found a laptop with detailed plans."

He opens the folder carefully. "Also, thanks to Lena, forensic accountants have a head start in confirming that this wasn't Sebastian's first operation. He orchestrated similar schemes at other companies before joining yours."

The detective pauses, genuine regret crossing his features. "And I was actually building a case file on him years ago, based on anonymous tips and financial irregularities at Meridian Corp."

"The story Lena was working on." The pieces fall into place with sickening clarity.

"Yes. I was almost ready to bring it to the DA when I got shut down." Adams sets the folder on the coffee table between us.

"Lena tried to expose him. She lost her career over it. Everyone thought she was just being paranoid." My voice cracks as the weight of it hits me. "*I* thought she was being paranoid."

Adams taps his pen against the folder, the small sound sharp in the silence. "Now we know why no one believed her. Sebastian has a pattern of cultivating people at all levels—government offices, judges, law enforcement. He uses blackmail, bribes, and considerable social manipulation." He meets my eyes. "Your sister was right all along."

Lucy turns on the couch, mumbling something unintelligible. I cross over to her, my hand finding a spot between her shoulder blades, rubbing small circles until her breathing evens out again.

When I return to my seat, the detective's expression is hesitant. "Mrs. Samson, you have some difficult decisions ahead. The DA is prepared to pursue full charges against Sebastian, Eva, and everyone else involved in this conspiracy." He sets his coffee aside. "But I need to be honest with you—it would mean a lengthy, very public trial."

"And Lucy might have to testify," I finish, the words sticking in my throat.

"Potentially. We'd use video testimony, closed sessions, whatever protections we can arrange. But this case is..." he searches for the word, "unprecedented in its complexity."

I feel caught in an impossible choice, my throat tightening as I look between my sleeping daughter and the detective's patient face. Justice for Peter means putting Lucy through more trauma.

"What's the alternative?" I ask quietly.

"Sebastian has already approached the DA through his lawyer, looking for a deal." The detective's tone remains neutral, professional. "He'd plead guilty to financial crimes and conspiracy charges in exchange for avoiding the murder charges. Still significant prison time, but it would limit public exposure and potentially spare Lucy from testifying."

Six months ago, I might have taken the easier path. But I'm not that woman anymore—the one who'd let others define her boundaries, who'd learned to doubt her own instincts, who'd give up parts of herself to keep the peace.

I look directly into the detective's eyes, my voice emerging stronger than I expect. "Peter was murdered in cold blood while his doctor, who should have protected him, watched him die. Sebastian and Eva manipulated the legal system to steal my daughter." I straighten my spine, my voice growing steadier with each sentence. "Judge Morris abused his position to hand my child to strangers. I want them all prosecuted to the fullest extent of the law."

Adams holds my gaze longer than before, the corner of his mouth lifting slightly.

"But," I continue, "I need guarantees about Lucy's well-being. I want child psychologists involved at every stage. I want her protected from media exposure. And I want alternatives to having her testify in person if at all possible."

"I'll talk to the DA personally," he says, closing his notebook with careful precision. "We'll make it work."

The door swings open, and Lena comes in, her cheeks flushed with cold or excitement or both. "Jules!"

I rise to meet her, surprised by the energy radiating from her despite the late hour. "What is it?"

Lena's words tumble out rapidly, her hands gesturing in that familiar way they do when she's breaking a story. "Megan's exposé—it's running in tomorrow's Tribune. Front page, above the fold. Everything we uncovered about Sebastian—the financial crimes, the custody manipulation, the evidence of Peter's murder. It's all there."

Detective Adams stands, frowning. "The press already has this?"

"Megan was my colleague at The Tribune." Lena lifts her chin, suddenly resembling the fierce journalist she'd once been. "The public needs to know how deep this corruption goes."

The irony isn't lost on me. Lena, whose journalism career ended when she tried to expose Sebastian years ago, is now instrumental in his final unmasking.

Adams runs a hand through his hair, his expression shifting from pleased to worried. "Look, I appreciate good journalism, but this could complicate things for the prosecution."

"How?" Lena crosses her arms, defensive.

"Defense attorneys love media coverage. They'll claim Sebastian can't get a fair trial, that the jury pool is tainted." Adams glances toward Lucy, still sleeping peacefully. "They might push for a change of venue, delay tactics, anything to muddy the waters."

My stomach drops. "You're saying the story could help Sebastian?"

"Not help him, exactly. But it gives his lawyers ammunition." Adams pulls out his phone. "I need to call the DA tonight, give her a heads-up before she reads it in the morning paper."

He moves toward the door. "The good news is we have Eva's confession and solid physical evidence. The story won't destroy our case, but it means the DA will need to be extra careful." He stops and looks back before he leaves the room. "Don't worry. It may take some time, but we have a strong case."

Justice for Peter. Accountability for the corruption that nearly destroyed us. It doesn't feel like victory—not yet—but like the first clean breath after breaking through water's surface.

A whimper draws my attention to the couch where Lucy stirs. Her eyelashes flutter against her cheeks, hands reaching out before her eyes even open.

I move to kneel beside her, taking in the details I'd missed in the days we'd been apart. Beneath the dank odor of the office—body odor and cigarettes—clings the faint scent that is uniquely Lucy, the sweet-shampoo of her hair.

"Mommy?" she murmurs, voice thick with sleep.

I gather her into my arms, her small body fitting against mine as perfectly as it always has. "I'm here, sweetheart. I'm here, and I'm not going anywhere."

Her arms wind around my neck, holding on with surprising strength. Against my shoulder, her voice is muffled but clear: "Are we going home now?"

Home. Not the house Eva had contaminated. Not the life Peter and I had built. Something new, forged in fire, that Lucy and I will create together.

"Soon, baby, but not quite yet," I whisper against her hair. "We're going to stay with Aunt Lena for a little while."

Lucy pulls back to study my face, her dark eyes searching mine with that uncanny perception children possess. "Because the bad people were in our house?"

The simplicity of her understanding catches me off guard. No need for complex explanations about crime scenes or evidence collection, or the fact that I can't bear to sleep in the bed Peter and I once shared—not in the house Eva had claimed and transformed, making me an intruder in my own home.

"Yes, because of the bad people."

She nods solemnly, then brightens. "That's okay. Aunt Lena has the good cereal."

Despite everything, I laugh—a real laugh that bubbles

up from somewhere I'd forgotten existed. "She does have the good cereal."

But as I meet Lena's eyes over Lucy's head, I know our journey is far from over. The truth will be in tomorrow's paper, and then will come the real test—learning to live with it.

38

Two weeks after Sebastian's arrest, I stand on the porch of our house, the key trembling between my fingers. We've been staying at Lena's since that night at the sheriff's, giving the forensic team time to process the crime scene that was once simply our home.

Sunlight filters through maple branches, casting dappled shadows on the brick walkway Peter laid three summers ago. Such a normal thing to remember. Such a normal place to be. Except nothing is normal anymore.

Lucy's hand tightens in mine, her small fingers pressing into my palm with surprising strength. She hasn't spoken since we pulled into the driveway.

"Are you sure you're ready for this?" I ask, crouching to her eye level. "We can go back to Aunt Lena's if you want."

She shakes her head, lips pressed together in that determined way that reminds me of her first day of kindergarten—when she was trying so hard to be brave.

The lock turns with that familiar click. I push the door open and the scent hits me immediately—harsh lemon cleaner barely masking something beneath it. Eva's perfume. The cleaning crew couldn't scrub away everything.

Lucy freezes at the threshold. Her eyes dart from the coat rack to the staircase, while her fingers twist her rabbit's ear. Nibbles hasn't left her side since our reunion.

"Is Mommy Eva coming back?" she whispers.

Her innocent question cuts deeper than any weapon Eva wielded against us. Despite five sessions with Dr. Brenner, Lucy still sometimes slips and calls Eva "Mommy." Each time, it feels like losing her all over again.

I pause, searching for the words Dr. Brenner suggested. Simple truths. No emotional overload.

"No, sweetie. Eva isn't coming back. She's in the hospital now, and then she has to go somewhere else because of the bad choices she made."

Lucy's eyes remain fixed on the staircase. "Is it okay that sometimes I miss her?"

I press my palm against her cheek. "Your feelings are always okay. All of them. Even the confusing ones."

We step inside together. The living room furniture sits where it always has, but a subtle wrongness pervades everything. Eva repositioned the throw pillows, replaced our blue curtains with beige ones, and removed certain photographs from the walls. It's our house reinterpreted through someone else's vision—like looking at your distorted reflection in a carnival mirror.

Lucy drifts toward the kitchen, her sneakers squeaking on the hardwood floor. On the counter, a burgundy lipstick stain marks the rim of a coffee mug that the cleaning crew must have missed. Lucy touches it with one finger.

"She made me hot chocolate with tiny marshmallows," Lucy says. "But she got mad if I asked for too many."

I take the mug and place it into a paper bag I brought specifically for Eva's possessions. The police took most evidence, but these intimate traces remain—breadcrumbs of a woman who studied our lives to steal them.

"Let's check out your room," I say. "We can see what we want to keep and what we want to change."

Upstairs, Lucy's bedroom bears the most obvious evidence of Eva's interference. Unfamiliar pictures cover the bulletin board above her desk. Books I never bought line the shelves. A flowery comforter has replaced her beloved purple butterfly one.

Lucy walks to her bed and sits on the edge, bouncing slightly. "She said butterflies are for babies."

"What do you think?" I ask, joining her.

She pulls Nibbles closer. "I still like butterflies. And I'm not a baby."

"No, you're not." I brush a strand of hair from her face. "Your butterfly comforter is safe at Aunt Lena's. We can get it tomorrow."

She slides off the bed and moves to her desk. Her finger traces a drawing that makes me shudder—three stick figures holding hands. The middle smallest figure is Lucy. The figure on the right has scribbled hair, somewhat resembling Sebastian's. The figure on the left has been labeled "Mommy Eva" in Lucy's wobbly handwriting.

"Can you tell me about this picture?" My voice sounds steadier than I feel.

"Eva helped me make it." Lucy's voice drops to a whisper. "She said we could be a family together. That you were sick like Daddy was."

I take a slow breath. "And how did that make you feel when she said that?"

"Scared." Her eyes, so much like Peter's, meet mine. "And mixed-up. Because sometimes I remembered you weren't sick, but then she would show me the special book..."

She moves to her bookshelf and pulls out a leather album I've never seen before. My fingers feel cold and clumsy as she hands it to me.

"This is Eva's special book," she says.

I open it slowly. The first image punches the air from my lungs—Lucy as a toddler in front of our Christmas tree with Eva kneeling beside her. But I was there that day. Peter took that photo of Lucy and me.

Page after page reveals the same sickening alterations. Family photos where Eva has digitally replaced me or Peter. In some, I've been erased entirely. In others, her face has been expertly pasted over mine.

"These pictures aren't real," I say, struggling to keep my voice even. "Eva changed them using a computer."

Lucy frowns, touching a particularly convincing fabrication of Eva helping her blow out birthday candles. "But I remember this happening."

"You remember your birthday, and blowing out candles. But it was me next to you, not Eva."

Confusion clouds her features. "How can I remember something wrong?"

I close the album gently. "When someone shows us a picture over and over, and tells us a story about it, sometimes our brain starts to think it's a real memory. Eva told you so many stories that your brain got confused about what really happened."

Tears fill Lucy's eyes. "She lied to me?"

I set the album aside with deliberate care, as if the fabricated memories within might somehow contaminate the air around us, and reach for Lucy. She comes willingly, her small body folding into mine like a puzzle piece finding its proper place. Her weight settles against my chest, warm and solid and real—a tangible reminder that she's here, that she's safe, that we're together again despite everything Eva tried to steal from us.

"Yes, she did. And that was wrong." I search for words she can understand. "Eva is sick in her mind—not like Daddy was sick in his body. She wanted so badly to be your mommy that she convinced herself it was okay to pretend and lie."

Lucy picks at a loose thread on her rabbit's ear. "Why couldn't she just be my friend?"

The simple question knocks the wind out of me for a moment.

I take a deep breath, then answer, "Eva wanted to keep you all to herself, instead of loving you the right way—by letting you be who you really are."

We sit quietly, Lucy processing in her own way while I breathe in the familiar scent of her hair—strawberry shampoo and that indefinable essence that is purely Lucy. Scents I feared I might never experience again.

"What do we do with all this?" I ask, gesturing to Eva's alterations to her room—the photos, books, decorations.

Lucy slides from my lap and pulls a box of art supplies from her closet.

"When I feel mixed up, Dr. Brenner says I should draw how I feel," she announces, setting the box on the floor. "Can we make a new book? With real pictures?"

Tears sting my eyes. "That's exactly what we should do."

"And can we get my butterfly blanket back?" She tugs at the flower comforter with distaste. "And the pictures of Daddy? She put them away. She said they'd make me too sad."

"Did they? Make you sad to look at Daddy's pictures?"

Lucy shakes her head, dark curls bouncing. "I like

remembering him. He made pancakes shaped like Mickey Mouse."

"He did," I smile, blinking back tears. "And he could never get the ears right."

"They looked like blobs!" Lucy giggles—the sound so achingly familiar it physically hurts to hear it.

This moment holds more healing than a dozen therapy sessions—not a dramatic rescue or police interrogation, but my daughter remembering her father with joy instead of the manufactured grief Eva tried to create.

"I have an idea," I say, standing up. "Let's put all of Eva's things in some boxes for Detective Adams. Then tomorrow, we'll get your butterfly comforter and our real photos from Aunt Lena's. We'll make your room exactly how you want it."

Lucy nods, her face brightening. "Can we paint it too? Eva said pink was better, but I still like purple."

"Any color you want." I begin gathering Eva's additions to Lucy's room, placing them into a box. "Your room, your choice."

We work together, piece by piece sorting through the remains of Eva's deception. With each item we evaluate, Lucy grows more certain, more herself. The confusion doesn't vanish—Dr. Brenner warned it would take time—but Lucy's natural instinct for truth begins to reassert itself.

As afternoon light slants through the windows, we move downstairs. Lucy stops at the mantelpiece where our family photos once stood, now displaying generic decorative items.

"Where are our real pictures?" she asks.

"Right here." I open the storage ottoman where I'd hidden a box during my preliminary visit yesterday. "I saved them all."

We unpack the frames one by one: Peter cradling

newborn Lucy in the hospital. The three of us at the beach last summer. Lucy's preschool graduation with Peter kneeling beside her, their matching smiles radiant. With each photograph we return, the house becomes more ours again.

Lucy places the final frame—Peter pushing her on a swing, both caught mid-laugh—in the center of the mantel.

"There," she says with quiet satisfaction. "Now it looks like our house again."

I wrap my arm around her shoulders, feeling the steady rise and fall of her breathing against my side. "Yes, it does."

Later, after heating up SpaghettiOs at her request, I tuck her into our makeshift fort in the living room. Neither of us is ready to sleep in our bedrooms yet. The couch cushions and spare blankets create a cave-like sanctuary that feels both new and safe.

"Mommy?" Lucy mumbles, eyelids heavy. "Are we going to be okay?"

I smooth her hair back, struck again by how much she resembles Peter when she's sleepy—the same slight furrow between her brows, the same curve of her cheek.

"Yes," I tell her, with certainty that surprises me. "We're going to be okay. Different than before, but okay."

"Different can be good." Her eyes flutter closed.

"Different is how we move forward," I whisper as her breathing deepens into sleep.

I settle beside her, listening to our house at night. The familiar creak of the heating system. The ticking of the grandfather clock Peter restored. The distant hum of the refrigerator. Home sounds. Our sounds.

The photographs on the mantel catch the last glint of evening light. I focus on Peter's smile, frozen in time, and something loosens in my chest. He can't come back to us. That loss remains. But his memory—authentic and untarnished—is ours again.

My phone buzzes on the coffee table. Detective Adams. I slide my thumb across the screen to answer, careful not to disturb Lucy.

"Juliette," he says, his voice unusually hesitant. "I'm sorry to call so late."

"It's fine. What is it?"

A pause. "Eva's asking to see you. Says she has something important to tell you about Sebastian—something she wouldn't tell us."

Lucy stirs in her sleep, murmuring something unintelligible before settling again. I watch her face, peaceful in slumber, and think of the album filled with stolen, fabricated memories.

"Tell her," I say quietly, "that she'll never see either of us again."

I end the call and turn off my phone. Eva's had her last chance to manipulate us. Tomorrow will bring its own challenges—more therapy, preparing for the trial, rebuilding our lives. But tonight, we've reclaimed what matters most: our truth, our home, each other.

It's a beginning.

THE HONEST LIE

COMING SOON

Turn the page to enjoy a preview
of Stephanie Kreml's next thriller!

1
———

The Winstons bring panic into my office like an unwelcome guest. Her shallow breathing and his tight shoulders disrupt the quiet I've cultivated between white walls and carefully spaced furniture. They perch on the edge of my white leather sofa, neither fully committed to staying nor brave enough to flee.

"Dr. Thorne…" Janet's voice wavers. Her fingers twist a tissue into a tight spiral. "Maybe this was a mistake."

I cross my legs at the ankle and straighten my spine. A practiced posture. My silk blouse stays crisp while outside, Los Angeles wilts in the August heat.

"Nothing about seeking help is a mistake, Janet." I keep my voice measured. "You're here because something valuable is at stake."

Sunlight glints off my wedding band. Twenty one years with Damian. I twist it once, a habit, and refocus on the couple before me.

Robert's jaw tightens. He's the resistant one—they always come in pairs. One desperate for healing, one dragged along, convinced they can fortress their secrets behind silence.

"We've tried everything else," he says, adjusting his tie for the umpteenth time since sitting down. "Three other therapists. A weekend retreat. Even that... what was it, Jan? That app that sends you prompts to discuss?"

"Couple Connect." Janet blinks rapidly, mascara threatening to streak. "It just made things worse."

I make a note with my fountain pen. The Winstons exchange glances at my leather notebook. They expected tablets, perhaps. Everyone does.

"You've come to me because conventional approaches have failed." I let the statement settle between them. "My methodology is different. It's not comfortable. But it works."

Awards for my podcast, *The Honesty Mandate*, hang on the wall beside the couple. Janet's eyes flick to the accolades, then back to me.

"I've listened to all of your episodes," she says. "Twice. But Robert—"

"I'm here, aren't I?" Robert cuts in, defensive already. His expensive watch catches the light as he gestures sharply. "But let's be clear, Doctor. The texts were nothing. Just some messages with a coworker. Janet's blowing it completely out of proportion."

Robert's shoulders hunch forward, his hands minimizing with each word. Classic deflection.

Janet inhales sharply. The tissue in her hands shreds as she picks at it with her fingernails.

"Nothing? You told her she understood you in ways I never could. You told her you thought about her at night. You deleted the messages so I wouldn't see them!" Her voice rises with each accusation, color flooding her cheeks. "Six months! This went on for six months!"

"Here we go again," Robert says, slumping back into the sofa. "It wasn't physical. Not once."

Across from him, Janet's gestures expand, her pain seeking space. Two people, two entirely different perceptions of the same events.

"Robert," I say, my voice cutting through their escalating tension, "fidelity isn't merely the absence of physical intimacy with others. It's the presence of complete emotional transparency with your partner."

His eyes narrow. "So what then? We're supposed to have no privacy? Tell each other every stray thought that crosses our minds?"

I lean forward. "Privacy is about the bathroom door. Secrecy is about hidden text messages." I hold his gaze until he looks away. "There's a difference."

Janet's shoulders soften marginally. Someone seeing her pain, validating it.

"Dr. Thorne," she says, her voice quivering, "I don't think I can ever trust him again." A tear breaks free, trailing mascara down her cheek. "But maybe some things are better left unsaid. Maybe knowing everything just makes it worse."

I breathe in slowly. This challenge to my methodology arises in almost every first session. The belief that secrets protect us. That partial truths can build whole relationships.

"Pain hides in shadows, Janet. Secrecy is where it gains its power." The words feel worn with use but no less true. "What you don't know can absolutely hurt you. It's already hurting you."

Robert shifts uncomfortably. "Look, I've apologized a hundred times. I've given her my phone, my passwords. I'm sleeping in the guest room. What more can I possibly do?"

"You can tell me why," Janet says, suddenly direct, her

pain flaming into fury. "Why her? What was I not giving you that she could?"

Robert's face flushes. "This is pointless. We're just going in circles." He reaches for his jacket draped over the arm of the sofa. "I knew this wouldn't work."

The session teeters on collapse. Janet stands, gathering her purse. "This was a mistake. We can't fix this."

She clutches something in her purse—a small silver frame partially visible from where I sit. A wedding photo, the corner catching the light. A deliberate choice to bring it. A reminder.

I can't let them walk out. Not when they've come this far. Not when I know I can help them.

I rise and step around my desk—breaking my usual pattern. I take Janet's hand, feeling the dampness of her tissue against my palm.

"Janet, look at me." My voice softens. "Pain hides in shadows. Bring it into the light, examine every inch of it, and it loses its power." I squeeze her hand gently. "Not today, not tomorrow, but gradually."

Her breathing steadies. I turn to Robert, who has paused halfway to the door.

"And Robert, that requires your complete transparency. Everything. No matter how small, no matter how painful."

He swallows. "What if... what if the truth makes her leave anyway?"

An honest question. Finally.

"Then it will be her informed choice. Not one made on false premises." I hold his gaze. "Isn't she worth the risk of your complete truth?"

The silence between them changes in quality. Robert's breathing slows. Janet crumples up what remains of the tissue.

Slowly, she lowers herself back onto the sofa. After a moment's hesitation, he follows.

She wipes her cheeks, smearing the mascara further. "Twice a week, then?"

I return to my chair and open my leather planner.

"Tuesdays and Fridays. 1:30 p.m." I write their names in precise script. "We'll start with individual sessions next week to establish baselines, then move to joint sessions."

They nod, the fight temporarily drained from them. Janet's hand brushes against Robert's arm—the first voluntary contact I've seen between them. Small victories.

After they leave, I straighten my desk, adjusting my pen to lie parallel with my notebook. Order restored from chaos. My methodology works, even in the most resistant cases.

Through my window, the skyline gleams in the midday sun. Below, the Winstons emerge onto the sidewalk, walking with careful distance between them, but still together. For now.

My calendar sits before me, full of couples navigating their way back from betrayals large and small. The afternoon stretches ahead—three more sessions before I can return home.

Home to Damian. To our glass and steel house with its clean lines and emptiness that still echoes sometimes, three years after Celia's death. To the quiet routines we've built around that absence.

My phone chimes softly. A text from Damian: *Picking up dinner from Zarape. The usual?*

I type back: *Perfect. Home by six.*

Simple. Predictable. True.

I close my planner with a sense of satisfaction. Another couple choosing truth over comfortable lies. Just as I've taught thousands to do. Just as I live my own life.

2

———————

My last clients for the day leave at five thirty. I scribble a final note about the Winstons' defensive patterns before locking my office door, pleased with how all the couples today faced uncomfortable truths head-on. Progress, even with the resistant Winstons who arrived sitting as far apart as they could on the couch.

The evening air caresses my skin as I exit the building, my lungs expanding gratefully after hours of recycled air. The city's skyline burns amber in the setting sun, its rhythm shifting as office lights blink out one by one. I slide into my car—a silver sedan chosen for reliability over statement—and join the stream of vehicles crawling toward the suburbs.

Tonight marks twenty-five years since Damian first asked me to dinner. Tomorrow, our wedding anniversary. Twenty-one years of marriage—the last three shadowed by grief but strengthened by our commitment to honesty through the darkest moments.

I pull into our driveway fifteen minutes later. Our

modernist home stands against the deepening blue sky, its clean lines and expansive windows reflecting Damian's architectural sensibilities. Through the glass, I glimpse him moving between the kitchen and dining room, wine already breathing in a decanter on the counter. My shoulders relax at the sight, the tension of holding space for others' pain beginning to dissolve.

As I step into our entryway, my nose twitches. A scent, unfamiliar and distinctly feminine, hangs in the air. Not Damian's usual cologne, but something sweeter, with floral notes. I pause, inhaling deliberately, cataloging it like I would a client's inconsistent statements.

"Nay? Is that you?" Damian's voice carries from the kitchen.

I hang my coat in the closet, the unfamiliar scent lingering in my nostrils. "Yes, just got in."

Damian appears with wine glasses in hand. He smiles with the same warmth that has greeted me every evening for two decades, yet tonight it feels wrapped in tissue paper —beautiful, but carefully protected. His dark hair shows more silver at the temples than when we first met, but the same intelligence remains in his gaze. He's changed from his work clothes into a soft blue polo.

"Zarape outdid themselves," he says, leaning in to kiss my cheek. "The mole smells incredible."

Up close, his familiar scent reasserts itself, but the other scent clings subtly to his shirt collar, impossible to ignore now that I've noticed it.

"You smell different," I say, accepting the wine glass he offers. "New cologne?"

His blinking quickens for a split second—the microexpression so brief I might have missed it without years of professional training. "Oh, that. Had lunch with a potential investor today. Wore heavy perfume. She was practically bathed in the stuff." He laughs, the sound slightly higher than his natural chuckle. "Couldn't escape fast enough."

I sip my wine, rich and velvety on my tongue. "Successful meeting?"

"Promising," he says, turning back toward the kitchen. "Nothing concrete yet."

I follow him, watching as he arranges the takeout containers on our dining table. His architectural firm has been pursuing several high-profile sustainability projects lately, consuming more of his time than usual.

"How was your day?" he asks, spooning the chicken mole into shallow bowls. "Anything interesting?"

"Had a first session with a new couple. They're still in the blame phase, but at least they showed up, which means they want to save their marriage." I sit at my place, the table set with the minimalist dinnerware we selected together years ago. "The husband had an emotional affair. Claims it was 'nothing.'"

Damian places bread between us and sits across from me. "What constitutes nothing? Texting? Flirting?"

"Six months of intimate messages he deliberately hid from his wife." I tear off a piece of tortilla. "He deleted them, but she found snippets in the cloud backup."

Damian's spoon freezes halfway to his mouth. "Technology makes it harder to keep anything private, doesn't it?"

"Private or secret?" I counter, watching his face. "There's a difference."

His forehead creases slightly as he lowers his spoon. "I suppose from your professional standpoint, there shouldn't be secrets between spouses at all."

"Not if they want true intimacy. Secrets create distance." I taste the mole, savoring the complexity of chilis and chocolate. "Privacy is about having space for yourself. Secrecy is about hiding parts of yourself from someone who deserves to know you fully."

Damian nods, his finger tracing the stem of his wineglass. "Even if knowing might hurt them?"

"Especially then. Buried pain festers."

"And what about that new couple?" he asks, his gaze shifting to the window. "What's your approach with them?"

"The usual. Individual sessions first, then bringing them together once I understand each of their narratives."

"And if his version conflicts with hers?"

"That's where the work happens. The truth usually lies somewhere in between." I study the way he focuses on rotating his wine glass rather than meeting my eyes. "You seem unusually interested in this case."

He takes a long sip before answering. "Just thinking about how complex relationships can be. Sometimes people have reasons for keeping secrets."

The words settle in the space that separates us, heavy and unexpected. The muscles between my shoulder blades tighten—the same tension I feel when a client contradicts their previous session's story. It's an unusual position for him to take—Damian has always supported my methodology, my belief in radical honesty.

"Justifications, perhaps," I reply. "But rarely *good* reasons."

He nods too quickly. "Of course. I'm just playing devil's advocate."

We eat in silence for a moment. I focus on the flavors of the mole to ground myself as my mind catalogs this aberration in his usual pattern.

"By the way," Damian says, his knuckles blanching slightly around his spoon, "your book edits looked solid.

That opening chapter on the fallacy of protective lies really hits hard."

I set down my spoon. "You read my manuscript?"

"Just the introduction." He beams at me, though his forehead remains tight. "Couldn't help myself. It was on your desk when I brought you tea yesterday."

"I thought you were saving it for when it was published." I keep my voice neutral, the same tone I use when clients reveal unexpected information. "You've always said you preferred to read my finished work."

"I got curious." He refills our wine glasses, the bottle clinking against the rim of mine. "That opening paragraph about twenty one years of complete honesty caught my eye. Seemed appropriate with our anniversary tomorrow."

The timing of his interest strikes me as convenient. An unfamiliar scent. An unusual defense of secrets. Now reading my manuscript after specifically saying he wouldn't. My internal alarm system—honed through thousands of clinical hours—pulses quietly.

Damian raises his glass. "To twenty one years of complete honesty—just as you wrote in your introduction."

His words have a rehearsed quality, like when clients practice what they'll say before their session. I've heard this precise cadence countless times—the voice of someone assembling a narrative they want me to believe.

I weigh each discordant note against our years of trust. Tomorrow's celebration hovers in my mind, making me second-guess the whispers of doubt that have crept in. Maybe I'm seeing shadows where there are none.

We've built our marriage on honesty—it's not just my professional methodology but our shared value system. If something were wrong, Damian would tell me.

I clink my glass against his. "To us, and to never hiding anything, no matter how small."

I study his face as I say it—a professional habit I can never fully turn off. His eyes meet mine steadily. No pupil dilation, no microexpressions of discomfort.

Damian takes my hand across the table, his thumb brushing over my knuckles. "You're all that matters to me."

The moment passes. Damian asks about my final edits for the publisher, and I push the tiny doubt aside. Our conversation flows back into familiar patterns as we clear the dishes together, his hand occasionally brushing against mine.

"I was thinking," Damian says as he stacks plates in the dishwasher, "we should do something special tomorrow night. Not just dinner at Geoffrey's. Maybe drive up the coast afterward, spend the weekend at that bed and breakfast you liked."

"The one in Santa Barbara? With the garden?" I hand him the last plate. "Don't you have that pitch on Monday?"

He waved his hand. "I'm all set. And twenty one years deserves more than just a few hours at dinner."

I smile, warmth spreading through my chest. "It would be nice to get away."

Later, as we get ready for bed, I watch Damian's reflection in our bathroom mirror. He moves with the ease of long familiarity—hanging his watch on the small hook I installed years ago, aligning his toothbrush in its holder. He catches me watching and smiles, his eyes crinkling at the corners in the way that first attracted me to him all those years ago.

I watch him perform these nightly rituals—evidence of our synchronized life, the embodiment of the principles I teach my clients every day. Whatever small anomalies I noticed earlier must be just that—anomalies, not patterns. Not secrets.

As Damian slides into bed next me, I turn off my lamp

and concentrate on his warmth as he drapes his arm across my waist. I focus on our weekend plans rather than that lingering scent.

But as sleep approaches, a hardened kernel of doubt nests beneath my breastbone—too small to justify voicing aloud, yet impossible to dissolve completely. My body knows something my mind isn't ready to acknowledge.

3

———

I wake with last night's doubt still alive in my body, a physical presence I can't shake. Damian's side of the bed is empty, the sheets cool to my touch. Through our bedroom window, morning light cuts sharp-edged rectangles across the hardwood floor. I adjust my pillow to align perfectly with the edge of the mattress, straightening the comforter until its hem runs parallel with the bed frame.

My phone buzzes with a calendar notification: "Podcast Interview 10 a.m." Three and a half hours to prepare for my conversation with Maya Scholz, host of "Hard Truths," a self-help podcast with over two million subscribers. The timing couldn't be better, in the lead-up to my book launch week after next.

Downstairs, a note waits for me, propped against the coffee maker.

Early meeting with Mark about the Gallo project. See you tonight for dinner at Geoffrey's. Happy Anniversary. - D

I trace his handwriting—confident strokes that flow like the architectural sketches littering his desk. Today marks twenty-one years of marriage. Twenty-one years of building truth between us. I press the note against my sternum, as if the paper could absorb the unease that started last night.

After a quick breakfast and shower, I stand in front of my closet, considering options. I select a white silk blouse, running my fingers over three others before choosing the one with the most structured collar. The graphite pencil skirt has precise seams, no fraying at the hem. I add minimal jewelry—silver earrings, my watch. Then I fasten my mother's silver necklace, its tiny locket cool against my skin on the hollow between my collarbones. Inside, invisible to everyone but me, rests a snippet of Celia's hair.

The podcast studio occupies the fifteenth floor of a downtown high-rise. The receptionist—young, with a carefully neutral affect—leads me to a waiting area where framed magazine covers line the walls. My own face looks back at me from last month's *Psychology Today*: "Dr. Naomi Thorne: Truth's Fierce Advocate." In the photo, I look more certain than I feel this morning.

Maya Scholz emerges from the recording room. She's shorter than I expected—early thirties, dark hair cut in a precise bob, eyes that dart quickly over me before settling on my face.

"Dr. Thorne," she says, extending her hand. Her shake is firm, assessing. "I'm delighted you could make it. We've been trying to get you on the show for months."

"My publicist mentioned your persistence," I say, matching her grip. "I've listened to several episodes. Your series on cognitive dissonance in family systems was particularly insightful."

Her eyebrows lift slightly. A small smile forms, her shoulders relaxing by a fraction.

The sound engineer—a man with tattooed forearms and headphones around his neck—makes adjustments to my microphone as Maya outlines the format: fifty minutes, beginning with my background and methodology, then applications of my honesty approach, and finally discussing *The Honesty Mandate*, both the podcast and the book.

"Any topics you'd prefer we avoid?" she asks.

"None," I say. "My work is about facing uncomfortable truths, not avoiding them."

She nods, a flash of something—anticipation, maybe—crossing her features. The red recording light blinks on, and Maya's posture shifts. Her voice drops half an octave as she welcomes her audience and introduces me.

The first twenty minutes flow smoothly. I walk through my definition of radical honesty, distinguishing it from mere cruelty. I share case studies (anonymized, of course) and explain how habitual dishonesty corrodes relationships from within. Maya asks questions that let me elaborate on key sections from my book, sometimes finishing my sentences with apt paraphrases.

"Your approach has gained significant traction," she says. "What draws people to your methodology in particular?"

"We're drowning in deception," I say, shifting forward in my chair. "Think about it—you scroll through Instagram and see carefully filtered lives. Politicians lie without consequence. In our daily conversations, we say 'I'm fine' when we're falling apart, 'I love it' when we're disappointed." I pause, noticing a couple of strands of hair have fallen from Maya's otherwise perfect bob. "These small lies —they create hairline fractures in who we are."

"And you practice this approach in your own life?" she asks. "Complete transparency in all relationships?"

"Yes. Ask my husband about the time I told him his anniversary gift was 'functionally thoughtless.'" I give a small laugh. "Not my proudest moment, but our relationship is stronger for that kind of candor."

She chuckles. "I imagine that didn't go over well."

"The truth rarely does, at first. But discomfort passes. Hidden issues that remain unaddressed don't."

Maya glances at her notes. She taps a finger twice on the desk and shifts in her chair. The hairs on my arms rise—something's coming.

"Dr. Thorne, you lost your daughter a few years ago," she says. "Did your 'radical honesty' approach help you through that grief, or were there moments when a comforting lie might have been kinder?"

The air in the room changes. My mouth goes dry. The studio walls seem to close in by several inches. Three seconds pass in silence. Five. I'm aware of the sound engineer watching me through the glass partition.

"I apologize if that's too personal," Maya says quietly.

I tug at the edge of my sleeve, smoothing a wrinkle that isn't there. "No need to apologize. My work doesn't exist separately from my life." I inhale. "After Celia died, people offered what they thought would help—that she was 'in a better place' or 'looking down on me.' I..."

My voice catches. An image flashes: Celia's bedroom door, still closed. Three years later, and neither Damian nor I have cleared it out.

"What actually helped," I continue, forcing steadiness into my words, "was acknowledging the brutal reality. Damian and I didn't hide our anger from each other, or our guilt. We didn't pretend to be okay."

Maya leans in. "Your critics suggest your approach lacks nuance. What about telling a terminally ill child they'll get better? Or telling someone with dementia that their deceased spouse is 'just at the store'?"

I reflexively clench my fists under the table, nails

digging into my palms. The sharp pain grounds me, allowing me to open up. Taking a deep breath, I force myself to relax and spread my hands flat against my thighs.

"Those examples confuse compassion with deception," I say. "Children understand more than we give them credit for—they sense when adults are lying. And with dementia patients, reality eventually intrudes. Then they suffer fresh grief, along with the disorientation of having been deceived by someone they trusted."

Maya's gaze doesn't waver. "Isn't some truth just hurtful, though? A way to unburden ourselves at someone else's expense?"

I recognize the moment for what it is—the fulcrum on which this interview will balance. I could acknowledge the complexity, the gray areas my philosophy sometimes struggles to address. My publicist's voice echoes in my head: *Your certainty is what people respond to, Naomi.* Book sales depend on clarity, not equivocation.

But something in Maya's question resonates with my private doubts. That unfamiliar scent on Damian's collar from yesterday. His unusual defense of secrets. The note this morning, when he could have simply wished me happy anniversary in person.

No. I can't afford uncertainty, not now.

I sit up, straightening my shoulders. "Truth can hurt, temporarily. But lies poison relationships permanently." The words come out confident, practiced. "When my daughter died, people thought they were being kind by offering spiritual platitudes. But what I needed was someone to sit with me in the terrible reality—not try to paste over it with pretty lies."

My conviction hangs in the air between us. Maya nods, her expression a mixture of respect and lingering doubt.

"What a powerful perspective," she says, shifting

toward her conclusion. "Dr. Naomi Thorne's new book, *The Honesty Mandate*, releases a week from Tuesday. Thank you for joining us today."

The red light blinks off. As I gather my notes, my fingers aren't quite steady. The papers slip from my grasp, and I fumble to collect them. Maya doesn't miss this.

"That was excellent," she says, her professional edge softening. "Really compelling. The personal elements will resonate."

I manage a smile. "I hope so."

"Your publicist mentioned a launch event next Friday?"

"Yes, at The Omni downtown. You should come."

We exchange a few more pleasantries while the sound engineer finishes his work. As the elevator descends to the parking garage, I let gravity do what I'd been fighting— pulling the tension from my body floor by floor. My phone shows three missed calls from my publicist.

"You nailed it," he says when I call him from my car. "Maya texted that you were 'absolutely compelling.' Perfect for the promotion materials."

"She asked about Celia," I say, starting the engine.

"As we expected. But you handled it perfectly. Your consistency is your brand, Naomi."

After he hangs up, I find myself staring at my phone's lock screen—Celia at seven, grinning with a gap where her front teeth should be, her hair in messy pigtails.

What would she make of who I've become? The question rises unbidden, sending a tremor through my carefully constructed certainty. I've built a career telling others how to face their painful truths. But there's a difference between acknowledging grief and actually moving through it.

Maya's questions about nuance follow me home, mingling with the memory of Damian's unusual behavior yesterday. Two anomalies don't make a pattern, I remind myself. But they do merit attention.

Tonight's anniversary dinner will be a chance to reaffirm our commitment to integrity. Twenty one years deserves celebration. Whatever doubts have surfaced, I need to press them down, examine them carefully. Our marriage isn't just a personal relationship—it's the living embodiment of my professional philosophy.

It has to be as honest as I've claimed. The alternative would unravel everything.

ABOUT THE AUTHOR

Stephanie Kreml writes mysteries and thrillers after working as an engineer, a physician, and a life science consultant. She lives with her family in Austin, Texas.

For more information, visit
www.stephaniekreml.com/

ALSO BY STEPHANIE KREML

The Dr. Samantha Jenkins Mystery Series

Truth Unveiled

Neglected Truth

Truth Promised

Misguided Truth

Coming Soon

The Honest Lie

www.ingramcontent.com/pod-product-compliance
Lightning Source LLC
Chambersburg PA
CBHW021244190726
48289CB00005B/1488